# Protecting the Source

## 2027

### Steven E. Browne

"An action-packed roller coaster ride!"
        Ru Emerson, Author
        Spellbound, Night Threads


"A real grabber! I was totally mesmerized."
        Deborah Spector, Best-selling Author
        Too Close for Comfort, Magic Moment

Wilton Place Publishing,
P.O. Box 291
La Cañada Flintridge, CA 91012

COVER ART BY NEAL THOMPSON
DESIGN AND LAYOUT BY SCOTT WILLIAMS

Acknowledgments
I want to express my deep, heart-felt thanks to my family; Michele, Nikole, Kris, and Kate who cheered me on.

I am a very lucky man.

### How it began

I was working on a textbook back in 1992, trying to meet a deadline for different manuscript. I was also working a day job and trying to make time for my family. I thought I had it under control.

Then *IT* hit me. I tried to ignore it. I had too many commitments to be fooling around with a demanding novel. But the story haunted me. It invaded my dreams and kept me up at night. I stopped working on the textbook long enough to write everything I knew about the story, then I went on with my hectic schedule.

I began to work on a new textbook, but was dogged by the pillar of light and Rick Peters' unearthly challenge. I stopped again and threw another 100 pages into the computer.

Another year went by. When the second book was off to the printer, it was time to finish the story. It took a while to get the details in place, but it was worth the effort.

I hope you enjoy reading it as much as I enjoyed "passing it along."

Steven E. Browne 9/6/95

### 2020 Update

There were several thousand copies printed for the first edition. They're long gone now. Forced to stay home during the pandemic, I decided to update the technology and make some slight improvements for clarity.

Actually, I found the story more relevant now than in 1996 when I finished the first draft.

Steven E. Browne 5/2020

# DEDICATION

To Michele, without whom there would be no words.

# IT BEGINS

NEWPORT LAMBORGHINI DEALERSHIP
BEACH, CALIFORNIA
SATURDAY, APRIL 11, 2026
12:18 P.M. Pacific Standard Time

It'd been a slow morning at the Newport Beach Lamborghini dealership. A few people had wandered through the showroom, but so far, the day had proved dull and uneventful. Harold Gray flipped through the Los Angeles Times. Another article about the "2027 Crazies" caught his attention.

Five homeless people claimed they'd seen the end of the world as they fished off the Santa Barbara pier. A bright shaft of light was going to cause a series of cataclysmic earthquakes and volcanic eruptions. Harold shook his head. 2027 was not going to be pretty.

The showroom door opened and portly Rick Peters sauntered in. Harold immediately recognized the paunchy stockbroker. Rick had dropped by each Saturday for the past several weeks. The man was obviously taken with the white Spyder sitting in the center of the showroom.

Harold had tried to sell him the car, but Rick continued to haggle over price. Wasn't that always the case? The people with money were the least willing to give it up. This man had everything else: two luscious girlfriends, a high-paying job and that oh-so-common privileged attitude.

"Good morning, Mr. Peters. Nice to see you again." Harold grinned broadly as he folded the paper.

Rick circled the desk and stood behind the salesman. "Let's take the Lamborghini out, Harold."

"Are you going to make that purchase today, Rick? You look like you've made a decision."

Peters smiled. "I have a feeling something spectacular is going to happen this weekend. It could be a car purchase. Then again it might be a spur-of-the-moment vacation to Grand Cayman."

Harold rose and pointed at the paper. "Record high Dow Jones average this week. It's not like 2020. I hope the bull market is proving to your advantage."

A smile crossed Rick's lips. "It was a stressful five days, but in the end, it worked out for the best."

Rick made it a rule to never volunteer financial information, especially in a week when he'd lost over seventy grand. Trading wasn't as fun as it used to be. Keeping up with a wildly moving market seemed empty, unimportant. He hoped a new car might breathe some life into his stale attitude.

A quiet voice told him this car would take him where he wanted to go. Rick intended to ignore the subtle instruction, but he'd been looking for a sign, some message about what he should be doing with his life. Even his dream of striking it rich had lost its luster. The voice told him to take a test drive near the commercial area of Long Beach.

"Will Patty and Sue be joining you today?"

Rick chuckled. It was physically impossible to ignore Patty or Sue. Separately they were attractive; together they could take a man's breath away.

"No, Patty and Sue won't be here today. They're in Malibu."

And Rick would be joining them in a couple of hours. Another exhausting night at the beach was in the cards. Rick enjoyed being around Patty and Sue. They helped him forget his life had no purpose.

Rick pulled out of the dealership in the shiny new convertible and immediately became one of the ultra-elite. Harold kept constant eye contact with him. There was a potential sale here.

"You look good in this car, Rick. It suits you."

"I think there's a rattle in the back."

"I don't hear it."

"Can't have rattles in a Lamborghini, Harold. Knocks the price down at least ten thousand."

Rick could afford the Spyder, but the payments would eat into his party budget. What was the sense of living if you couldn't party, especially if he continued make bad financial decisions?

It was a classic Southern California weekend. Surfers dotted the coastline. Vans of chattering families filled the beach parking lots. Late morning riders unloaded their tenspeeds in preparation for traveling the bike path. A group of vacationers shaded their eyes and squinted in an attempt to see who was driving the $300,000 car.

The voice in his head said turn right. Rick silently obeyed. He aimed the car north, leaving the beach behind.

"Handles well in traffic," offered Harold.

"Seems a little sluggish," said Rick hoping to get a deal.

Rick loved the car. If he churned a few more of his accounts, found another wealthy, unsuspecting client, and wrangled a decent interest rate, he could absorb the additional cost without affecting his other expensive pleasure pursuits.

Yet, he knew that even if he had this impressive car in his garage, something was missing in his life, something deep in his soul that would not be still, would not go away.

A bright orange glow above a four-story brick building caught his attention. He slowed the car to get a better look. Fifty-foot flames shot into the sky.

Rick pointed through the windshield. "Can you believe that!?"

Harold twisted his head and spotted the orange blaze. "Pull over! Let's take a look."

Rick swerved to the side of the road and stopped.

"It's the billboard!" Rick yelled. He squinted at the brilliant light. This was no ordinary fire.

Harold was concerned. "What should we do?"

"Look closely, Harold. The flames aren't smudging the support posts and the smoke doesn't go anywhere. This can't be a real fire. It must be a new type of ad."

Rick craned his head to get a better look. A second check confirmed his suspicion. The black plume raced upward only to fade a few feet above the ad.

"They've done an amazing job." Rick muttered as he opened the car door. "Come on, Harold, let's check it out."

As he entered the adjacent office building and punched the elevator button, a sense of excitement ran through Rick's body like an electric shock. Harold barely made it into the elevator before the doors closed. At the fifth floor, Rick ran down the hallway trying each door. Finally, he found one that was unlocked and burst into a dental office.

"I'm sorry, sir, we're closed. Dr. Heyes is here for an emergency procedure."

Rick raced past the dental assistant and darted into one of the examination rooms.

"I'm with him," pointed Harold following Rick.

A nervous patient sat alone in a white leather recliner.

"I'll only be a minute." Rick slapped the drill out of his way. "We've got a problem out there."

The elderly man struggled out of the chair and joined the two men at the window. "What's happening?"

"Look!" Rick pointed to the roof across the way. Atop the adjoining building was the engulfed billboard. The large rectangle contained a Boeing 777, in flames, heading to the ground. Rick could smell the acrid odor of melting plastic. Screams filled his head as images outside the window played liked a movie.

"Mayday! Mayday!" the copilot yelled.

The pilot struggled with the controls as smoke filled the cockpit. "More power! Open it up!"

"We're at full power!" the copilot shouted back.

The rear of the plane had been sheared off, leaving a gaping hole. Luggage flew from the overhead bins. Magazines, snack trays and backpacks whipped around the cabin, smashed into terrified faces, then disappeared out the back of the plane. A flight attendant screamed as he was sucked down the aisle and disappeared into the hungry void.

"Sir? Can I help..." Doctor Heyes stopped mid-sentence. "What the hell is that plane doing!?"

Rick continued to focus outside the window, unaware of the dentist's presence.

The jet plunged from the sky. Two more rows of seats ripped from the flooring. Six shrieking passengers flew out the back, their arms flailing. Smoke poured from the mortally wounded aircraft.

Rick stared at the billboard in disbelief. What was happening outside this window? What was happening to him? The cries and moans from the passengers pulled his attention back to the animated rectangle. The jet burst through a bank of clouds, skimmed across an angry ocean, then vanished in a plume of seawater.

The image changed to a future edition of the Wall Street Journal. Details concerning the dramatic crash of a commercial flight off the coast of New York filled the front page. Although rescue craft were on the scene within an hour, over one hundred fifty passengers had gone down with the fuselage.

The bulk of the article was about a financially troubled defense company called Dynotech. Seven of the company's key executive, who held crucial information about the corporation's upcoming ten billion-dollar government contract were on the plane. Three executives and four master scientists had broken a long-standing ban against having more than two senior employees on the same flight.

The article continued describing what happened when the news of the missing men hit Wall Street. The market reacted immediately and Dynotech's stock plummeted. Miraculously, the men were rescued hours later and, as a result, Dynotech's stock came roaring back. Alongside the story was a detailed graph that tracked the defense company's precipitous slide and rapid recovery during the day of the crash, three weeks from Friday.

Rick turned from the window. "Paper! Pencil! Hurry!"

He grabbed a pen from the dentist's pocket and copied every number from the graph onto a patient's chart as the others watched the billboard. He noted the names of the executives, the airline and the flight number: 755. After double-checking the information, he looked up, realized where he was and quickly headed for the door.

Rick tucked the patient's file under his arm and turned in the doorway. "That was an incredible sight. Thanks for your help."

Harold followed right behind. The dentist and patient continued to stare out the window.

Back on the street, Rick felt his heart pounding. He glanced over his shoulder at the billboard. A blank space stood silently where the 777 once poured smoke into the sky.

He turned to Harold. "What do you think?"

"What's to think? It was a plane crash and a newspaper," shrugged Harold. "I have to admit the effect was spectacular."

Rick was stunned. "Effect?"

"Sure," said Harold, "It had to be one of those new electronic ads. It looks real, but it's an illusion. I bet this was an unannounced test."

Rick stared at Harold. There was no need to go any further with this discussion. What occurred in that large rectangle was no computer graphic. It was too real, too special to be man-made. He glanced down at the dental chart. The numbers seemed right. Dynotech was in financial trouble.

Rick slid behind the wheel, then glanced over as Harold slumped into the passenger seat.

Harold sensed Rick's eyes on him. "That wasn't an ad, was it?"

Rick shook his head. "No, Harold, I don't believe it was."

"The dentist saw it."

"Doesn't matter."

"Have you read about the '2027 Crazies'?"

"No. Who are they?"

Harold swallowed. "There have been a series of reports about people claiming they've witnessed the end of world. Five of them vanished yesterday."

"I don't know anything about that, Harold. And I certainly haven't seen anything like the end of the world. What I do know is that Dynotech is an existing defense company and it's in deep financial trouble." Rick unconsciously chewed his lip. Good or bad, something big was in the air.

"Let's go back, Harold. It's not the right day for this."

The evening with Patty and Sue was canceled. Rick spent the rest of the afternoon at his computer. He Googled all available information about Dynotech. The results were alarming. The men mentioned in the article were senior executives of the Dynotech corporation. Information about intense contract negotiations and company's shaky financial position were also confirmed. Apparently, this deal would make or break the highly leveraged firm.

By midnight Rick had verified every fact he'd seen, including the flight number and its arrival time in New York. At three a.m. he dragged himself to bed and dreamed of terrified people being sucked out the back of the plane. He woke in a cold sweat. Could he have seen the future? If he had, if the stock prices were anywhere near correct, he was going to be obscenely rich.

MARQUIS TOWERS
WESTWOOD, CALIFORNIA
SUNDAY, APRIL 12, 2026
11:45 A.M. PST

"Rick, you sound like a crazy man," said Curt Smith.

Rick and Curt had been friends for over fifteen years. They met their sophomore year in college and traveled Europe together after graduation.

Sunday morning Rick was at Curt's door seeking advice. Rick grabbed some orange juice from the refrigerator and they parked themselves in Curt's den.

Curt patiently listened to Rick's story, thought a moment then pointed a finger at him. "You didn't happen to see the end of the world, did you?"

"No. It was nothing like what the people in Santa Barbara described."

"You head about them?"

"Yeah."

"Then you must know they're nowhere to be found."

"They probably hopped a freight train."

"They've been fishing the pier every day for two years and now they're gone."

Rick rubbed his forehead. The "2027 Crazies" were clouding the issue Rick wanted to discuss.

"Curt, four people stood at my side and saw the same thing I did. When I got home, I researched it all. Every name and date checked out. This morning, I went on linkedin. The pilot and co-pilot are employees of Northwest airlines. I'm certain this is an important message. I just can't figure out what it means."

"It means you need some rest."

Rick ran his fingers through his full beard. "Come on, buddy. Stay with me on this." He pointed at his friend. "You know what I think?"

"You're going on a talk show?"

"It means I'm going to discover a purpose to my life."

Curt groaned. "Oh Rick, how many times do I have to tell you? Your purpose in life is to make more money than you can spend and get laid as much as you can stand."

Rick shook his head. "Wrong. There has to be a greater purpose in life."

Curt paced cup on the coffee table. "What's wrong with sex and money?"

Rich shrugged. "Can't you be more original? What about your soul? What about giving, self-sacrifice, you know, lofty ideals."

"I prefer sex and money."

"I know. It's pretty obvious."

Curt leaned back and checked his watch. "Why don't you fly down to Mexico this weekend. Bring Patty and Sue."

"You're annoying me, Curt."

"I've got the name of a great psychologist. He's very reasonable."

"Now you're pissing me off."

"Okay, okay. Tell me this: What happens if this amazing vision is accurate?"

"I'll be rich."

"My point exactly. All anyone wants to be is rich and sexually satisfied. If your little episode proves correct, you'll be halfway there."

"And I'll know I saw the future."

"Who else have you told? In other words, who else considers you a major nut case?"

"Northwest Airlines."

"What?!"

"I had to let them know. It was the least I could do."

Curt was shocked. "What have you done, Rick? Did you call them from your place?"

"Yeah, but I only said that a particular flight on a particular day might be sabotaged."

Curt stood and walked across his living room, stopping in front of his huge picture window. It was an exceptionally clear day.

"What were you on, Rick?"

Rick shrugged. "I had some coffee, that's it."

"And the night before?"

"Couple of beers. Nothing out of the ordinary." Rick held his hands up. "I know. I know. You're thinking I had one of those crazy nights with Patty and Sue, but it's not true. The Dow hit another record high last week and I managed to lose over seventy thousand dollars. I was in no mood to party."

Curt tapped the window with his index finger. Rick had been contemplating his purpose on Earth, looking for something to justify his existence. He hoped Rick's desire to be needed hadn't gotten him into trouble. This was not the time claim he saw a vision or to call an airline about a terrorist threat.

"Are you sure you didn't have some kind of nightmare, or imagine it in a daydream?"

Rick was on his feet, pacing. "Curt, this entire event took ten, maybe fifteen minutes. I went up elevators, talked to an old man and copied an entire page of detailed financial information. This was not a chemically induced state. There were people around me, moving, talking, reacting. It was no dream. I could never make this up."

He grabbed the cordless phone and began dialing.

Curt was concerned. "Who are you calling?"

"The sales guy at the Lamborghini dealership. He'll tell you what happened."

Curt cocked his head. He'd never seen Rick so intense. "Lighten up, Rick. You don't have to call the guy."

"I'm going to prove it to you. Hi, Harold. It's Rick Peters. Quite a day we had yesterday. I was telling a friend of mine about the billboard...you know, the billboard that was on fire. What do you mean? We went into that dentist's office...you can't be serious."

The line went dead. Rick redialed. No one answered.

Curt stared at his friend. "Guess you should have bought the car."

"He said he didn't see anything and he doesn't want to talk to me again."

Curt folded his hands together. "Would you sit down? You're making me nervous."

Rick completed several more passes before landing in one of the high-backed chairs.

Curt leaned forward. "Rick, the plane will land safely and you'll never know how thoroughly you were investigated. Whatever happened, whatever you think you saw, it's over. Neither of us will ever understand what it was about."

"You're wrong, Curt. The plane is going to crash."

"If it does, you're in trouble. How long were you on the phone?"

"Three, maybe four minutes." Rick paused a moment, realizing what Curt was saying. "There's no way they can blame me. I called to warn them, not threaten them."

"There's so much scary stuff going on," said Curt, "The Middle East peace agreement has unraveled. The Feds have granted the National Security Agency limited jurisdiction over domestic intelligence. There've been a dozen '2027 Crazies' incidents in the last month. If you called the airlines, you're on a list. Luckily, for your sake, the plane will land safely. Don't invest any money. You'd be better off buying lottery tickets."

Rick gritted his teeth. There was no way he could turn down an opportunity like this. It was the chance of a lifetime.

"Are you listening, Rick? The plane is going to land safely. They always do."

Rick sighed. It was a good thing he didn't tell Curt about the voice that told him to go to the dealership or to drive up the street where he discovered the billboard.

Curt stared at his friend. "You're running with this, aren't you?"

"Every name checked out. The flight number matched. The departure time was the same. The pilots work for Northwest Airlines. It is going to happen, Curt. I saw the future. I don't know why. I don't know how. But I'm going to be rich. Not just wealthy. I'm talking about tens of millions."

Curt understood. Rick was in debt, not excessively, not dangerously, but he lived beyond his means. Patty and Sue were always on his arm. His expansive wine collection and antique-filled, ocean-view condo did not come cheap.

"Want a beer?" Curt had heard enough about the amazing billboard. Maybe Rick was playing a prank. Whatever was going on, it would sort itself out.

Rick left Curt's place certain the billboard incident was real. He double-checked the information, this time using different search engines. The results were the same. Dynotech was floundering and the flight was scheduled to arrive at 7:15 a.m. two weeks from Friday.

On Tuesday afternoon, he called the patient whose file he'd swiped at the dentist's office, pretending to be a policeman. This time he used a pay phone.

"Mr. Greystone, this is Detective Jackson. We're investigating a complaint from a Dr. Heyes. He's a dentist in the South Bay area. Did a stranger burst into the office Saturday during your procedure?"

The voice on the other end hesitated, as if trying to remember the incident. "Well, yeah, there was this nut who stormed into the examination room. But I already talked to one of you guys."

"Which guys, Mr. Greystone? Who did you talk to?"

"One of your men who's investigating the end of the world thing. Scared the hell out of me. Don't you guys communicate with each other? I told him everything."

"We have one more question, Mr. Greystone, if you don't mind: Was there anything happening outside the window?"

The old man paused again before replying. "Um, something happening outside? Let me see, outside…"

The man was stalling. The phone made a strange clicking sound. Rick hung up. He called the dentist.

"Dr. Heyes, please."

"Who may I say is calling?"

"Bob Terrance," said Rick, "I came in last Saturday morning with my friend. He'll remember. It's important."

"Just a moment."

The government was investigating the billboard incident. Was this bigger than he suspected? Did someone else report it?'

"Hello?"

"Dr. Heyes, I came into your office Saturday afternoon. There appeared to be a fire on the roof across the way. Do you remember?"

"I certainly do."

Relief flooded Rick's body. Finally, someone admitted seeing the billboard.

"Then you saw the plane crash and the Wall Street Journal."

"I saw you steal one of my patient's files."

"What about the billboard?" asked Rick.

"I want that file returned."

Rick heard the familiar click.

"Consider it done. What about the fire, the plane? You never saw them outside your office window?"

Again the pause. "What was your name again?"

Rick replaced the receiver and quickly left the area.

It didn't concern Rick these people were denying what had occurred. He was not going to let this opportunity slip by. Rick opened accounts at ten brokerage houses. Papers were filed and forms completed. At the end of the week, Rick had access to over eight million dollars at two points above prime.

Four trips to the mysterious billboard revealed nothing. The blank space had been replaced with a beer ad. Returning from his last visit, Rick stopped at the Lamborghini dealership. Harold quit the day following Rick's test drive. No one had heard from him since.

Two days before the plane was supposed to go down, Rick and Curt had dinner. Rick was confident his plan was going to work.

"Everything is in place. My only concern is that this might not turn out as profitable as I had envisioned."

Curt sipped his Black Russian. "You seem different."

"How so?"

"You were pleasant to the waitress and you haven't ordered a drink." He leaned in. "Have you seen any more burning billboards?"

"No. And everyone I've talked to either denies seeing the plane or refuses to talk about it."

"After those guys in Santa Barbara disappeared, no one is talking about visions. Doesn't that bother you?"

"They're scared to admit what they saw. Probably the '2027 Crazies' thing has them spooked."

"Exactly. What about the Lamborghini salesman?"

Rick shrugged. "Quit. Gone. I guess he flipped out."

Curt stared at his friend. Nothing about Rick's story made sense. Maybe this was how people went insane. Little by little their grip on reality slipped away.

"I'm not going insane," said Rick.

Curt was startled. He knew he hadn't said anything, but he ignored the coincidence

"Did you go back to the billboard?"

"Several times."

"What did it say?"

"Buy Bud Light."

Curt laughed heartily, nearly choking on his drink. "And did you?"

Rick shook his head and wrapped his hands around his water glass. "I'm betting everything on Dynotech."

"Rick, can I be honest?"

"Of course."

"This is a really, really bad idea. If you're wrong, you'll lose everything including the condo. Let it go. Just be glad you tried to save some lives."

"Curt, I've done my homework and now, I'm ready to reap the rewards."

"I think it's great you had a powerful experience, but please, don't waste your money."

"You think I'm crazy."

"You're being unreasonable. You wouldn't buy Google stock when I told you to, but you'll risk everything for this?"

"Curt, I saw the future and I'm going to do something about it."

VANDENBERG AIR FORCE BASE
LOMPOC, CALIFORNIA
SUNDAY, APRIL 12, 2026
9:00 P.M. PST

Greg Slocum approached his short, squatty boss with caution. Slocum could never tell if White was in a good or bad mood.

"Who do you want first?" he asked.

Lance White continued to stare at the ceiling of the hangar. He was about to interrogate five homeless degenerates. God, he hated this job. After fifteen years in the intelligence business he'd been reduced to the level of a gang member.

"Bring me the oldest," snapped White.

Slocum nodded and disappeared.

White circled the empty folding chair. One of these derelicts would tell him what happened at the end of that pier.

He'd survived three attempts on his life and four major Administration upheavals, yet he was removed from the field because he was considered a throwback to the simple, violent nineties, unable to adapt to the newer, kinder era of spying. When the Agency began its investigation into the "2027 Crazies," White volunteered to lead the small department. The suits allowed him a last chance to prove he could operate in a changed world.

The incident in Santa Barbara caught his attention and he moved in quickly. The gray van swooped down on the pier late Saturday evening. Within an hour five men were sitting inside a small hangar on the Vandenberg Air Force Base.

The first of the foul-smelling men was escorted to the chair. His blindfold was roughly removed.

"What's your name?" asked White, leaning into the derelict's face.

The man's body shook. Sitting in his underwear, he was cold and hungry. The man knew no one was going to save him.

"Edward Brand."

"How long have you been having seizures, Edward?"

Brand looked around, then returned his focus to White. The undersized agent produced a small scalpel.

"I don't have seizures," said Brand, wondering if he or any of his friends would survive the night.

"You had one Friday night. You dreamed you saw the end of the world."

Brand might be homeless, but he was far from stupid. What did this man want to hear? A slap across the face shook him from his thoughts.

"I asked you a question."

"I saw what the others saw. There was a pillar of light in the middle of a field. A tall man ran at it, tried to run into it, but someone killed him before he could get there. Then all hell broke loose. Volcanoes, earthquakes...."

The knife etched its way across his thigh, cutting several inches into his flesh before Brand realized what was happening.

"Tell me the truth, Brand."

"You're crazy!" yelled Brand.

"Yes. Yes, I am."

7811 ADMIRALTY WAY
MARINA DEL REY, CALIFORNIA
FRIDAY, MAY 8, 2026
3:05 A.M. PST

When Rick woke, it was dark. Dawn was hours away. He wandered his Marina condo, unable to sleep. Flight 755 was airborne, heading for New York City. If the billboard proved correct, in a few hours his life would soon be permanently changed to one of leisure and excess.

At four a.m. Rick brought his steaming coffee into the darkened living room. Cable News Network played silently on his wide screen television. He tried to settle into his favorite suede chair, but was too restless to sit. Back on his feet, he continued to pace. One minute after four. Fourteen minutes to go.

He'd bought millions of dollars of Dynotech options over the last two days. If all went according to plan, his long put would make him well over two hundred million, that is if the price fell to 30 like the numbers in the billboard predicted. Then, after selling those options, he'd take a long call with a

50-dollar strike price with some of his money, and buy Dynotech stock with the rest of his winnings just before the executives were found alive. No sense drawing too much attention to himself. Five hundred million for a day's work would do nicely.

He abruptly stopped pacing. What the hell was he doing? Even if the billboard was correct to the penny, why had he put his entire future on the line?

The digital clock at the top corner of the television changed as weather forecasts and political reports filled the screen. Four-ten came and went. Rick stared at the display, then checked his smart watch. It was four-eighteen when he slumped into his chair. All that preparation and hard-earned cash at risk, for what? A chance at being fabulously wealthy? Now what was he going to do? His life was over. His career was over. There was nothing left.

Rick groaned. What the hell happened that Saturday morning? What had he done? Once his clients found out he'd blown their money on Dynotech, he'd lose his license.

Only a month ago, he was reading boring prospectuses and baby-sitting spoiled clients; stealing from the rich to pay for his expensive obsessions and cover his growing debts. Now he'd set himself up to fail and for what? To prove he saw a vision of the future? How crazy was that?

Maybe Patty and Sue were free tonight. He could use a little diversion. God, he could use a big diversion. It'd probably be his last one.

At four-twenty, there was an important news break. A Boeing 777 had exploded fifteen miles outside New York City, disappearing from radar screens over a stormy Atlantic Ocean.

Rick pounded the coffee table with his fist. "Bingo!"

He leapt from his chair, grabbed his briefcase and raced out the door.

4156 PACIFIC COAST HIGHWAY
LONG BEACH, CALIFORNIA
FRIDAY, MAY 8, 2026
5:45 A.M. PST

The trading pit of Weisman and Maduff was sleek and modern. Monitors hung across the front of the room displayed the prices on the New York, American and NASDAQ markets. On either end of the room hung two large flatscreens, one showing CNBC, the other Bloomberg News.

Rick ran into the room, threw his coat on the desk and put on his headset. This was going to be a great day. He glanced around at the other traders preparing for the day's work. They had no idea within the next few hours Rick Peters was going to be a multi-millionaire.

He smiled and stretched. Firing up his computer, Rick thought about the Lamborghini he would soon own, the beach house he'd always wanted and the spectacular resorts he'd never visited. There was a lot of catching up to do.

The moment the market opened, trading in Dynotech was halted. The expert on the exchange floor refused to open the stock due to an order imbalance. Far too many people were trying to sell the troubled security. Needing to keep the stock trading, he bought fifteen thousand shares at forty-nine dollars with some of his remaining funds. Over the next hour he sold those shares taking a temporary loss, then bought more long puts with everything he had left.

He noticed the numbers he'd written on the dental chart weren't entirely accurate. The price fluctuated between fifty cents and a dollar off the billboard's figures, but the difference was hardly enough to worry about. The important issue was the plane had crashed, the stock was plummeting, and he was going to be a very wealthy man.

"Having fun?" asked Brad Eisner, a broker who'd worked alongside Rick for the last three years. Brad couldn't help but notice the unusual trades Rick had been making. He rarely ordered more than two or three transactions during the course of a week. Rick had bought more options in the last two days than in the last six months. Not only that, Rick had changed.

He had a new confidence about him, a determination Brad had never seen.

Rick covered his microphone with his hand. "Brad, this is the going to be the best day of my life. The good news is, tomorrow will be even better."

Brad nodded and turned back to his station. Maybe Rick was on drugs.

It didn't take long for others on the floor to take notice of Rick's unusual activity. Pictures of empty life rafts and bodies of the pilot and copilot played on the monitors hung from the ceiling. Rick ignored the images. Instead, he kept a constant watch on CNN and Dynotech's stock price.

A mangled teddy bear floated next to a piece of bobbing luggage. Dynotech's stock price drifted lower. It was now at thirty-six dollars a share, a drop of over thirty percent.

The brokers following Rick's early morning lead lost their nerve and bailed. Even the seasoned professionals in the room couldn't stand making money on a heart-breaking disaster. The images on the televisions didn't help. The stock took another sickening dive to thirty-three dollars and seventy-five cents and was still falling.

Rick watched the Dynotech price as a family of six clung to a cluster of seat cushions. Two of the young children were dead, but the father stubbornly held onto them, refusing to let the tiny bodies slip beneath the waves. A businessman who'd lost his legs in the crash was airlifted to New York. He died before the wheels touched ground.

At precisely one fifty-five in the afternoon, Rick reversed his tactics, sold hi long puts at 30 and bought thirty million dollars of long calls. He purchased six million shares of Dynotech with his profits.

Ten minutes later, news came that all Dynotech employees had survived the catastrophe and were being flown to the mainland. Found in a sinking life raft with their watertight briefcases, the fiercely devoted group vowed to stay with each other until they were rescued. With the news of the scientists' survival, Dynotech's stock soared.

Families converged on the airline terminal. Most were greeted with the worst news. College students, grandmothers and newlyweds had succumbed in the icy waters off the East Coast. Newscasters pressed forward, trying to get that precious interview from the grief-stricken relatives. Rick ignored the television and stared at the stock display. Dynotech continued its upward movement.

CNN ran a story about a young writer who'd begged his best friend to get off the jet, claiming the airliner was doomed. The friend had laughed hysterically. He was going home to his parents after three months living in France and refused to leave the plane.

When the scientists were found, Rick was already rich, but with his reinvestment, his net worth shot up.

"What are you going to do after this stellar performance?" Brad asked, as Dynotech's stock rose above where it opened earlier in the day.

Rick smiled. Nothing he'd ever experienced compared to this exhilarating feeling. "Brad, I'm going to live like a king. I'm going to travel the world, meet and woo attractive women and push every envelope I can find. I am going to live life to its fullest and never again worry about my future. I might even find the woman of my dreams."

Rick glanced at the clock. Five minutes to go. His hands were slick with perspiration, his shirt was soaked, but he executed his last trades with professionalism. Like a pitcher striking out his last batter to clinch a no-hitter, Rick pulled in his final one hundred million quickly and efficiently. He looked up at the strip of lights that danced across the front of the room. Dynotech was trading two dollars above its original price. His total win was over five hundred million dollars.

"That was some nice work," said Brad, envious of Rick's newfound independence.

"Thanks, Brad" said Rick, chuckling to himself.

Rick had been given a powerful gift. He'd seen the future, believed in what he'd experienced and despite others' doubts he had the foresight to use that information to the utmost advantage. A few more days like this and he would be one of the wealthiest men in the world.

Brokers crowded around. Old-timers slapped Rick on the back and shook his hand while younger members of the firm looked on the celebration in awe. Rick Peters was a hero.

Brad watched as Rick basked in the glow of admiration and victory. How he wished he could trade places with this man who'd waited patiently for the right moment, then acted so decisively and accurately. Rick Peters was in total control of his surroundings.

Then Brad sensed a change. Rick was staring at the television monitors, detached, unfocused. His mouth dropped open, sweat returned to his forehead. Brad glanced at the screens. They were all displaying the same dark, ghost-like images. A shadowy figure ran through a dense forest, dodging trees and rocks. Suddenly the man burst into the open field and the picture became clear.

Rick was no longer in the trading room, but at the edge of a large meadow. The sky hung black and starless. Powerful winds ripped at his clothes. Splintered branches flew through the air. Directly ahead of him in the middle of the open space stood a monumental pillar of yellow light, illuminating the area with a ghostly, pulsating glow. The colossal cylinder flowed like a vertical river into the darkness above.

An earsplitting groan filled the air as the ground heaved upward and cracked beneath the searing yellow pillar. Rick ran into the meadow and headed toward the light. A rainbow of bright flashes filled the air. A revolver was in his right hand. Something whizzed by his head. He looked back toward the forest. Twenty soldiers were advancing toward him. A single figure, apparently the leader, ran in front of the rest, heading directly at Rick.

"The light. Go into the light," said a familiar voice.

Rick turned. The pillar grew, its pulsating became frantic, more powerful. Bullets ricocheted off unseen boulders, zinging incredibly close.

To the left of the column appeared another dark figure. This man was a civilian, his face twisted in an angry scowl. He squinted through the swirling dust, as if looking for someone. He spotted Rick, and in one quick motion he produced a handgun and began firing. The wind howled. Trees swayed.

Rick turned to run in the opposite direction, only to face the line of onrushing troops. The lead man stopped abruptly and raised his M-16.

"The light. Get to the light. It's your only chance," whispered the voice.

Rick started back toward the pulsating light but a powerful force pushed him sideways. Pain shot up his side as a bullet entered his chest. He stumbled, then fell to the ground.

The soldier came to Rick's side. "It's over, Peters. We can't let you go on."

"Into the light," Rick heard himself say. "Bring your men. You have to continue into the light."

"You know I can't do that."

"You must!"

The rest of the troops surrounded the undulating column, guarding it, as if to block anyone to approach it.

"Tell them. Tell them," repeated the voice. "Tell them to go into the light."

The wailing of the cylinder abruptly stopped as it was sucked into the dark sky. Soft warm sunlight flooded the meadow. The winds stopped and for a brief moment there was silence, peace, loneliness.

Then, with a thunderous roar, the rip in the Earth widened. Rick was lifted above the scarred Earth, high above his body. He watched the area beneath him mangled by a series of monumental earthquakes. To the left, a dormant volcano erupted, spewing deadly lava half a mile in the air.

Rick continued his ascent. One area after another was engulfed in violent volcanic and seismic disruptions. Here and there small islands of safety could be seen, but the majority of the continent was wracked with devastation. Tidal waves swept across oceans. The Earth's crust buckled and cracked. Cities were leveled, then swallowed. Great lakes disappeared into the Earth, only to shoot back into the sky as scalding clouds of super-heated steam.

As Rick floated above the Earth the voice spoke for the last time.

"Go to the Jet Propulsion Lab, take position 19C, watch Sagittarius and wait for a sign."

Brad stared at the television monitor in amazement. The column of light was enticing, hypnotizing. As he watched Rick stumble to the ground on the monitor, he heard a moan and thump. Looking to his side, he saw Rick on the floor. Brad knelt at his side.

"Into the light," Rick said weakly. "You have to continue into the light."

"What are you talking about, Rick?"

"You must... go... into the light..."

Rick was in pain, his face ashen.

"Call an ambulance!" yelled Brad.

No one moved. The traders continued to watch the global devastation play out on the monitors. Brad reached over a paper-strewn computer station, grabbed the nearby receiver and dialed 911. Rick's body jerked. The fallen broker grabbed his chest, then his body went limp.

SOQUEL PARK
PACIFIC PALISADES, CALIFORNIA
THURSDAY, MAY 14, 2026
7:55 P.M. PST

The softball diamond was deserted. Rick waited in the parking lot to see if he'd been followed. Satisfied that he was alone, he cautiously walked down the small hill then around the chain link fence. For another fifteen minutes, he nervously waited at home plate, a leather briefcase at his feet.

The sun dipped behind the horizon. Darkness began to overtake the brilliant red sky. A flock of birds flew overhead. Scuffling noises from a group of trees caught his attention. Rick swiveled and peered into the darkness.

"Curt? Is that you?"

The lawyer walked around the fence onto the dusty field. Rick's smile surprised him. He expected to see a harried, frightened man. Instead, he found his friend very much at ease, almost happy.

"Rick, I'm surprised. You don't look like a man who's had a heart attack and is being investigated by two government agencies."

Rick shook Curt's outstretched hand. "Not to worry, it's only going to get worse."

It had been a harrowing forty-eight hours for Rick. Reporters, Federal Aviation Administration, Securities and Exchange Commission investigators, the FBI and media-hungry politicians had begun to focus their attention on him. He was lucky to make out of his condo unnoticed. Hopefully, Curt would be carrying the answer to his dilemma.

"I've been in more pleasant situations. By the way, my friend, it wasn't a heart attack."

"Another vision?"

Rick nodded.

"Care to talk about it?"

"Do you really want to know?"

"Sure."

The words passed Curt's lips before he considered the possibility Rick might possess news he really didn't want to hear. The Dynotech story had proved uncannily accurate. This next tale could be unnerving as well.

"I've joined the '2027 Crazies' club."

Curt's stomach leapt to his throat. It was going to happen. He kicked at the loose dirt around home plate. Damn it! Why this century? Why now? But wait, maybe Rick could be reading it wrong. Maybe it wasn't going to happen.

Rick shook his head. "Curt, there's five hundred million in a bank account that says I'm right. It's going to happen, just like that plane fell from the sky. You didn't believe me then. You don't have to believe me now. There is a chance it can be stopped, or at least changed."

"That's why you had me get the false I.D.s? You're going to try and stop it?"

Rick paused a moment. Was he making a mistake talking to Curt? It was hard to tell. He stared into his friend's eyes. Curt was a lucky man. He'd always been satisfied with who he was, even when he was being a total jerk. Rick envied his friend's self-confidence, that unquestioning acceptance of personal faults and gifts. Rick had always doubted his own worth, and that skepticism had brought him to this dusty softball field, with an unbelievable amount of responsibility. Curt needed to be a messenger, but Rick had to be the hero.

"Did you get the documents?"

Curt pulled a large manila envelope from his leather pouch. "How long have we known each other?"

"Fifteen years, four months, but who's counting?"

"In all that time, have I ever failed you?"

Rick smirked. "There was that brawl in Ensenada when you slipped away with Gail."

"Besides that."

"You've been there every time, Curt." It was difficult for Rick to control his voice. "I can't tell you how important that's been to me."

"You sound like you're going to die."

"It won't be much fun."

"Rick, I know the FAA and SEC are investigating you, but they don't have any real evidence. It's not a law in this country to be rich. I'm a damn good lawyer. Let me get you out of this."

Rick shrugged. If it was as simple as dodging the SEC and the FAA, he would have bought his way out of the situation.

"Curt, this isn't about the plane or Dynotech. I have to move quickly without question."

Curt handed Rick the package. "Everything you need is in the bag: Driver's license, high school and college diplomas, social security card, birth certificate, credit cards. There are a few more odds and ends that will help the transition." Curt chuckled. "I decided your resume needed an extra kick, so I gave you a Ph.D. in Astronomy."

Rick's eyes met Curt's. The lawyer had no idea how much that would help...or did he?

"I really appreciate this, buddy."

A troublesome thought crossed Curt's mind. If the fate of the world was in Rick's hands...

Rick's laughter echoed across center field. "You don't have a choice on that one, buddy. As far as I know, I'm your only hope. Even the brokers who watched it on the monitors won't talk about it. I'm no James Bond, but I'm the only person who's standing between you and a very unpleasant future."

"It's that bad?"

Rick wanted to tell his friend the truth - chances were they'd both be dead before the end of 2027 and most likely nothing could stop the onslaught heading their way. One positive piece of information remained. Rick had discovered the future was pliable. It had shape and direction, but wasn't etched in stone. The prices on the billboard were not dollar-accurate. The Dynotech execs rescued minutes later than the billboard indicated.

"It'll be all right, Curt, thanks to you. This package is half the battle."

"Really?"

"Yes, really."

A visible relief swept over Curt's face. "Did you get enough cash for yourself? I heard they'd seized most of your accounts this morning."

"I'll be fine."

"I guess Patty and Sue aren't going with you."

Rick shook his head slowly, his lips pressed together. "I'm on my own with this one, buddy."

Curt tried to detect if there was some sort of pain or loss in Rick's face. He couldn't tell if his friend was at peace with his situation or panicked, but he couldn't read him at all. One thing was certain, he'd never seen his friend so focused.

"Rick, if you disappear, they'll do everything they can to find you. One of the brokers talked to a reporter about what he saw on those television monitors. They altered his voice and hid his face, but he basically confirmed the bright light story. People are really freaking out. I'd leave the country if I were you."

Curt didn't want to get into the moral issues of the situation. Rick had made over almost half a billion dollars while one hundred and fifty-three people died. Though Rick had done nothing wrong, he would never be right.

Rick rubbed the back of his neck. "I'll have to get as far away as possible."

There was no sense telling Curt his plan. If he knew Rick's destination was a mere twenty miles away, it would jeopardize both their lives. Walking away from his condo, Patty and Sue, the job, even his numerous personal possessions didn't bother him, but leaving Curt was painful. For the first time in his life, he realized what a friend this man had been.

"Take care of yourself, Curt. And from now on, try and make every moment count. It's going to get ugly."

DOUG'S RESTAURANT
HARTFORD, CONNECTICUT
SATURDAY, MAY 9, 2026
10:45 P.M. EST

Kim Callaway and Renee Stoner sat at the mahogany bar and surveyed the dance floor. The music throbbed as bodies rubbed and tempted one another. It was a good night for love in the city of Hartford. There were several popular pick-up places in Connecticut's largest city, but Doug's was considered the best hunting ground for upscale movers and shakers.

Renee made an appearance at least once a month hoping to find her knight in golden armor. Kim rarely ventured near this or any of the other meat markets. Her Saturday nights were usually spent reading or occasionally bowling with a few friends.

Kim scanned the faces surrounding her. All she saw were beautiful men trying to find the best-looking woman for a night's pleasure. Renee could have her pick of these exquisite samples of the male species. Her wavy blonde locks and plainly visible curves fit into the bunny image that men loved to capture and conquer. Kim, on the other hand, looked out of place. Her loose-fitting clothes were hardly fashionable and her one hundred sixty pounds placed her at the bottom of every man's wish list.

Renee shoved her elbow into Kim's side. "Don't be so nervous. You're fine."

Kim knew a woman had to be seductive or rich in order to snag the type of man who frequented this establishment. Once you had them, you had to put out either physically, financially or both.

"Of course I'm fine," she lied. "I'm always fine."

Another gorgeous man headed toward them. Like a heat-seeking missile, he locked eyes on Renee and closed the distance between them. Kim was fascinated by the activity Renee created. Guys loved the way she looked, drawn to her like a moth to a flame. Never hinting she was interested, Renee would chat with them, subtly investigating his financial and personal background.

Kim did not have the packaging or the personality to tease or entice, nor did she want to. Her had no intention of living a glamorous life with a high-powered lawyer or otherwise-occupied businessman. Her search was for an honest, sane man who would treat her kindly. She did not see anyone in the room who could fit her needs.

Kim checked out the new arrival. This one was different. Less pushy than the others, Kim felt something unsafe about him. She came to the conclusion he was not a good person. Though the music blocked most of Renee's conversation, Kim caught a few choice words that flowed from his mouth: "beautiful," "could be a movie star," "saw you from across the room."

Renee made pleasant conversation, occasionally scanning the dance floor or glancing over to Kim. No doubt about it, Renee was a brilliant actress.

A series of images filled Kim's vision. One moment she was watching Renee chatting away with an exquisitely chiseled male, then Kim found herself in a large house. As her eyes grew accustomed to the darkness, she heard people upstairs. Her body drifted up a wide staircase.

"She's in trouble," whispered a voice in her head. Kim turned to see an empty hallway. "She will die. Don't let her go home with him."

"Who are you? Where are you?" she asked.

There was no answer. Kim continued up the staircase, then floated into a candle-lit bedroom. A tall man stood over a naked woman. The room was deathly silent. He traced the blade of a knife down her chest. The woman begged for mercy, but Kim could not hear her words. The knife rose above the man's head.

Screams filled Kim's ears. The knife fell, then rose again. Over and over he struck. The anguished shriek turned to a sickening gurgle, then stopped altogether. He stood and removed the rest of his clothing. Rubbing blood on his body, he mounted the lifeless corpse.

Kim was about to vomit. She drifted out of the room, back to the top of the stairs. Although she never saw the man's face, his body and movements were extremely familiar.

Unwilling to believe what she'd seen, she peeked back into the room. He was still in the midst of his passion, unaware of Kim's presence. It was the man at the bar, the easy-going man talking to Renee.

She was back inside the music-filled room. It took Kim a few moments to regain her composure. When she finally was able to deal with reality, she looked over to find Renee staring at her. The stranger was still babbling about his fabulous Sunday morning breakfasts and how successful he was.

Renee grabbed Kim's arm and pulled her away. Kim passed at least two people who staring at the dance floor with horrified expressions.

Renee dragged Kim to the relative quiet of the lobby, then stopped and whirled her around.

"Kim, you won't believe this. I saw someone being stabbed. Swear to God. This poor woman was...it was horrible. I saw someone being killed."

Kim was in shock. "I saw the same thing!"

Renee's grip tightened. "What does it mean? Oh, God, what should we do?"

"I don't know, Renee, but he looked like that guy over there." Kim nodded toward the bar. "The guy who's trying to pick you up."

"Jason? No, it didn't look anything like him. He's the nicest guy I've met here in six months."

She had to be kidding. If it wasn't him, it was a perfect likeness.

Kim grabbed Renee's shoulders. "You can't ever see him again."

"What are you talking about?"

"It was that guy, Renee. Wasn't it obvious? If you meet him somewhere else, promise me you won't go anywhere with him. Promise me right now."

"It wasn't him."

"Renee...."

"All right. All right. I won't go anywhere with him. I promise. Okay?"

RICHLIEU CEMETERY
WEST HARTFORD, CONNECTICUT
SATURDAY, MAY 30, 2026
11:28 A.M. EST

Renee's funeral was held in a pristine Connecticut cemetery. Kim stood in the back of the crowd as the mahogany casket disappeared into the ground. Her friend had been brutally murdered, stabbed more than twenty times, then dumped on the side of a road.

Why did she go back? Was she fascinated by what she'd seen in the bar? Kim glanced around at the two hundred solemn faces. Did any of them know Renee saw her own murder? Had any of them seen the vision? Kim turned from the grave and began walking back to her car feeling very much alone.

A powerful gust of wind pushed her from behind, causing her to stumble. An afternoon thunderstorm? No, the wind was too forceful, the sky too dark. She noticed trees being bent over, some touching the ground. Instead of maples and oaks, she was surrounded by tall pine trees. The grass was long and uncut. It waved furiously as the wind whipped it from side to side. The maelstrom increased in intensity. This was not New England.

Kim walked on, hoping the illusion would disappear. She was certain her car was close by. She managed a few steps and found herself at the edge of a large meadow. Directly ahead stood a towering column of pulsating yellow light that flowed like a golden river into the darkness above her. Energy surrounded the edge of the flowing column. Bright flashes filled the air. Powerful gusts of wind tugged and pulled at her. She felt weak, sick to her stomach.

Then she was being dragged across the field toward the pillar by a strong, tall man. She tried to fight, but her body would not respond. Looking down, she saw her leg had a bloodstained bandage wrapped around it. Her left arm was paralyzed. Her shirt sleeve was missing. Long, ugly gashes the length of her biceps had been crudely sewn together. Waves of pain washed over her body.

The wind increased in strength. Branches flew through the air. The pillar's beating had become more frantic, more powerful.

Kim was just at Renee's gravesite. What was she doing here? The burning in her limbs was so intense, she was about to pass out. Was this some of dream, some sort of hallucination?

"Into the light. Into the light," demanded the familiar whisper. "Fill the chamber with lead, it will destroy the ship."

To the left of the column appeared a dark figure, his face contorted in a loathsome sneer. He pulled a handgun from his belt and began firing. The man carrying her continued on track, running directly at the pillar of light.

"Into the light. Into the light," pleaded the voice. "Shoot the heart, the red heart. It's your only chance."

Dirt flew in her face as she crashed to the ground. The stranger at her side gripped his chest in pain. The wailing reached an unbelievable pitch, then the cylinder of light abruptly disappeared into the darkened sky. The wind stopped, and for a moment there was silence.

With a tremendous roar, the ground shook and split. Kim was lifted high above the scarred earth, high above her body. The area beneath her was torn by a series of incredibly powerful earthquakes.

"Prepare for the fight. You will need strength. You will need a Casull. You need Rick Peters. Go into the light."

Kim found herself lying on her back, staring up at a circle of faces.

"She's waking up."

"Are you all right?"

Kim struggled to sit up. Helping hands gripped her arms. "What happened?"

"Three of you fainted," said an elderly woman. "Fell to the ground screaming. We were so worried."

Kim glanced around. "There were others? Where?"

"They are over by that headstone."

Kim stumbled to the tall grave marker. "I'm sorry to bother you, but do you know a man named Rick Peters?"

The two women glanced fearfully at Kim. Without a word, they stood up and ran to a waiting car.

Kim sat on the cold marble, trying to gather her thoughts. Several people approached her, but she waved them off. She was tired, her arms and legs hurt. Her ears were ringing.

If Renee had listened to the voice, she would still be alive.

Apparently it was time to prepare for battle and find a Casull, whatever the hell that was.

# HIDING

ANGELES NATIONAL FOREST
LOS ANGELES COUNTY, CALIFORNIA
THURSDAY, JUNE 4, 2026
1:15 P.M. PST

Rick gripped the revolver with both hands and squeezed the trigger. Unable to control the recoil, Rick's hands rose in the air and hit him in the forehead.

"Damn."

Hank Evans couldn't help but chuckle. Obviously, Rick had never fired a gun before, certainly not this one. "First time with the Casull?"

Rick rubbed his head. "I didn't think it was that powerful."

Hank pointed at the shiny revolver. "The Casull is a big gun. It'll take time to get used to it. You might consider doing some exercises to increase the strength of your arms and upper torso. If you want to use this weapon effectively, you've got to be in control of the gun and your body. You sure you wouldn't like to work with a smaller piece? This thing's a cannon."

"That's probably why they wouldn't let me shoot it at the Van Nuys range."

Hank pushed his cap back on his head. "They were right to turn you away. This sucker'd blow a hole through their back wall."

"That's what they said. As for using another gun, I have no choice. I've bet a friend I could out-shoot him with this one. I've got eight hundred dollars on the line."

"I hear you, buddy. Okay. Let's get to work."

By three p.m. Rick's shoulders and arms were aching, but there'd been substantial improvement. Rick had hit the target, once.

"Mind if I ask you a question?" asked Hank as they walked back to their cars.

Rick's heart raced. It had only been a month since he'd "disappeared." He'd carefully molded his personality to the identity Curt provided. Could Hank have noticed that his new student was the notorious stockbroker Rick Peters? There was one way to find out.

"Ask away, Hank."

"Where'd you get the Casull?"

Rick tried not to show his relief at not being discovered. "Gunbroker.com."

"Of course, I should have known."

Rick pulled three crisp twenty-dollar bills from his wallet and handed them over. "I'll master this thing yet."

"You'll do fine, Rick. I must say, you're one of the most intense students I've had in years. First-timers usually back away when they feel that recoil. I'm impressed."

"It's important that I win this one." Rick made a mental note of the lie. Ultimately, his freedom could depend on his remembering what lie he told to whom.

Hank scratched the back of his head. "I guess that puts a little added stress on the situation, doesn't it?"

Rick shrugged. If Hank only knew.

"I want to thank you for taking such an interest in my situation. Don't think it isn't noticed."

"Not a problem, Rick."

Rick returned to his place in the quiet community of La Cañada, a small, unassuming town a dozen miles north of Los Angeles. The shooting lesson was the first time he'd ventured out other than to open a checking account and arrange to have his groceries delivered. He wished he could visit Patty and Sue, or even strike up a conversation with the attractive brunette at the bank. Apparently cold showers were going to become a way of life.

Rick cooked a simple meal and ate alone. Silence wasn't so bad; it was the waiting that was driving him crazy.

HOP BROOK APARTMENTS
NAUGATUCK, CONNECTICUT
SATURDAY, JUNE 13, 2026
4:15 P.M. EST

Kim Callaway's safe and secure job as an online advisor for Verizon Wireless was no longer an acceptable life choice. During the last four years she'd been saving money for an extended vacation to the Bahamas. Those funds were now earmarked for physical training, weapon purchases and daily needs. The thought of finding a strong, pleasant man who cared for her was shelved.

The Thursday after Renee's funeral Kim stood in front of her mirror and argued with herself.

"You're quitting your job, really?!?" she admonished the reflection.

"You saw what happened to Renee. You have no choice. You have to prepare."

"I don't have to do anything. I can find a decent man. I can go to the Bahamas. I can live my life any way I want. I do not have to believe this nonsense."

"Are you telling me you want to continue living the same way you've done for years? You want to keep dreaming about meeting some guy who doesn't exist, and if he did, wouldn't pay the slightest bit of attention to you if he saw you? Who are you kidding? This is a perfect reason to shake yourself out of your slump. Turn off the radio, turn off the television, get social media out of your life and turn on your mind. This is your wake-up call."

The following morning her job of helping strangers find the best cell phone package had come to an end.

"You're quitting?" Kim's supervisor, Dale Masters, was shocked. Quiet, sedate Kim Callaway was the last person he expected to seek higher ground.

"What's the problem, Kim? I know having to pay for your medical insurance hurts, but we all had to kick in."

"I can't work here any longer." She let the silence fill the room without attempting to fill it.

Dale knew he was losing a talented employee. It would take a minimum of three operators to replace her. "Would you care to explain why?"

"No."

"Are you getting married?"

"No."

"Tell you what, I'll double your vacation and let you have an opportunity at the next slot for weekend supervisor."

The threat of leaving was creating an opportunity for advancement. How absurd. She'd watched several of her incompetent co-workers climb the corporate ladder and disappear into the executive offices. Obviously the company appreciated aggressive behavior over cooperation.

"I'm leaving, Dale. It's nothing personal."

Now he was challenged. What would it take to make her stay?

"How about a raise, a dollar an hour on top of everything else I've offered. As a bonus, I'll let you coordinate training for freshmen operators. That'll get you off the live lines. You could teach these new people a lot."

"Thank you, but no. I should tell you, though, I could have used that money last year."

Kim paused. Dale knew he had her. The idea of a raise had finally sunk in.

Kim continued. "I believe I have enough vacation to cover my resignation if I give you notice today. I've never called in sick...."

"You know that doesn't matter, Kim." Now he was angry. She was playing with him.

"Guess I should have lied, like everybody else." She said it to herself as much as to Dale.

"I guess so."

Kim walked out of the brick building without looking back. The search for her Prince Charming would have to wait.

JOURNEY'S END ROAD
LA CANADA, CALIFORNIA
MONDAY, AUGUST 17, 2026
4:15 P.M. PST

The dream haunted him. He'd be fine for weeks, then when he wasn't thinking about it or regretting his abrupt change of life, it would catch him by surprise. It usually happened at night, while he was asleep. It hit him at work on one occasion. Luckily no one saw him slumped over his desk. It happened once in the evening, when he was taking his evening walk. That time, he found himself lying on the side of the road. He quickly brushed himself off and hurried back to his house.

Each time the experience was as painful as the first. The pillar was just as bright, the storm just as intense and the results just as fatal. In his small bedroom, at work, even the night on the deserted street, he'd awake drenched in sweat.

Rick suffered alone. Although it remained painfully apparent that this was the path he was supposed to follow, the solitude was unnerving.

Usually his evening walk was uneventful. Rick would travel the darkened streets of the small town. As he walked, he'd smell the fresh scent of the pines. He'd stare into the living rooms and kitchens of his unsuspecting neighbors. They were the lucky ones, these families and couples who lived normal, boring, frustrating lives. He was, alone, betting everything he had so that someday, he might join them.

Maybe, if a miracle occurred, he could get married, start a family. The temptation of leaving this self-imposed isolation constantly beckoned him, but he knew better. The vehicle that had brought him his so much money continued to warn him of the impending challenge. Rick gave up his freedom to gain a future...maybe.

When he returned home, he'd prepare for the next day. His Casulls would be cleaned, carefully inspected, then replaced in the hall closet. Eventually, there would be a day when he'd need them. The question was, would they make a difference?

HOP BROOK APARTMENTS
NAUGATUCK, CONNECTICUT
FRIDAY, NOVEMBER 27, 2026
4:18 P.M. EST

Kim's Callaway's life had changed radically. Her plump figure morphed into a svelte hard body. Daily workouts designed to increase endurance rather than muscle caused her teenage figure to reappear, which in turn had attracted an incredible number of men. But Kim had no time in her life for suitors.

The only person she'd spent any substantial time with over the past months was Randy, a middle-aged man who worked the lines for the phone company. He'd called a week after she quit and asked her to accompany him to a family picnic. She going to refuse, but changed her mind when he mentioned that there would be target-shooting.

The date turned into seven months of visits to a secluded firing range. A gun fanatic, Randy taught Kim how to handle everything from a .22 to an Uzi submachine gun. He also advised her on purchasing her revolvers. Once Callaway became proficient with firearms and bought her two .454 Casulls, she stopped seeing him. Saturday afternoon outings with Randy were replaced with endless laps around the high school track and solitary shooting practice in the forest.

Economically, times weren't much different than when she was working. She never had money to waste. She continued her trips home for free meals and spent practically nothing. Her apartment was cheap, and though her purchases of running shoes, sweats and Casulls set her back almost a two thousand dollars, if she was careful, her savings would last for at least three more years.

Her father did not understand her sudden change in appearance. Lord knows what would happen if he found out she'd dated a forty-year-old gun fanatic, or worse, that she'd quit the phone company. Employment was treated as a divine blessing in Arnold Callaway's house. Everything was sacrificed for THE JOB.

Kim kept her private life just as secretive. Still, each visit home started with a mini-inquisition. Her father would call her in to the living room, and with the ever-present television playing in the background, he'd quiz her about her life.

"I don't understand why you've lost so much weight. You dating some guy?"

"I went on a diet, dad."

"Why?"

"A voice said I should get fit before I died of heart disease. Do you know what the leading cause of heart disease is?"

"Poor eating habits?" he offered.

"Television. You should throw that thing away."

Arnold squinted at his daughter. "What's gotten into you, Kim? You seem to have acquired quite an attitude."

"Must run in the family. Seriously, why don't you get out more?"

"And miss these great games? That's what weekends are for, watching football."

"And baseball, and basketball and hockey...Dad?"

"Yeah?"

"That guy just stole a base."

She left him trying to figure out who stole what. She headed for the kitchen where her mother was preparing dinner.

Grace Callaway loved cooking. It was a creative art that not only nourished the body, but also the soul. Some of her best ideas came to her when creating a special meal. She heard Kim enter the kitchen but did not look up.

"Terry called for you yesterday. She wondered why you hadn't returned her messages. She was worried about you."

Kim had purposely avoided her few acquaintances. She'd quit the Saturday night bowling league, dropped her gun-toting Randy and exercised in the early morning or late evening to avoid running into the neighbors. Her answering machine took all her calls.

"Are you all right, Kim?" asked her mother.

Kim pulled a wooden spoon from a drawer and sipped at the soup. "Needs a bay leaf. Maybe two. Mom, I'm fine. I've just been busy."

Grace stopped stirring and looked at her daughter. The softness had disappeared from Kim's face. Her clothes hung loose. There was a determination in her eyes, but all was not well.

"When are you going to tell me, Kim?"

Damn. Her mother always knew when she was up to something. "Not right now, Mom."

"When?"

"Soon. Soon enough."

"It's not good, is it, Kim?"

"What makes you say that?"

"I know a lot more than you think. If you need someone to talk to..."

"Thanks, Mom. But this one I've got to do alone."

"You'll tell us when you're going to leave, won't you?"

"I'm not going anywhere."

"Just don't leave without saying good-bye."

The drive back to her apartment was depressing. Nothing seemed right. Being a recluse was no better than being a frumpy twenty-four-year-old heavyweight. How long could she wait before giving up and exploring the life she knew she could have?

LANCE WHITE'S APARTMENT
WESTWOOD, CALIFORNIA
FRIDAY, FEBRUARY 19, **2027**
10:13 A.M. PST

When the last of the "2027 Crazies" failed to supply Lance White with information concerning the pillar of light, his life as an NSA agent virtually disappeared.

There was an occasional report that someone had seen the oncoming Armageddon, but each time White investigated a report, he was stymied with quick denials. He never got another opportunity like the homeless men in Santa Barbara. He'd kept his budget alive by his manufacturing fake witnesses, people who didn't exist, but whose falsified files indicated that the "2027" scare was far from over. Until something substantial occurred, Lance White was in a holding pattern.

The brokers who'd seen the pillar of light and Rick Peters running toward it, recanted their stories. The others who'd confided in friends they'd witnessed a similar event, would not repeat their tales. White only had one hope: to find the elusive stockbroker who'd disappeared last May. He had a feeling that Rick Peters' fortune had something to do with the five homeless men.

He tried to convince the Agency to allocate resources to find Peters, but his superiors were unwilling to give him the needed computer access or manpower to make the search worthwhile. All White could do was wait, but he knew the right moment would come along.

ANGELES NATIONAL FOREST
LOS ANGELES COUNTY, CALIFORNIA
TUESDAY, MARCH 9, 2027
1:15 P.M. PST

Rick squeezed off six rounds from the Casull, popped the cylinder, jammed six new shells into the gun from his speed loader, slapped the gun closed and fired another six rounds.

Hank Evans was impressed. "That's some damn good shooting, Rick. I don't think there's much more I can show you."

Rick was pleased. He'd ripped the center out of the target and fired twelve rounds in less than seven seconds.

"Say, would you like to join me this weekend? I'm goin' up to Bakersfield. They've got a big competition and I think you'd knock their socks off."

Rick lowered his head. Wouldn't that be the best? Getting out of town and competing with some of the state's best shots? He'd worked hard to hone his shooting skills. It would be quite an accomplishment if he won.

"I'm afraid I can't, Hank."

"Come on Rick, you're really good. Let's show them your stuff."

"I'm sorry, Hank. I have to work. Trust me, I appreciate your asking. It means a lot to me."

"You sure you don't want to try?"

Rick nodded.

"Well, if you change your mind, give me a call. I've got friends who'll put us up if that's a problem."

Rick put his arm around Hank's shoulder. "Maybe next time, Hank. I've got this commitment...it's pretty important."

His job was so important he gave up everything. This commitment was getting on his nerves. When was something going to happen? Was anything ever going to happen?

BARNES AND NOBLE BOOKSTORE
HARTFORD, CONNECTICUT
TUESDAY, MARCH 9, **2027**
1:18 P.M. EST

If anyone asked Kim Callaway why she chose to browse the large bookstore near the University of Connecticut that afternoon, she'd probably say it was just something she felt like doing. She'd been using that special sense to guide her through the loneliness and frustration of waiting. Nothing of substance came of the trips to shooting ranges or state parks or libraries.

She'd spent the last hour in the New Age section, looking at titles about Roswell alien encounters, astrology guides, angel sightings and traveling into the final bright light of death. Sensing nothing special, she left the area and wandered to the travel section.

At the foot of the bookshelf was an assortment of picture books covering a range of wilderness areas from Tibet to Antarctica. She checked a few of the texts, but her interest dissipated. She turned and headed for the door.

Halfway to the exit she spotted a brilliant reflection in the front window. It came from the section she'd just left. She turned and was nearly blinded.

In a flash the light was gone.

An observant clerk noticed the young woman shielding her eyes with her forearm and came to her side.

"Can I help you? Are you okay?"

Kim ignored him and hurried back to the travel section. She scanned the titles. It was here somewhere. It had to be. Damn. She'd waited all this time, but she wasn't ready. It had to be in front of her. It had to be...

It was a picture book - "The Teton Wilderness" written by Dorl Carpenter. Kim grabbed the book and opened it. Her hands shook as she turned the pages. Containing colorful photos of the jagged peaks of the Tetons, lazy moose eating in the Snake River drenched in sunset reds, the tourist town of Jackson and the rugged back country of the Rockies filled the book, but the book contained no obvious sign, no animated vision, no coded message. Kim's excitement faded. She turned to the last two pages, a large fold-out aerial photo of the Jackson Hole area.

The light returned with a glare so intense she nearly dropped the book. This time she forced herself to look directly at the glare. In the center of the ski slopes, atop a small triangle of trees between two wide ski runs, was the source of the light.

And then it was gone.

Kim walked to the counter. "I'll take this."

The clerk scanned the book. The computer beeped angrily.

"It appears this book is not in our data base. Strange."

"Just tell me how much." Kim wanted to leave. She had to pack. She had to go.

"I'm not sure," said the clerk.

Kim removed her wallet, pulled five twenties out and placed them in front of the register.

"That should cover it."

She leaned over the counter, ripped the book from the man's hands and ran from the store.

# WARNINGS

OFF THE PACIFIC COAST
MARINA DEL REY, CALIFORNIA
SATURDAY, **SEPTEMBER** 11, **2027**
2:15 P.M. PST

The sailboat turned into the wind, its yellow fabric flapping wildly. Moments later the canopy reinflated and the boat resumed its journey across the blue-green Southern California waters. Rick and his date, Barbara Whitten, had been navigating the waters off the coast for several hours. When the turn was completed, Barbara noticed the bow was no longer pointing toward the open ocean.

"Heading back?" Barbara asked as she threw her braid of silky brown hair behind her.

Like I have a choice, thought Rick. He could not go back. The past held no protection. The future was his only hope.

"The marina's upwind." Rick pointed to the shoreline. "It'll take a while to get back to the harbor."

Barbara nodded, then turned her attention to the hypnotizing waves. Despite her initial reluctance to accept this blind date, she'd found Rick to be agreeably pleasant. An excellent sailor and a gentleman, the handsome green-eyed man created a warm emotional hum within her that she quickly grew to enjoy.

At first she thought the sensation a whim, but when Rick left her to settle the boat rental, the harmonious envelope vanished. When he returned, the warmth returned with him. Heading back to land was a disappointment not only because her unusual date was coming to a conclusion, but because the soothing feeling would end as well.

Rick adjusted the rudder and maneuvered close to the wind. He sensed the brunette shift her attention away from the water.

"What do you see, Barbara? Can you figure it out?"

She answered quickly, without thinking. "I see a man who's not sure what lies in his path. He has a tremendous challenge ahead of him and is going to meet it head on, very soon.

Rick was startled by her response. "That's very perceptive, Barbara. I'm impressed. You never did tell me what you did at the Foundation."

"I'm a historian and senior military analyst. I've also authored numerous articles on infantry weapons and their impact on recent military campaigns."

"Unusual field of study."

"For a woman, you mean."

"Not really. I meant for anyone," said Rick. "How do you research such a subject?"

"I visit skirmishes: Syria, Kashmir, Indonesia. I interview soldiers and observe them in action. I'm also considered one of the best marksmen in Southern California."

"I'll remember that."

Twenty-five miles in the distance, a line of dark clouds had formed over the Angeles National Forest. A late summer storm was approaching the Los Angeles Basin.

Rick pointed inland. "Looks like some weather up in the mountains."

Barbara nodded. "It'll be in the Valley this afternoon."

"And we'll probably drive right through it," said Rick.

"Most likely," she agreed.

It had been an unusual day for Rick. He'd stopped socializing eighteen months ago, when he assumed his new identity. He'd limited his personal contact to a handful of people at the Jet Propulsion Laboratory, where he worked. He rarely ventured out in the daylight and did his shopping online. Groceries were purchased using Instacart and delivered to the house.

Today he was out in the world, sailing with a woman named Barbara Whitten. He was here at the insistence of a co-worker. Initially he'd refused, continuing to protect his privacy, but when Rick heard about the unusual circumstances concerning her availability, Rick agreed to take her sailing.

Once a few words had passed between them, Rick realized the twenty-eight-year-old woman was intelligent and confident, someone he would have ignored in his former life. During those days, he would never consider talking to a woman who wasn't tan, passive and narrow hipped, despite his own two hundred and fifty pounds of softness. His pounds and prejudices were long gone.

Barbara accepted the afternoon rendezvous out of desperation, an action as foreign to her as sailing. Poised and conservative, she had a plan for every day of the week. It was not uncommon for her calendar to be filled in by the hour. But today's rectangle remained blank and unscheduled. One arrangement after another fell short of confirmation. The annoying space remained open. By Wednesday, she'd given up, figuring the day was meant for relaxation or a surprise event planned by one of her friends. Nothing happened. No one called. At nine that morning the couple who lived down the hall came knocking.

"A blind date?" Barbara was amazed at the audacity of her good-intentioned but meddlesome neighbors, "You arranged a date for me without asking?"

"You're the one who's been moaning about having nothing to do," countered Ted. He was tall, well-built, and enjoyed women as well as men. "We took care of it. What are friends for anyway?"

Barbara's frustration was obvious. She crossed her arms. "The last time I went out with one of your friends I was surrounded by every computer nerd in Southern California."

"Oh, lighten up," snapped Ted, waving his hand in the air, "I've heard that story ten times. Besides, Gary promised me that Rick's totally human. You might even like him."

"And what does that mean?"

"It means you're a picky military brat who wants a strong, tough guy who always gives in. Hard qualities to find in a man. Well, we found him."

Gary nodded seriously. "He's a professional. He's well-mannered, has a good job, is a straight-ahead guy who has been working much too hard."

"He's homy," commented Barbara.

"Aren't we all," Ted replied without missing a beat.

"Stop it," groused Gary, thwacking Ted on the arm. "Rick's a delight. You'll see. Come on, girl, get a move on."

On other day, at other time, Barbara would have refused to be a part of this unplanned encounter and chased her friends out of her apartment. But her inability to fill the maddening space in her appointment book forced her to agree. She had to do <u>something</u>. Three hours later, she was sailing the Pacific with a handsome bachelor who made her feel respected as well as desirable. It was as if the day had been planned in heaven.

With other men she'd dated, each word would be analyzed for clues about the man's education, his family history, relations and income sources. She especially took notice of personal hygiene traits. Rick was triggering a completely different response. His personal background, education and financial statement held no interest for her. Could she be in love after two hours? Barbara turned and looked at him again, but something foreign and threatening grabbed her attention.

"Watch out!"

Rick turned to spot a sizable yacht crossing their wake, mere yards behind them. Scattered about the deck of the expensive cruiser were dozens of bronzed bodies, in the skimpiest of swim suits. Although much too close, the boat powered harmlessly past their stern. With a moment's glance, Rick recognized the situation. He'd been on that boat and others like it many times. He probably knew most of the people onboard. As the yacht turned and ran alongside the small sailboat, Rick heard his name being called. Two women waved energetically from the bridge.

"Rick! Over here!"

Patty and Sue. Their glistening bodies motioned for him to maneuver closer, but Rick kept the rudder steady. There was nothing on that boat that could help him. Today, as yesterday and the day before, he was on a different course.

"Rick!" The two women jumped up and down insistently, their tanned breasts nearly coming out of their postage-stamp bikinis. "Where have you been? Come over and party."

Rick shrugged and looked over to Barbara. "Old friends."

"They certainly look friendly," Barbara commented. She wondered if the image of the two stunning women and Rick entwined in a boat cabin was the result of her being in the sun too long.

"Bring your date! She's cute!" called Patty, putting her arm over Sue's shoulder. "We love to share, remember?"

Yes, he remembered. Patty and Sue were always ready for anything, anytime. As the large boat turned, the women removed their bikini tops and waved a provocative farewell.

Barbara thoroughly enjoyed the show. It wasn't often she saw the randy, uninhibited ocean-going lifestyle she'd read about.

"Are they really old friends?" She didn't know anything about Rick. He could be playing mister nice guy for the day.

"It was another time in my life," he replied.

"Why'd you leave? Did you run out of money?"

Rick laughed. "Money is the least of my problems." He hesitated, checking his words. "I made a decision about my lifestyle last year, made some personal sacrifices." He pointed toward the retreating yacht. "You can only go so far on that boat."

"And how would you explain those extremely friendly women to your children?" asked Barbara. It couldn't hurt to test his feelings about kids, potential husbands and fathers liked them.

Rick squinted in the bright sunlight. The yacht was heading west, probably on its way to Catalina Island. If he guessed right, they'd be anchoring not fifty yards from where Natalie Wood drowned.

"I don't think that issue will come up," he said.

"Not having kids?"

"Oh, I want a family. But it's out of the question right now."

Barbara's interest was aroused. "What's stopping you? Lack of a suitable spouse?"

"I have a very important task to accomplish and have no idea how long it'll take. I was hoping you might have an inside track on that information."

"Me? Why would I know anything about your future?"

Rick let out the sheet a bit and turned the bow away from the wind. "Gary told me about the difficulty you had filling your social calendar today. It appears this a very unusual event for you. I was going sailing for the first time in a year and a half. I thought there might be more to this meeting than just a pleasant afternoon."

Barbara was confused. What was Rick talking about? She held a sensitive post at the Pasadena Foundation. Though she'd never been involved in a suspicious situation, there was always a first time.

"I'm afraid I can't help you, Rick."

Rick nodded knowingly. "The day isn't over," he said with confidence.

He was such an attractive, even-tempered man. No one had ever made her feel so comfortable.

"You don't know when this assignment will be completed?"

Rick leaned back on the side of the boat. "No. And there's no way to find out when it will start."

"Why don't you ask? You could be on the verge of completion."

"Who do I ask? I'm not even sure what the project is."

Barbara smiled. If nothing else, Rick was an interesting man. Was he telling the truth or avoiding the issue?

"I happen to know a fortune teller who might be able to help. We could stop on the way back to my place."

Rick smiled. "Now there's a different approach. Sure, let's give it a try."

"What if you don't like her answer?"

"It wouldn't bother me," grunted Rick as he pulled in the sail to start a new tack, "But it might cause you to alter your way of thinking, perhaps change your life."

Barbara laughed. Sonya was a reasonably accurate psychic, but she'd never revealed anything drastic or disturbing. "I doubt I'd be troubled by your project."

The boat was left at the marina. Rick and Barbara returned to Rick's white Fiat.

"Want the top down?" Rick asked as he opened the door for her. "I hate leaving the ocean and it's such a boring drive back to the Valley. With today's beach traffic it'll probably take hours. A little wind would take the edge off."

"It's a great day," said Barbara, enjoying the gentle hum Rick created in her. "Go ahead, put the top down."

Despite the heavy traffic, the never-ending wall of cars continuously parted, allowing them to cross the city with ease. Barbara directed Rick through the downtown area, up the Golden State Freeway into the city of Burbank. A mile down a surface street, the Fiat pulled to the curb. Rick raised the top and secured it with Barbara's help.

As they walked past a park toward a small cluster of commercial buildings, Rick noticed an aging military aircraft towering above a local park entrance. A shiny spot on the fuselage of the F-104 Starfighter cast a circular reflection on a nearby building, an occult bookstore.

"If we're lucky, Sonya will have an opening," said Barbara, oblivious to the jet or its reflection. "She's very good."

"How do you know she's good?" Rick continued to examine the reflective spot on the side of the run-down storefront.

"When she was fifteen, her father threw her out of the house because she refused to stop reading the Tarot. He was a fiercely religious man and considered her hobby blasphemous. Most of her clients still swear by her and travel hours to be with her. She's that good."

Once inside, Barbara talked to the clerk while Rick examined the store. The walls were covered with paperbacks about the famous psychic Edgar Cayce, psychology through visualization, and the prophecies of Nostradamus. In the center aisle were herbs and dozens of metaphysical self-help manuals. Rick picked up a book. He skimmed through a few pages and was captivated by an article about coincidence, how it doesn't exist, that every action is either planned by someone or is a result of someone else's decision.

By the time Barbara returned, he was examining a two-thousand-dollar crystal ball.

"Rick," she said apologetically, "I didn't mean to drag you here against your wishes. If you're not comfortable, you can back out."

A far-off rumble indicated the storm was reaching into the Valley.

"I have no problems with this," he replied. "Would you like to join me?"

Barbara searched Rick's green eyes for some clue as to what he was thinking, but became lost in his gaze. It took more than a little effort to pull herself out of her semi-trance. How could she place so much trust in a man she'd only known a few hours? Was she being set up for a horrible experience?

Rick shook his head. His light brown hair was still matted from sea salt. "No need to worry, Barbara. I'm not at all dangerous, not today. There's only information to be gained. That's why you brought me here, isn't it?"

Barbara was surprised he'd read her so easily. She made a mental note to be more aware of her expressions and body language.

"I think I'd like to know some more about this mysterious responsibility of yours."

"And so you shall," he replied with a small grin.

For clairvoyant Sonya Glenhurst, this day was similar to other Saturdays. Her schedule was filled from early morning to late afternoon, with the exception of one cancellation.

Her clients were varied and pleasant. No Earth-shattering revelations were made and no terminally ill cases had presented themselves. Her next clients were in the hallway. She immediately recognized Barbara Whitten, one of her regulars.

"Barbara. I didn't expect to see you so soon."

"Hi, Sonya. Actually, this visit isn't for me. I'd like you to meet my friend Rick. He's your client."

Rick nodded and offered a small smile. "Good afternoon, Sonya."

"No last name, Rick?"

Barbara looked at him. It was his decision.

"Peters. The name is Peters."

A puzzled look swept across Barbara's face, until he winked at her. Her confidence returned. Perhaps Rick feared telling Sonya his real name, an understandable reaction when visiting a mystic for the first time.

As Sonya shook the strong man's outstretched hand, a soothing sensation descended upon her. There was something familiar deep within his emerald eyes. She decided she liked him, but felt that he posed an unusual challenge. A sharp crack of thunder shook the building.

"I hope the rain will wait until we're finished." Sonya pointed to the ceiling. "It makes a racket on the metal roof." She motioned toward an open door. "Please come in."

The only furniture in the dark room was a wooden desk and several folding chairs. Barbara and Rick sat next to each other. As Sonya walked around to the other side of the desk, her long, paisley skirt made a rustling sound that echoed off the plywood paneling. A soft pool of light fell from a small lamp onto the desk.

Once she was settled, Sonya folded her hands and looked directly at Rick. "I thought you should know the client scheduled for this time canceled half an hour ago."

Barbara nodded, drawing Sonya's attention from Rick. "Yes, they told us at the front desk."

"He said someone needed the time more than he did."

"Maybe he was using that as an excuse to get out of the appointment," said Barbara as she tried to get comfortable in the metal chair.

"Perhaps." Sonya shifted her focus. "What do you think, Rick?"

"Some coincidences are far more important than they appear," he said.

"That would mean they weren't coincidences, wouldn't it?"

"That's right."

"Rick was thinking of starting a family," Barbara heard herself saying. "Before he can pursue that goal, he has an important assignment to complete. His question concerns when that job will be finished."

"Is that correct, Rick?"

He glanced at her deck of faded cards that sat conspicuously upon a red silk scarf.

"Barbara suggested you might be able to identify the start of this situation."

"A great deal of what happens in this room depends on you."

She wrapped her fingers around the cards and offered them to Rick. He accepted the timeworn deck without comment.

Barbara watched Rick skillfully manipulate the cards. When finished, he placed the cards between Sonya and himself. "I believe they're in the proper order."

Sonya took the deck and dealt fifteen cards, five groups of three, then returned the remainder to the indentation on the scarf. Her broad hands adjusted the cards, putting them into neatly organized rows. Slowly, her expression changed from professional contentment to one of confusion.

"I'm stunned. Every card here is a major arcana." Her voice became laced with mistrust. "Rick, do you know what you're going to be doing?"

"Let's say it involves a number of serious problems and most likely several deaths."

"Have you told anyone about this project?"

"Barbara was the first. You're the second."

"Rick, this is the most intense grouping of cards I've ever seen. Are you aware how unusual this situation is?"

Rick nodded. "The task is of great importance. No doubt the cards reflect that. I hope they can be specific about times and dates. By the way, what is today's date?"

Sonya looked at her watch. "September 11th."

"An easy date to remember." Rick pointed to her wrist. "Do me a favor and check your watch next time you find yourself in a strange place. It may provide a clue for us."

"I'll keep that in mind," she said, becoming wary of Rick's intentions.

Could he have rigged the deck? She took one last look at the cards, then began. "You will be confronting a great force, a force larger and stronger than yourself. There will be a battle, but it will not take place here." Her eyes swept the desk then pointed to the upper left card. "The confrontation will occur soon."

"How soon?"

"I cannot tell. It could be any time over the next three months. You have been training. This will prove helpful. The discipline you have acquired will increase your chances of success."

Rick scanned the cards. They reflected a yellowish incandescent light from the desk lamp, taking on an eerie glow. Reaching out, he tapped the nearest card. "The waiting is over, isn't it?"

"Yes, the waiting is over, Rick," said Sonya staring blankly at the cards.

"Will there be anyone else involved?"

"Others are considering the call. Most do not believe. Only a few will come to your side. Three will be women. One will be severely injured. There will be many deaths."

Barbara was shocked. She'd never heard Sonya utter a negative word.

"Battle? Deaths? Are you sure?"

Rick ignored the interruption. "Is Barbara one of the women?"

"She has not decided. There is another female. She is traveling to meet you. You will need each other to survive. Do not leave her side."

"Where will I find her?"

Sonya's eyes were closed tight. "She is not in this city."

"Is there anything else?"

"Handguns are very important. You must keep at least one, maybe two with you at all times. Casull is the name of the gun."

Barbara recognized the name of the firearm, one of the most powerful revolvers, far more potent than Dirty Harry's famed .44 magnum. Why would Rick need a Casull?

A blinding yellow flash filled Sonya's mind. As the glare subsided and her vision cleared, she was no longer with Barbara and Rick, but standing in a dark, windswept forest. Through the tall, narrow trees she saw a bright light. Walking toward the glow, she noticed movements in the shadows.

The glare increased bringing more light into the forest. Sonya spotted Marines scurrying for cover among the pines. She continued toward the source of the illumination. The closer she came to the light, the stronger the wind became, until a tumultuous howling filled her ears.

When Rick's hand touched the cards, Barbara was also transported to the strange forest, experiencing everything along with Sonya. She tried to force her mind to return to the safety of the bookstore, but the images overtook her. Her ears filled with the deafening roar. She moved to the edge of the forest to see a large, flat meadow covered in white billowing mist. The sky hung black and starless.

Powerful winds ripped at Sonya's hair and clothing. Thick branches flew through the air, smashing into the forest. Howling wind gusts shifted direction every few seconds, bending weaker trees to the ground then releasing them, only to push them down again.

Directly ahead of her, in the middle of the meadow, stood a monumental pillar of yellow light, illuminating the clearing with pulsating glow. The colossal cylinder flowed like a vertical river into the darkness above.

Sonya checked her watch. It was eight-thirty in the morning. The date was September 14th.

The ground heaved upward with a tremendous groan and split directly beneath the searing yellow pillar. The earthquake knocked Sonya off her feet. As she waited for the Earth to stop moving, she realized she was not afraid. She was a protected observer. No harm would come to her.

When the shaking stopped, Sonya stood and walked toward the mesmerizing light. Someone rushed past her. No, it was two people. One of them was hurt. The injured person appeared to be a woman. The pair struggled toward the sparkling column with difficulty.

Shots rang from the nearby trees, some from where the Marines had taken cover. Bullets ricocheted off unseen boulders. The man carrying the injured woman was Rick Peters.

Bolting from a different direction came another figure. Sonya sensed something familiar about the man, something about the way he ran. It took her a few seconds for her to realize it was her father, Major Walter Glenhurst, racing toward Rick in an obvious attempt to intercept him.

Elongated shadows on nearby trees made the chase look like a bizarre puppet show. The wind howled. Trees swayed. The gusts shifted direction, throwing Rick and his partner off balance. The two stumbled, then regained their stride.

Major Glenhurst stopped and raised his M-16. To the left of the column, a third man appeared, firing a handgun. Rick veered to the right, but the change in direction did not protect him. He fell to the ground. Mortally wounded, Rick attempted to continue, crawling toward the column. The woman did not move.

Glenhurst shouldered his weapon and ran to the fallen man. Kneeling next to him, the Major gently restrained Rick from moving. His hands were slick with sweat. Dark runnels of sweat tracked his face.

"It's over, Rick. We can't let you go on."

"Into the light," gasped Rick, "Bring your men. You have to continue into the light."

"I can't do that, Peters."

"You must!"

Rick made an attempt to stand, but had no strength. Slumping back to the ground, he saw Sonya watching over them. He painfully turned his body.

"Sonya, tell him. He will die. You will die. Everyone will die. He must go into the light."

The wailing of the cylinder abruptly stopped and was drawn into the black sky. Soft warm sunlight flooded the meadow. The winds stopped, and for a brief moment there was peace, loneliness.

Then, with a wail louder than the wind, the rip in the Earth widened. The ground rocked as a massive shock wave rolled across the area. Sonya was lifted to safety, high above the Earth. She watched as the area beneath her was twisted and mangled by a series of powerful earthquakes. Glenhurst, Rick, everything was swept into a giant hole. She continued her ascent. Within seconds she could see hundreds of miles in all directions.

One area after another was engulfed in violent volcanic and seismic disruptions. The entire continent was consumed with devastation. There was nowhere to hide.

Sonya was back in her darkened room, sitting behind her desk. In front of her, the remarkable grouping of cards remained untouched.

Rick waited a few moments to regain his bearings while Sonya and Barbara calmed down. Once they were aware of their surroundings, he spoke.

"Are both of you okay?" he asked quietly.

Sonya checked her body. She felt no pain. Her hair was in place. Everything appeared to be the same as it was before the vision began. Barbara did not move.

"I'm all right," Sonya replied after making a second check. "How about you, Barbara?"

The dazed brunette managed a nod.

"Good," said Rick, satisfied neither of the women had been harmed. "It's always a shock, no matter how many times you go through it. I've had this vision at least once a month for the past year and a half. I know if I can reach that light, I can avert the disaster that follows."

Despite being a professional fortune-teller, Sonya had never witnessed a spiritual occurrence. She made her predictions using personal information offered by her clients, common sense and, as a last resort, indications from the cards. She was not convinced what she'd just experienced was a supernatural event.

"It was a dream, Rick. There's no need to panic."

Rick sat back in his chair. "I am not panicked, Sonya, nor am I asleep. What you saw was no dream. It will happen. I need to know how much time I have before it begins. That's why I'm here."

Barbara's heart was pounding. She'd been near many skirmishes, bombings and full-scale assaults, but she'd never witnessed such widespread destruction.

"That's about to happen?"

"Not exactly," Rick replied with a reassuring calm in his voice, "The future constantly changes. It swerves and redefines itself. As people change their minds and then their actions, the oncoming reality is in flux until the present arrives. I will have to confront those men sometime soon. Hopefully, we can come to an understanding before the pillar of light disappears." Rick's attention shifted. "How long, Sonya? Could you tell?"

"I have no idea... wait! It was eight-thirty on the..." She looked down at the date window on her watch in an attempt to jog her memory. "It was September 14th! Three days from today."

Rick's shoulders relaxed. His face took on a completely different appearance, as if he'd moved onto another level, like when one completes a task and a fresh challenge is faced.

"I had a feeling it would be soon. Now, Sonya, think carefully. Could you tell anything about the location?"

"It happened so fast. But those mountains... I thought it was somewhere near Colorado or Montana."

Rick threw his hands in the air. "Of course! The Rockies. I assumed those mountains were the Sierra Nevadas. This is very exciting."

"What happens now?" asked Barbara, almost afraid to hear the answer.

Rick silently admired Barbara's courage. Scared and confused by the realistic vision, she'd maintained her composure, fought her fear and continued to be involved. Personal growth was considerably more impressive than a half-hearted execution of God-given talents. But this was not the time or place to discuss his future plans.

He stood, towering over the women. "It's time for me to go. Thank you, Sonya."

"I hope this was helpful, Rick," she sighed, relieved the session was ending.

Rick looked deep into her brown eyes. "You recognized that soldier," he said kindly. "Talk to him, Sonya. I have to reach that light. Tell him what is going to happen. He'll listen to you. Our lives depend on your going to him. Don't let us down."

The thought of telling her father she'd witnessed a psychic vision brought a cold fear to her heart. There was no telling how violent he would become.

"I'll do what I can," she said, hoping the tall man wouldn't pursue the matter.

Rick turned to Barbara. "Let's go." With a quick movement he was out of the room. Barbara caught up to him outside the store.

"I was not impressed with that silly trick," Barbara said angrily. "You took advantage of my friend and scared the hell out of me."

A brilliant flash of lightening ripped across the dingy sky followed by a mighty clap of thunder.

"I did not force you in there. And I specifically warned you that it wouldn't be pleasant. As for what is or isn't going to happen, much of it is up to you."

"I'm not falling for this mumbo-jumbo, Rick. And no, it wasn't pleasant in the least. What is it with you? Do you enjoy making fools of strangers?"

Rick stopped at the side of the car, frustrated with her inability to believe. What more proof did she need? A goddamned program?

"What you saw was my future, Barbara. If Sonya doesn't talk to that Marine, that's where I'll be stopped, killed, ambushed. And if I'm stopped, you and everyone you know will be dead. That's what you saw, Barbara. You saw the end of the world; at your own request, I might add."

"And I'm supposed to believe this preposterous story, Mister Peters?" she shot back with equal attitude. "What kind of idiot do you think I am?"

"Get in and I'll explain everything."

"In the car? With you? You've got to be kidding."

"Suit yourself," he said unlocking the door as fat drops of rain fell from the dark, angry clouds.

Barbara hesitated, then sat in the front seat, leaving the door ajar. By the time Rick settled into the driver's seat, he was drenched.

"What's going on?" demanded Barbara as rain blew into the car. "Why have you done this to me?"

Rick ran his hands through his soaked hair, then turned to face her.

"I haven't done anything to you. Are you going to keep the door open?"

"Until I find out who you are, yes."

"Fine. My name is Rick Peters. I used to be a stockbroker. Close the door, please. I can't afford to get sick."

Totally soaked, Barbara complied with his request.

"Thank you," he said, rubbing his hands on his chest to dry them. "I suppose you'd like to hear the story."

"I think it would be appropriate."

There was a reason Barbara entered his life. With so little time left, he would need all the help he could find. According to Sonya, there was a possibility Barbara might be involved in the final event.

As the storm raged outside the car, Rick told her about his Lamborghini test drive, seeing the prophetic billboard, and how he'd used the information to make hundreds of millions over the course of that exciting day.

Barbara gasped. "You're that guy who made all the money when that jet crashed off the coast of New York."

"That's me."

"You blew up the plane."

"Yeah, right. You must be kidding. I blew up a plane hoping five powerful Dynotech executives would miraculously survive and that the company's stock would plunge and then recover in six hours. Who would believe that story? I am amazed at the crap people will accept as true simply because it's said on television. No, Barbara, I didn't have anything to do with the plane or the explosion. I had a lot to do with that day's stock trades. I noticed that, as my co-workers joined in or bailed, their decisions affected the stock's movement. That's what give me hope I might have a chance of reaching that pillar, especially if Sonya talks to that Marine. That's also why, if you go to the authorities, I could be stopped before I reach that meadow.

"I made over nine hundred million dollars in a few hours, but at the end of the day, when I was about to become a happily retired man, I saw what you saw today, only without the girl. My guess is she's changed her mind about going to the meadow."

Barbara frowned. "Let me see if I've got this right. You experienced a vision, made millions, and now you have to save the world because of a second prophecy?" Barbara shook her head with a smirk, "You don't expect me to believe this crap, do you?"

Rick's expression turned fierce. "I'm not <u>asking</u> you to believe anything. In a couple of days you'll have plenty of proof, if that's what you need. It makes no difference whether you believe it or not, this planet is going to self-destruct if I don't get to that light.

"It's not my fault this is going to happen and it's not my fault you went into that room and saw what you did. I'm just trying to do the right thing. I believe what you saw will occur, just like I believed the stock market would react the way I was shown. Faith is the key, Barbara. You don't believe and are afraid. I totally accept it and I'm petrified. The difference is that I'm going to do something about it."

He grabbed his keys and started the car. "If I don't get to that light, you're never going to find a husband or have a family." He pulled into traffic. "It's time to take you home. I've got some packing to do."

The fifteen-minute ride was made in silence. Rick fumed over Barbara's inability to accept what she'd experienced. How could she deny being on that plateau? She must have felt the wind and the earthquakes. He took in a breath. If his next few days were filled with skeptics like her, he'd never get to that light.

Barbara was lost in thought. Should she believe this man? Was he really the Rick Peters who'd disappeared eighteen months ago or was he making that up? If he was the fugitive stockbroker suspected of causing over a hundred and fifty deaths, shouldn't she turn him in to the authorities? But if she turned him in, didn't that mean she believed him? Most disturbing of all, why couldn't she fill her appointment calendar today? How deep did this conspiracy reach?

Rick walked her to the entrance of her building.

"Good-bye," Barbara said quickly. She turned to unlock the security gate. Rick held her shoulders and gently pulled her around to face him. His deep green eyes captured her as he spoke.

"Barbara, if you're considering calling the authorities, please, wait a day or two. See what happens. You'll have plenty of proof this is true before Tuesday. Just have a little patience, please."

There was a desperation in his face she could not ignore. She wanted to believe him, but the idea of the world coming to an end within the next four days wasn't a concept that she could accept.

"I won't tell anyone, Rick. I just pray that you're wrong."

Rick nodded. "You won't regret your decision."

He turned and left her alone. Barbara unlocked the gate to find Ted and Gary waiting for her in the rain-soaked courtyard.

"I told you he was different," said Ted.

GLENHURST RESIDENCE
OCEANSIDE, CALIFORNIA
SATURDAY, **SEPTEMBER** 11, **2027**
8:25 P.M. PST

Sonya Glenhurst was amazed at how well her visit with her parents had progressed. She'd bought a feminine Laura Ashley dress for the occasion, something she would never wear under any other circumstance. Though she feared confronting the Major, he almost looked pleased when he opened the door. A few more wrinkles and a sprinkling of gray hair gave him a look of sophistication.

Nancy Glenhurst was overjoyed. She'd never seen her daughter look so pretty. For the next hour, the three Glenhursts talked about the neighborhood, traffic, the recent thundershowers and military cutbacks. The reunion went smoothly as Sonya carefully avoided any sensitive subject, especially that of her Tarot readings.

She lied and told her parents she worked as an accountant for a small Burbank manufacturing firm and that she belonged to a Presbyterian church. That information brought a smile to the Major's face.

A pleasant dinner was followed by more reminiscing of Sonya's early childhood. After hearing about her father's impending maneuvers, Sonya excused herself and headed for the stairway.

"Why don't you use the downstairs bathroom," suggested her mother.

"Would you mind if I glanced into my old room?" Sonya asked politely. "It's been such a long time."

"Go ahead," said the Major, delighted with how much his daughter had matured. There'd been no talk of mystics or those damn cards. Maybe she'd left all that heresy behind and become a normal woman. Could it be his little girl had finally grown up?

Sonya walked up the stairs and glanced through the first doorway on the left. What used to be her only refuge was now a sparsely furnished sewing room. There was no indication she'd ever lived there. Tiptoeing down the hallway, she crept into her parents' bedroom and opened the closet. On the floor was her father's dark green duffel bag, always packed in the event he was called into service at short notice. The bag had been in the same place for as long as she could remember. She pulled an envelope from inside her dress and carefully slipped it under his shaving cream and tee shirts. Sonya closed the closet door and stood alone in the room.

"What are you doing?" came her father's voice from behind her.

"I couldn't help myself, Dad. My room has changed so much, I felt lost, so I came in here. It's exactly how I remember it."

"Come on downstairs," he said, putting his arm around her. "There's nothing up here for you."

As they returned to the living room, Sonya thought her heart would burst. I'm okay, she thought. He can't read my mind.

"Did the room bring back memories, Sonya?" asked her mother as Sonya returned to the flowered couch.

"Yes. I can't tell you how wonderful it was living here, Mom." Her palms were beginning to sweat again. Although she was no stranger to confrontation, she was terrified of her father's temper. "What about boys? Are you seeing anyone?"

Her mother wanted to know about the boys in her life. Boys. She was twenty-seven years old, for God's sake. There were no "boys" in her life, but this was the opening she needed. She hoped her nervousness would not affect her voice.

"There is someone," she said, choosing her words carefully. "He's tall, very good looking and has the most gorgeous green eyes."

"Really?" said Nancy Glenhurst, delighted to hear her daughter had found someone in her life. She'd always worried Sonya would remain single because of her weight. Maybe this relationship opened the possibility of having a son-in-law, even grandchildren.

"Actually," continued Sonya, "He's taken on a very large project. He's traveling right now."

"Oh? Where?" asked Nancy Glenhurst.

"Wyoming," Sonya replied, her mind flashing to the incredible destruction she'd witnessed. "Dad, you're going to be meeting him soon."

"Me? Where?"

Sonya wasn't sure she wanted to ruin the most entertaining evening she'd ever spent with her parents. Her father was taking the time to listen to her as if he actually liked her. With the next few words, all that security and love would evaporate.

Maybe Rick Peters had pulled a cruel trick on her. Maybe she'd experienced an illusion, seeing something that wouldn't necessarily come true. Maybe she just wanted her father's acceptance. Forget this saving-the-world crap. All she wanted in life was to have people, especially her father, like her.

The reality of the situation sunk in. She'd spent the last three hours talking about the weather, lying about boyfriends, jobs and faking her religion while sitting in a ridiculous dress made for wispy blondes. There was no place for her in this house. It was time to act.

"You're going to meet him in a day or two, Dad. You'll both be in a meadow. It's going to be dark and very windy. He's going to run toward a shaft of light. Dad, you've got to help him. You've got to listen to him. Our lives depend on it."

Nancy Glenhurst was confused. "I don't understand, Sonya..."

"What meadow?" The Major's expression changed from that of a relaxed man to an angry, dangerous beast. Sonya wasn't talking about her boyfriend. She'd returned to his house to practice witchcraft.

"I understand what this is about!" he shouted. In a blur of motion he was on his feet, standing over his daughter.

"You have to help him, Dad. His name is Rick... "

He grabbed her arm and pulled her out of the chair.

"Peters. Rick Peters..."

"I thought we'd finished this," he said, dragging her to the front door. "You have some nerve, bringing your black sorcery into my home. If your mother wasn't here..."

Her shoulder ached from his vise-like grip. "Dad, you must help him!"

He glared at her with disgust as he opened the front door. "Get out of my house," he said menacingly.

Sonya stood in the doorway, refusing to leave. "Tell me you understand. Tell me you'll think about what I've said. You can't follow orders your entire life."

"Get out!"

She moved to one side, away from the opening. "Dad, there are situations where you must think for yourself, no matter what your commanders tell you. You have to let Rick Peters get to the light."

He grabbed her shoulders with both hands. Though he didn't use half his strength, he threw her out the door. Sonya stumbled, then fell on the front step. Emotionally shaken, she slowly stood up and glared at him.

"You have to listen," she said slowly. "The man's name is Rick Peters."

Glenhurst raised his hand to hit her.

"Walter!"

Nancy Glenhurst ran to shield Sonya from her husband. She quickly guided her away from the porch.

"Go, Sonya," she said forcefully. "You can never come back. It's not safe. It never was."

Sonya gave her mother a hug as tears streamed down her face.

"What about you?"

"I'll be fine."

"I love you, Mom."

"I love you too, Sonya. Now go!"

712 JOURNEY'S END ROAD
LA CAÑADA, CALIFORNIA
SATURDAY, **SEPTEMBER** 11, **2027**
8:35 P.M. PST

Rick returned to his small rented home in the foothills of the Angeles National Forest. For the next several hours he gathered and sorted his gear in the center of his living room - knapsack, water bottles, dehydrated food, waterproof matches, compass, maps, hunting knife, poncho, down jacket, survival tent and long underwear. Everything he could think of had been purchased online from Amazon.com. Last to join the equipment, kept in an unmarked box, were his two Casulls and boxes of 300 grain bullets.

As he sat on his tattered living room couch, Rick surveyed the neatly organized piles. A surge of panic gripped his chest and held him motionless. How was he ever going to get across that meadow? Why was he, an irresponsible playboy, picked for this selfless job? Sure, he'd been dissatisfied with his life, wanted to make his mark on the world, but who didn't? That was no reason to throw this insane responsibility on his shoulders.

Fear pulled his body into a knot, causing him to clench his hands. Even if he managed to avoid the mystery shooter, what was inside that pillar and why was he trying to reach it? Why hadn't he been told more? Who was in charge of this insanity?

He glanced down and noticed his clawed fists. He was resisting again. Damn, of course he was resisting. First, he'd been fooled into thinking he had magical powers. Now he had to avoid being killed by some stranger, only to jump into some stupid light. And for what? To save mankind? God, he wished someone else had been chosen, someone more able, more confident.

He ran his hands through his short hair. There was no turning back. For whatever reason, he'd been offered a chance. If he dealt with circumstances as they occurred, he might succeed, he might be able to return to some kind of life where he could walk the streets, go shopping or talk to people without constantly looking over his shoulder. Fearing the future only increased the possibility of failure. Just as the dream changed, his destiny would remain in flux until it became the present. There was hope. He had to continue to believe.

The tightness in his chest slowly dissipated. He took another breath and headed for the kitchen. After fixing a light dinner, he retreated to the back porch and ate while he watched the last of the storm's black clouds rush across the sky.

# SIGHTINGS

JET PROPULSION LABORATORY
PASADENA, CALIFORNIA
SUNDAY, SEPTEMBER 12, 2027
5:15 A.M. PST

Two short miles from Rick's house, nestled among a grove of pine trees, was the world-famous Jet Propulsion Laboratory. The sprawling complex provided a workplace for thousands of scientists, researchers and military personnel. Throughout the week the campus-like facility hummed with activity. On Saturday and Sunday, the action calmed. Parking lots were deserted, the buildings mostly vacant. Only a several hundred obsessed researchers and the weekend staff remained on the premises.

Yet, Rick Peters could be found at his station every day. From before dawn until dusk, Rick scanned hundreds of computer reports concerning background radiation in the constellation Sagittarius. He never traveled, never vacationed, never socialized. He was dedicated to his low-security, insignificant civilian job.

Rick's white Fiat slowed as it approached the sentry box. Security guards were an important part of Rick's life. These men always seemed to know what was happening in and around the company. It was good to be on friendly terms with them.

"Morning, Rick," came the upbeat greeting from Mike, the cheerful weekend sentry. The gate did not move. Rick slowed to a stop as the heavy-set man left his tiny glass booth, sauntered up to the car and leaned on the door.

"Somebody's been asking about you." Mike's eyes darted toward the complex. "An investigator was snooping around after you left yesterday, asking a lot of questions. Do you remember that stockbroker who made millions on the Dynotech scare a while back?"

"Vaguely," replied Rick, looking confused.

"I sure do. The guy made a boatload of money, was suspected of sabotaging a plane, and all of a sudden he disappeared with millions in cash. Well, get this, they think you know something about it, and if you want my opinion, they think you're the guy."

Mike snorted loudly, expressing his disbelief. "Can you believe that? I told them you'd be the last person to blow up a plane and you certainly weren't no millionaire."

Mike's expression turned serious. "Then the guy said the strangest thing. He asked if you'd ever talked about a column of light. He sounded like a one of those 2027 nutcases, if you know what I mean. Watch yourself, Rick. From what I hear, the snoop's been talking to upper management, and you know how jumpy they can be. Can't risk their government funding."

Rick smiled, looking totally unconcerned, hoping his nervousness didn't affect his voice. "Thanks for the tip, Mike. Let me know if you see him again."

Mike waved him past. "No problem. See you later."

The gate rose and Rick drove into the complex. This was trouble. If the SEC got their hands on him, it would mean weeks of questions, dealing with lawyers and the press. The Federal Aviation Administration probably had a few questions of their own about what happened to Flight 755.

More troubling was this guy knew about the light. Was he someone who'd come to help? It didn't sound like it. No one had come forth with any more Apocalypse stories since the men in Santa Barbara disappeared. Considering what Mike told him, it seemed his days at JPL were numbered.

Curt had done a great job of helping Rick disappear. Rick Bradley was a new identity that easily passed the standard JPL background check. Because he wasn't working a sensitive militarily position no one cared about his past. They were more than pleased someone had taken the boring, underpaid position.

Leaving his car in an unmarked parking space, Rick entered a three-story concrete building. There were other guarded structures containing highly classified equipment that spied on the world. Rick had no interest in looking down on the planet. His concern was in the distant reaches of space.

He opened an unmarked door and entered a small, cramped office. When he first took the job, the sticky hinges gave him trouble. After months of daily workouts, the door was no longer a challenge. He powered his way into the office without thinking about the former obstacle.

Along the beige walls of the small office were framed posters of the Earth reaching to the sky: Mount Everest, the Grand Tetons, the Matterhorn, the Himalayas and K2. The majestic formations were even more impressive when viewed against the monotone cinder block of his boring walls. Every day, Rick made it a point to look at the spectacular land formations. In those few moments, he reminded himself why he'd changed so drastically, why he kept such a rigid schedule, and why he would consider murder to maintain his freedom.

He filled a stained coffeemaker, flipped on the power and left the office. Down the hallway, he entered a massive machine room bursting with printers, oscilloscopes and flatscreen monitors. As he headed to his printer, he passed portly Keith Grunderson hunched over a computer terminal, surrounded by every kind of junk food imaginable. Grunderson, an ex-musician turned computer fanatic, continued to concentrate on his glowing display. Rick tore his pages from the printer.

An already burdened swivel chair complained as Grunderson turned at the sound of ripping paper. He put a half-eaten Snickers bar on top of a multi-million-dollar computer, flipped his long hair out of his face and motioned to Rick.

Rick folded the printouts into a thick, organized pile and approached his fellow researcher.

"How's it going, Keith?"

Grunderson pointed at a large radar-like device and swallowed. "Hey Rick, take a look at this, will you?"

Grunderson's rotund finger touched a circular screen filled with soft wavy green lines. The bends and turns of the contours looked strikingly similar to those on a topographical map. Grunderson pointed to a group of converging lines, then ran his finger down the middle of a large depression.

"Can you believe that?" he asked incredulously.

Rick shrugged his shoulders. "What is it?"

"I don't know," muttered Grunderson, "It showed up last night."

Rick chose his words carefully so as not to offend his fellow researcher. "I think you misunderstood me, Keith. I don't have a clue what this display represents."

Grunderson frowned. "Oh yeah. Sorry. This is a graphic presentation of gravitational energy in space. It calculates where the planets are supposed to be at any point in time. If there's a deviation, we can assume another object is out there, affecting them. The bigger the deviation, the more mass the object will contain."

Grunderson pointed to the center of the screen again. "Something's bending the contours. Right here. Big as a planet or with at least as much mass. Showed up about three this morning. I ran some computer tests, but everything checks out fine.

Rick stared at Grunderson's screen. The line was located in the center of the constellation Sagittarius, exactly where he'd been looking since the day he'd arrived at JPL.

"I don't know what to say, Keith. If I find anything in my data, you'll be the first to know."

"Thanks, Rick. I've been wrestling with this all night. It's driving me nuts."

"No problem."

"You want something to eat?"

Rick examined Grunderson's offerings. "No thanks. I just had breakfast. Maybe later."

Rick left Grunderson and returned to the office. Even if Grunderson's computer had located an abnormality in that quadrant of the sky, it didn't mean Rick's job was completed. Software glitches and erroneous satellite information were always factors to be considered. The possibility that the government might have located him cause more concern than Grunderson's wavy green lines.

He grabbed his coffee and went back to work. By nine o'clock, after he'd examining a quarter of the morning's two hundred pages, Keith Grunderson shuffled into the office.

"Got anything?"

"Nothing so far."

"Are you sure? My trough is growing and I'm concerned. I might have to send in a report. You know what happens to someone who creates a panic and it turns out to be false."

Rick looked up his fan-folded report as Grunderson ran his index finger across his neck. Then the portly scientist cocked his head.

"I can't believe you're using paper."

Rick pointed at the stack of printouts. "Patterns seem more obvious this way. Hey Keith, is your display real-time?"

"Just about. There's a one-to-two-hour delay depending on satellite use and downlink traffic."

"That could explain the difference. My data is stored overnight and output at four a.m.

Grunderson squinted at Rick. "Pretty low priority, my friend. And very eco-unfriendly."

Rick shrugged. "My guess is I won't confirmation of your sighting until tomorrow, if it exists."

Grunderson grunted and left Rick to his work. Another hour passed. Pages of data were flipped in a cadence that had become routine over the months. He was about to take a sip from his newly filled cup when a series of numbers jumped out at him.

This was news. Rick opened a file cabinet and pulled the previous night's report. A comparison of the two sets of data confirmed his suspicion. Something had changed during the night, something that had affected every number on the page by a factor of a thousand.

He turned to his computer and logged onto JPL's powerful supercomputer. This next series of commands would cost him his entire year of online time. Grunderson was right about this being a low-priority assignment. Hell, he was lucky to have an office. On the other hand, if there was any more security clearance required, he might never have gotten the job.

Rick instructed the computer to overlap the two days' data. The screen filled with a random pater of dots. Next, all duplicated data were eliminated. The result was displayed as a small diagonal line in the center of the screen.

Rick had the computer recalculate the data. The line reappeared in the same place. Now his calculations became a little quicker. He signed off the JPL computer and logged onto the operations center for the at the radio telescope facility called the Very Large Array in central New Mexico. He formally requested a scan in the constellation Sagittarius. The petition cited both his data and mentioned Grunderson's gravity experiment. Because Rick was an unknown in the scientific community, his request would probably be ignored until it was too late. No matter; he had to ask.

After terminating his connection, Rick composed a four-sentence warning and sent it to a classified electronic mailbox in Washington, D.C. The short message officially informed the National Security Agency that a highly unusual sighting had been observed in the vast canopy of space, along with coordinates and the equipment he'd used. Rick doubted this message would receive any worthwhile attention either. He wanted to use Keith's information, but he didn't have the credentials to send that kind of classified information. His brief communication would be one of thousands received during the day.

Before leaving the facility, he paid a visit to Grunderson.

"Keith?"

"What is it, Rick?"

"You don't have a software problem."

Grunderson looked up, amazed. "You found something?"

Rick nodded. "Straight line of radiation in the same area your gravity pull is located. They have to be related."

Grunderson whistled and pulled his hair back into a ponytail. "There's something strange happening out there."

"There's always something strange happening out there," replied Rick, wondering if his co-worker had any idea what he'd seen on his scope, "But this one is heading right at us."

"You know what, Rick?" said Grunderson, staring at the green wavy lines, "I had the same feeling."

TECHNICAL AND SCIENTIFIC DOCUMENT DIVISION
NATIONAL SECURITY AGENCY WASHINGTON, D.C.
SUNDAY, **SEPTEMBER** 12, **2027**
8:20 P.M. PST        5:20 P.M. EST

Located twelve miles outside the nation's capital was the operational center for the National Security Agency. Within those walls, hundreds of classified workers pored over tens of thousands of intelligence reports sent from all areas of the globe. Spies, satellites, drones, military operations and scientific installations funneled an incredible volume of information into the structure.

In one of the sparse basement rooms, newcomer Tom Ross occupied an innocuous desk. Transferred to the department the previous week, Ross had spent eleven long, intense months trying to be assigned to the Technical and Scientific Document Division. A snarl of red tape slowed the process. It wasn't until he threatened to leave the Agency that movement began. It was hard enough to get qualified personnel to work in the extremely dull department. The Agency didn't want to lose one of their few volunteers for that department.

An urgency in Ross' life surfaced during his junior year of college. He moved from being a permanent fixture at every college football, baseball and basketball game to one of the most intense physics students in the school. His sudden interest amazed his friends as well as his professors. The newfound dedication was backed with hard study and intelligence. It was the glowing recommendations from those professors that got him an employment guarantee from an NSA recruiter before he graduated.

By mid-June Ross had moved to Washington, rented an apartment and begun training for the promised assignment as a researcher in the TSDD. For almost a year he'd put up with inane rules and regulations without complaint. Ross hated the organization's internal structure, but there was no time to change years of bureaucratic entrenchment. He passed the final test and his clearance was approved. Now, he had to remain alert as he monitored messages from scientific installations around the world.

The rising water temperature of the Antarctic, recent floods in the Ukraine and unusual tremors in the North Atlantic did nothing to raise his interest, but when a message from Rick Peters arrived, Ross knew this was the reason he'd rushed to this boring, paper-filled room.

His instructors constantly told the recruits to be open to all of one's senses, not just the eyes. Ross' problem wasn't in identifying vital information. He had to figure out a way to get around established politics.

Ross had no clout or track record to push this warning to the next level of bureaucracy. What he needed was independent confirmation of Peters' data. If he requested an emergency hearing with this report, the watch commander would laugh him back to his desk. Ross put the message to the side and continued to wallow through hundreds more meaningless communications.

The salt in the Dead Sea was increasing. The smog in Athens was returning. Puffins were mating and Peters' message sat on the desk screaming for action. By eleven that night, the large room was nearly deserted. Only a skeleton crew remained. Twenty men would toil through the night until the senior staffers who worked the treasured eight-to-five shift began to arrive.

"Hey, Ross," chuckled Terry Nolan, the last of the swing shift. "You'll never get anywhere hanging around on a Sunday night. All the important stuff is transmitted during the week."

Ross waved him out the door. Lucky bastard. He wasn't saddled with a burden that forced him to this thankless job, a goddamned dream that refused to leave him or explain why it had followed him for months.

Once a week, Ross had seen this specific desk with an urgent message in front of him as a soft voice whispered, "Wait for more." Ross swore under his breath. It wasn't fair.

Why was he picked? But he couldn't argue with a frightening dream of a pillar of light, a dream that was as vivid as the one he'd had of his brother being decapitated in a violent car accident. The dream was so chillingly accurate that when Ross returned from his brother's funeral, he immediately changed his major and began his single-minded mission to become an NSA employee.

Ross examined another five hundred bulletins before he uncovered Keith Grunderson's notice of a powerful entity speeding toward Earth. Carefully reading the message, his excitement faded. This notification would not do.

Although the men used completely different equipment, the dispatches weren't independent enough to warrant a full-scale run at the agency's cynical management. Originating from the same facility at almost the same time, the reports appeared to be the result of a computer malfunction, rather than a startling discovery.

Ross stapled the reports together and put them aside. There had to be additional information coming. He had to find it before it was lost in the thousands of scraps of paper that passed through the room.

THE VERY LARGE ARRAY
SOCORRO, NEW MEXICO
SUNDAY, SEPTEMBER 12, 2027
11:17 P.M. PST      12:17  A.M. MST      2:17 A.M. EST

Conrad Wiley dreamed of this day. He stared at the message in his hand. An unknown researcher was urgently requesting a scan of the constellation Sagittarius, suspecting a large, abnormal mass was traveling through space at great speed. Wiley shook his head and laughed out loud. He'd known this moment was coming for over a year, since the day he watched his nineteen-year-old son being offered a tryout with the Seattle Mariners.

Wiley had had an unbelievably realistic daydream that a professional baseball scout would pick Jake from his undefeated high school team and offer him a two-year contract. The images were so real, Wiley almost believed it would happen.

Damned if the guy didn't show up wearing the exact clothes he saw in the dream. That night, Wiley saw an unusual computer program displayed across his bedroom ceiling. He carefully wrote the lengthy string of commands on a piece of paper, but as he was to discover, he'd missed bits and pieces. Over the past eighteen months he'd figured out the needed information and completed the program.

Now with this urgent message in his hand, his preparation made sense. The program was designed to override the Very Large Array's computer network, lock the twenty-seven active radio telescopes together and focus them on a predetermined set of coordinates.

Finishing the project last month, he'd debugged the program to the point where there was only one step remaining: a real-time test. If this supposed line of radiation was substantial, Wiley's program would back the discovery with additional data.

His hands shaking with excitement, Wiley typed a two-word command and the set of coordinates taken from the JPL message. With a press of the enter key, the computer abandoned its current program and began moving the large devices. Wiley sat back and waited for the results of the most expensive and audacious hijacking of a scientific facility ever attempted.

BEST WESTERN MOTEL
TETON VILLAGE, WYOMING
MONDAY, **SEPTEMBER** 13, **2027**
1:12 A.M. PST        2:12 A.M. MST        4:12 A.M. EST

Kim Callaway opened the door of her dusty pickup truck and stepped onto the gravel parking lot. The cold night air was a shock to her system. In the distance, bathed in moonlight, was Rendezvous Peak. It was on the slopes of that mountain she would discover the answers to her questions. Right now, all she wanted was a hot shower and to catch some much-needed sleep.

She trudged up the thick wooden steps and entered the Teton Village Motel. The young desk clerk tried to flirt with her, but Callaway was in no mood. Refusing his help, she carried her suitcase containing a change of clothes, down jacket and two revolvers to her room.

After thoroughly checking the layout, including the distance from the balcony to the ground, she concluded the room would suffice. Returning to the small bathroom, Callaway pulled off her wrinkled clothes and turned on the shower. As she stepped into the stream of water, she caught a glimpse of a stranger in the mirror above the sink.

Her thoughts raced to how she could get to her revolver when she realized it was her reflection. Oh boy, she thought, don't lose it, Kim. You're a little nervous, and frightened, but there's no reason to overreact.

Returning to the bedroom, she retrieved one of her Casulls and placed it on the counter next to the sink. She'd changed so much since Renee's funeral. Forty pounds had evaporated from her frame. Muscles rippled where flab used to hang. Her long, messy blonde hair was now short, neat and trim. The frumpy, twenty-five-year-old had been replaced by a newer, sleeker, more attractive model.

Hot water poured over her suffering body, washing away two days of hard driving. The steam cleared her sinuses and loosened her taught muscles. It felt good to be clean again. After drying off, she set up a makeshift alarm using the small bell she'd brought for hiking in backwoods bear country. She tucked her loaded revolver beneath the pillow and slid between the crisp sheets. The waiting was over, but the dream stayed with her.

Dinosaurs were everywhere. Gray scaly lizards foraged in the fern-like underbrush. A herd of lumbering brontosaurus wallowed in a shallow river. Pterodactyls flew in lazy circles searching for their next meal. The vegetation was green, tropical, lush. Kim had been here before. She'd watched these creatures meander the area, smelled the damp Earth and wondered how so many life forms could have vanished so quickly. The sky darkened, like on a humid New England afternoon before a thunderstorm. Strong winds began to blow, rapidly increasing in intensity, whipping from one direction, then another. The animals panicked and ran for cover. Even a gigantic allosaurus that lumbered from behind a cluster of tropical trees looked skyward, then thundered off into the distance.

With a blinding flash, a shaft of light extended from a circular cloud and sliced into the Earth. The beam gave off a desperate feel, like an animal caught, but still able to struggle. A cry for help echoed in her head. The wind ripped at her, tried to knock her down, pushed and shoved her. With another blinding flash, the light was gone.

As the cloud lifted and the winds subsided, Kim was left alone and vulnerable. Then the earthquakes started. At first they were small shakers, but quickly increased in intensity, knocking over trees, creating enormous landslides. A massive hole appeared and swallowed the swamp. On either side of her, mountains rose from the ground, spewing hot, deadly lava.

Forty feet above her towered the wide-eyed allosaurus. The carnivore lunged in her direction. As he was about to crush her, the beast disappeared into a newly formed sinkhole. Moments later, the enormous body was thrown into the sky, followed by a stupendous explosion that destroyed everything, including Kim.

She woke up, her heart pounding. Her body was soaked in perspiration, but she knew she was safe. The challenge was still to come. Closing her eyes, she fell back to sleep hoping she wouldn't have to dodge Marines and battle the short man in the steaming field. One of these horrible dreams was enough.

TECHNICAL AND SCIENTIFIC DOCUMENT DIVISION
NATIONAL SECURITY AGENCY
WASHINGTON, D.C.
MONDAY, **SEPTEMBER** 13, 2027
1:45 A.M. PST          2:45A.M.MST          4:45  A.M. EST

It was a long night for Tom Ross. Every obscure scientist in the world decided to transmit their useless information to him. Ross couldn't care less about the shrinking Arctic ice cap or the growing ozone layer. Where were the additional reports about the object in the sky? By five-thirty he'd nodded off several times, resting his forehead on his paper-strewn desk. Each time he woke, he circled the room and checked the hundreds of messages that had been texted, faxed or emailed to the station. A five-line notification from New Mexico sat in a pile of fan-folded computer paper for almost an hour as Ross dozed.

Moments before his weekday counterpart arrived, who would have taken the stack and tossed it in some overflowing carton, Ross checked one more time. This was it! A renegade scientist in New Mexico had commandeered the Very Large Array, forcing the complex to make a detailed scan of the Sagittarius area. Now he had something to work with.

Using the three concurring bulletins, Ross carefully composed a persuasive report, requesting a full-scale military alert and immediate, comprehensive scientific investigation. He also painstakingly outlined a series of defensive responses to the incoming target.

By maneuvering several KH-12 intelligence satellites to face away from Earth, infrared and visual data could be obtained quickly and accurately. Refocusing powerful space telescopes –Hubble, James Webb, and Spitzer could provide additional information for weapons targeting. The giant seventy-meter Deep Space Network radio telescope, located outside of Barstow, along with its counterparts in Australia and Spain, could find the intruder and track it. There was a prototype laser platform that was secretly launched in 2025 that could be used for a defensive attack. The Strategic Defense Proton Accelerator in New Mexico could be used in warding off the object.

Most effective plan would to have two coordinated attacks, ten seconds apart, utilizing all available ground forces, air and naval cruise missiles at precisely the same moment, ideally at 8:49 Mountain Standard Time on Tuesday morning. This event could overwhelm the object's defensive system.

By the time his presentation was finalized, the morning crew had begun to arrive. Ross waited for the change of command in order to present his findings. The day watch always carried more clout than the weekend crew. After a shave and thorough washing, Ross brought his presentation to the watch commander, Steve Hardin.

"What's up your butt, Ross?" demanded Hardin, squinting at the new recruit. Not only was the punk too smart for his own good, he was requesting a private hearing outside his shift. He was as green as they came, a college brat who'd been on the floor barely a week. Once the door shut, Ross began with a deadly serious tone that shocked the tough NSA veteran. Ross wasn't intimidated or interested in Hardin's best snarl. The department's newest member was intense, composed and prepared.

"We've received three independent sightings of extremely unusual activity in the inner reaches of the solar system. There is no time to waste on political formalities. We must move quickly and decisively." Ross stopped and took a breath. God, he hoped this bureaucratic stiff would listen to him or he'd have to find someone who would.

"The approximate speed of the object as of oh-three hundred hours was just over eleven million miles an hour. It's on a trajectory that will, if corrected slightly, put it on a direct intercept course with Earth. Sir, this object is traveling too fast to be a natural occurrence and should be considered a serious security threat. However, I believe if we handle the situation quickly and efficiently, our career prospects could be greatly enhanced, if you know what 1 mean."

Hardin grunted. Damned if this asshole didn't sound like a normal human. Using information to pursue personal advancement was the type of initiative he liked to see in a man. Granted, the only way to get noticed in this dismal department was to create a situation, but Ross would have to come up with something better than an alien assault to catapult out of the TSDD basement. Outer space crap was not tolerated within the NSA. It had been used once, with disastrous results.

"Ross," grumbled Hardin, irritated the fresh recruit had cornered him before his morning coffee, "You're about to lose all your leave for the next six months."

"Screw the leave," Ross shot back. "You don't want to see this shit, fine. I'll just zip it over to the National Research Organization. They'll know what to do."

Hardin slammed his fist on the desk. "Don't you threaten me or I'll have your stinking report buried so deep no one will ever see it, and you along with it. If I catch you sending anything to anyone, especially the NRO, I'll have you shot! Give me that report."

Ross tossed the papers to Hardin. The National Research Organization was created to oversee the Air Force and NSA's intelligence-gathering divisions. Threatening to send any information to the NRO was a direct insult to Hardin, but Ross had to do something to shake him up. If this old fart read the first two pages, he'd have no choice but to spring into action. Whether he'd bother to get off his fat butt was another matter altogether.

There were stories about Hardin losing sensitive reports, stuffing them in drawers, never to be seen again. Last Friday he'd caught a veteran trying to set up a meeting without involving the insecure commander. Hardin sent the poor guy down to interrogation. At times the NSA was a frightening place. If he went too close to his computer, there was a chance Hardin would have him killed.

"Why'd you stay all night?" asked the commander with a scowl.

"When I read Peters' report, I had a hunch he was onto something important. Grunderson's notification came next, but the men worked at the same facility and sent their information at almost the same time. So, I waited. When I got the VLA confirmation, I knew I had a valid reason to interrupt you."

Hardin leaned back in his chair. He was beginning to like this kid. Ross believed in himself and was willing to back it up with action.

"My predecessor was terminated because of an extraterrestrial scare," grumbled Hardin. "I don't intend to end up like him. Give me another confirmation and I'll kick it upstairs."

"What?" Ross was stunned. Hardin was refusing to take action. "Sir, the reports clearly indicate powerful radiation, infrared and gravitational signatures with identical trajectories. We can't afford to keep this to ourselves, sir. We need preparation and mobilization immediately."

Ross knew he'd lost it. He'd been up all night, and that had to be one of the sloppiest speeches he'd ever made. He sounded like a panicked cadet.

Hardin's voice turned kind, almost parental. "Tom, I'll decide what we sit on and what we'll run with. As soon as you get another confirmation, come back and talk to me."

Then the commander became the hardened career bureaucrat Ross had heard about: "But if this is your idea of a joke, you'll be sent to interrogation faster than you can type your name. Got it?"

"Yes, sir," said Ross stiffly.

"Get out of here."

Ross nodded and left the office. There was too much at stake to wait for another sighting. Once Hardin disappeared into the cafeteria, Ross casually typed a quick series of keystrokes on his computer. Acquiring communications with the Geostationary Earth Orbiting Deep-Space Surveillance (GEODSS) station in Hawaii, he left an urgent message on the bulletin board, along with the object's coordinates. Although he had no authorization or password, he sent the message hoping some alert serviceman would take notice.

As soon as the message was on its way, Ross moved away from the desk and busied himself with the new reports streaming into the station. Hardin reappeared with his coffee and squinted at Ross. Ross nodded and returned to his reading. A glance at the computer screen indicated he'd received a response from GEODSS. A curt thank you, we'll check into it was enough to bring him hope. Time was running out, not only for a military response, but also for Ross. A twin-engine plane with full tanks was waiting for him at College Park Airport.

Fifty minutes later, another report arrived. He ripped them out of his co-worker's hands and ran into Hardin's office.

"What the hell are you doing in here, Ross?"

"Another confirmation," Ross said breathlessly, "The object has been located by the Deep Space Network tracking station in Barstow."

Hardin grabbed the papers from his desk and the two in Ross' hands. "Stay here. I'm going to need you. Don't make any plans. You're not going anywhere until this is over."

"I'll be here, sir. I'm looking forward to working with you."

Ross danced a jig as soon as Hardin left the department. His work was done. There was no way he was staying in this tomb while a bunch of bureaucrats tried to figure out what he already knew. Five minutes later Ross was driving to the airport. GEODSS would eventually respond, and when it did all hell was going to break loose.

712 JOURNEY'S END ROAD
LA CANADA, CALIFORNIA
MONDAY, **SEPTEMBER** 13, **2027**
5:12 A.M. PST        6:12  A.M. MST      8:12  A.M. EST

Rick Peters woke early, loaded his camping gear into the Fiat and headed to JPL. Until he received his next instruction, all he could do was continue his daily routine, hoping some clue would present itself. Still he had to be ready to move at a moment's notice.

Once again, Mike held the gate closed as Rick approached. Rays of the morning sun sliced between tree branches as the guard walked to the car door. With an edgy foot on the accelerator, Rick kept an alert eye on Mike.

Rick was somewhat comforted by the bulge of his loaded Casull under his arm. The game was on. Anything could happen.

"They came back last evening," Mike said nervously. "I told them you didn't have a regular schedule, but they seemed to know your routine. Careful, buddy. I think your time's up."

"Thanks, Mike," Rick said lightly, glad he'd been generous to the guard over the past months, happier still that people couldn't read each other's thoughts.

The guard leaned into the car. "Hey, Rick," he said softly, "Are you the guy?"

Rick laughed loudly. "If I had that kind of money, I'd be lying on a beach, thousands of miles from here. No, Mike, it isn't me. Don't worry. They just made a dumb mistake."

"Didn't think it was you," Mike raised the gate. "Keep an eye out, though. They're serious."

Rick drove into the facility. If that money hadn't poured into his hands, he'd never be listening so carefully to his emotions, so carefully to the voices in his head. None of this made any sense. He was a stockbroker, for God's sake, not a superhero.

Rick parked his car parallel to the building making sure he had room to move in both directions. Today was not the day to get blocked in. Every minute he stayed at the facility increased his chances of being detained. Though he had no idea where he was going, he was damn sure he wasn't supposed to be hanging around JPL much longer.

Grunderson was at his post, as always. He shuffled over to Rick as soon as he realized his co-worker was in the room.

"Rick, come here," he said, dragging the tall man over to the gravity display. "Look!!" Grunderson's scope was one huge indentation of green throbbing lines. "We're in deep shit. Did you notify the NSA?"

Rick nodded. "I did, right after I talked to you. Fat chance they'll take it seriously."

"I sent a warning, too. Do you really think they'll ignore us? This thing is huge."

"Considering our world-renowned reputations, our emails are probably sitting at the bottom of some slush pile. They won't start moving until some famous Ph.D. finds it. Did you tell anyone else?"

"I called a friend over at Goldstone. They're going to look into it, but they couldn't break the dishes away. Those guys are booked for the next five years."

"They're going to get unbooked in a hurry once they realize what's heading in our direction."

Grunderson nodded in agreement, then a puzzled look swept across his face. "What do you think's happening out there, Rick?"

"I could be wrong, but I think this thing is heading right for us."

"I feel the same way. By the way, I also posted notices on several bulletin boards using both our data: Google's Astronomy Forum, Reddit, Yahoo, Space.com and NASA's site. There's a slight chance we could generate some action."

"Good idea, Keith. Let's see what happened last night."

Rick walked to his printer and tore off his report. He scanned the rows of numbers, then realized he'd expended his allotted computer time. "Hey, Grunderson, how much time do you have in your account?"

"A hundred hours, maybe more."

"Run my comparison for me, will you?"

"Sure." Grunderson scooted his swivel chair across the linoleum floor and stopped in front of his rack-mounted computer. It took a few minutes to transfer Rick's data to Grunderson's station and run the analysis. The line of radiation had extended one hundred twenty million miles. Its placement corresponded exactly with Grunderson's gravity pull. Ripping though the solar system at about nine million miles an hour, it would pass Mars before noon. Rick headed for the door.

"Where are you going?"

"I'm not sure, but I can't stay around here."

Grunderson nodded. "I was going to leave myself. God knows what this thing is going to do. Thought I'd enjoy my last few days in the country."

"Maybe we'll meet again," Rick offered, wondering if they should be talking about visions and glowing columns of light.

Grunderson nodded. "Our paths could cross. Either way, it was a pleasure working with you."

"Same here, Keith. Be careful."

Returning to his office, Rick gathered a few notes and stuffed them into his bag. He might have some quick explaining to do if they caught up to him. The phone rang. Rick suspiciously lifted the receiver. The voice on the other end didn't give him a chance to respond. It was Mike.

"They're on their way. Make yourself scarce."

As he hung up the phone, a bright reflection caught Rick's attention. He looked up expecting to see a gun pointing at his head. Instead, a circle of bright sparkles swirled around the poster of the Jackson Hole Ski Area. The luminous dots revolved faster and faster until they became a sphere of brilliant light resting directly on the picture.

Rick ran across the room and stared as the globe spun around a stand of trees separating two steep ski runs. He reached out to touch the ball, but it disappeared before his fingers could wrap around it. Close examination of the picture revealed no clue that the apparition had ever occurred. He checked the poster again, hoping to detect an overlooked burn hole or some other indication that pointed the way. But no, this damn affliction refused to be clear, refused to be specific.

Removing the frame from the wall, Rick smashed it on his desk, scattering glass across the room. Picking his way through the shards, he ripped the paper where he'd seen the revolving sparkles, stuffed the scrap in his pocket and ran out the door. When he reached the exit, he cautiously peeked outside. A blue sedan pulled in front of his white Fiat. Three men got out. One headed to the front door, one went around back, the third remained at the vehicle.

Rick backed into the building, located an unlocked office door and ducked inside. He waited for the first man to pass. Escape on foot wouldn't work. The Jet Propulsion Laboratory was located at the outskirts of a small, secluded town. His guarded car was the only way out. Rick drew his gun and boldly walked into the parking lot.

"Put your hands in the air and back away from the car," Rick ordered. The FBI agent dropped his gun, then raised his hands. He'd been caught off-guard. There had been no indication this was going to be anything but a simple interrogation of an eccentric scientist.

Rick moved swiftly. He quickly got in the car and started the engine with his free hand, without taking his aim from the agent. Shifting into reverse, he backed up, shifted again, then sped toward the exit. Mike didn't have time to raise the gate. The Fiat smashed through the barrier and fishtailed onto Oak Grove Drive. Once on the freeway, it only took him a few minutes to reach the Burbank airport, where he bought a one-way ticket to Jackson, Wyoming.

NSA BRIEFING ROOM WASHINGTON, D.C.
MONDAY, **SEPTEMBER** 13, **2027**
6:00 A.M. PST          9:00 A.M. EST

The nine a.m. National Security Agency briefing started thirty seconds past the hour. Tom Ross' report was last on the agenda. With a short discussion the group quickly agreed the sighting called for additional research. There was no pressing need to be alarmed. Someone had probably mistaken an experimental craft for a spaceship or someone was foolishly trying to get promoted. As the men began to file out of the room, an aide handed General Mark Binder a message. Binder immediately asked everyone to return to the table.

"I've received additional information on the space object. The existence of the phenomenon has been confirmed by a senior research associate from the Very Large Array in New Mexico. He also happens to be on our payroll."

Dunsmore frowned. "Isn't this the drill we went through last year? I don't have time to play another game like that."

"Someone could have created a diversion using a computer virus," offered Frank Wiser, the always-suspicious Executive Technical Advisor. "It wouldn't take a genius to plant such a program into several facility computers."

"This object, whatever it is, definitely exists," said Binder, his eyes drilling the others. "The sighting is secure, but the properties and composition of the entity are still undetermined. We've also discovered the five men who located the anomaly have disappeared. This includes our junior analyst who wrote the report in front of you. We will consider this phenomenon a major military and intelligence threat until proven otherwise."

Within minutes, the Joint Chiefs of Staff were informed of the discovery. Every available scientific institution was given the coordinates and ordered to identify the object, its manner of operation, strengths and weaknesses. Hourly briefings were scheduled until the matter was concluded. Two of the Agency's finest trackers were ordered to find and interrogate the suspicious scientists who'd first reported the object.

Lance White, who had been investigating the "2027 Crazies," was to lead the elite group of hunters.

# FUGITIVES

When Lance White's phone rang softly in his Westwood apartment, he knew something important was happening. Secure and scrambled, the line was only used for high-priority assignments. White listened carefully to the digitized voice. He was to leave his current assignment immediately.

The new orders were to locate and apprehend Rick Peters, Keith Grunderson or Tom Ross. Minutes later, White was traveling to the Southern California town of Pasadena, the location of JPL. Although Peters left the facility two and a half hours earlier, White would make a thorough search of his office. There might be a clue as to where Peters was headed. Supposedly Keith Grunderson was still at his post.

Until now, White had little to show for his year and a half s work. Most of the people who'd claimed to have seen the column of light changed their tale once the story of the missing homeless people hit the papers. His interrogation in the hangar had revealed little more than what he already knew: there was going to be a bright light that would signal the end of the world.

One of the brokers who claimed to have seen the light on the day that Rick Peters made his millions retracted his story. No one else wanted to talk about the light or the end of the world. The five homeless men were quietly buried in the Los Padres National Forest. As for White's career, it seemed his stepping-stone appointment had turned into a dead-end job. This new assignment delighted him. He was back in the field, where he belonged.

As White sped to the scientific installation twenty miles northeast of Los Angeles, files concerning Keith Grunderson,

Rick Peters, Conrad Wiley and Tom Ross were emailed to his phone. At the same time, other members of the crew from the Los Angeles office combed airline, hotel and car rental data bases, looking for a match on names and credit card numbers. By the time White was halfway to JPL, Tom Ross' flight plan had been located.

Flying out of College Park Airport, he was scheduled to arrive in Kentucky within the hour, but a search of the website flightradar24.com showed no plane with Ross' transponder in the air. He probably disabled the device.

A government plane was dispatched to intercept him, but White knew Ross wasn't headed anywhere near Kentucky. The itinerary was a lie. White was certain if there was a clue about where these people were headed, he'd find it. And if any of them men made a mistake, they'd be located that much sooner.

One of the Agency's Lear jets was put on standby at Burbank airport. Fueled and pre-flight checked, the plane would be ready to fly at a moment's notice. White wasn't about to leave Los Angeles just yet. He wasn't convinced that Peters had traveled from the area. If Grunderson was still at JPL and Ross was airborne, they could be meeting in or near Los Angeles. There were over a dozen airfields in the basin, several of them small and inconspicuous.

On the other hand, they could be working independently. Either way, White was going to gather them up like children. Once they were in custody, the Agency would probably let him direct the interrogation.

JET PROPULSION LABORATORY
PASADENA, CALIFORNIA
MONDAY, SEPTEMBER 13, 2027
8:50 A.M. PST          11:50 P.M. EST

In 2020 during the middle of the global pandemic the government released several UFO videos. Here was proof the planet had been visited by aliens. The technology displayed by these visitors was impressive, but never hostile. As a result, the military complex spent the majority of their resources looking no further than the outermost satellite for intelligence information. All the enemies that warranted attention lived and operated on the planet Earth.

This situation called for a radically different approach in thinking. Fifty-three highly classified and respected scientists were discreetly contacted, told of the find and asked for their help in deciding what this entity was and how to deal with it. All of them, regardless of their political affiliation, were stunned at the speed with which the government was responding. Reports of unusual activities in the heavens were routinely investigated then ignored because there was nothing to be done.

Even Keith Grunderson was amazed when two neatly dressed corporate officials paid a visit to his office early Monday afternoon.

"I told you," said Grunderson to the persistent JPL executives, "I was watching that quadrant because Rick was interested in the constellation Sagittarius. It's one of those things. A person starts working on a particular area of the sky, then someone else becomes curious and starts looking there as well. He was pretty intense about those coordinates. Watched them like a hawk. He was here every day, Saturday and Sunday included. But trust me, I don't have a clue what's out there. If 1 did, I'd be the first to tell you...wait, I did tell you. So did Rick."

The taller of the men nodded and asked his next question, one that Grunderson had answered at least four times.

"Where is Rick now?" said the balding man, holding out his phone which was recording every word.

"I don't know," snarled Grunderson, frustrated with this ludicrous waste of time. "He left this morning."

"Isn't that unusual for him to leave before noon?"

Grunderson looked at the ceiling, then back to the men. "Come to think of it, yes, it was strange. But, hey. I don't know where he went. Heck, I don't even know where he lives and I worked next to the guy for a year. I did hear someone say he was furious about something and quit. Broke the Oak Grove gate on the way out."

The two men did not respond.

Grunderson shrugged. "Look, this is taking too much time. I've got a batch of important measurements to send to the NSA. They're not going to like it if you're the reason they don't get their information. If you'll excuse me." Grunderson swiveled his chair and wheeled across the room to his computer station.

"Don't leave the facility," said one of the men as threateningly as he could. "There's a gentleman from the government who needs to talk to you."

"Fine with me," replied Grunderson, obviously annoyed. "I practically live here, if you didn't already know. Besides, I'm not going anywhere until I find out what this is all about. When is this government guy going to be here?"

"He's on his way."

"Great. I've got a lot of questions for him."

"I'm sure you do."

Satisfied Grunderson had no intention of leaving the facility, the irritating suits returned to the gravitational pull station to check on the progress of the object. A small crowd had gathered in the room.

As soon as the men's attention was focused on the display, Grunderson calmly walked to his car and left the facility. Returning to his tiny North Hollywood home, he grabbed a knapsack from his closet. Leaving the house, he rushed into his cluttered garage. Under a tarp, inside an old shoe box, was a shiny revolver. He stuffed the gun into the knapsack. If he moved fast enough, he'd be able to catch the last flight to Jackson Hole and be deep in the backwoods of Yellowstone National Park by morning.

JET PROPULSION LABORATORY
PASADENA, CALIFORNIA
MONDAY, **SEPTEMBER** 13, **2027**
10:20 A.M. PST        1:20 P.M. EST

Securities and Exchange Commission Special Agent Randall Klimer was ecstatic when Lance White called him at his Los Angeles office. He was going to be involved in a major investigation concerning the man he'd been trailing for the past eighteen months. During that year and a half, Klimer had scoured phone and computer records in the belief that Rick Peters had remained in the Southland.

If he could find Rick Peters, everything would change. The fortune Peters made during that day of trading created national headlines. That's when Klimer sensed an opportunity. Careful examination of the his Dynotech trades revealed Rick Peters had violated several SEC rules. Prosecuting this fugitive would separate Klimer from the bureaucrats working in the paper-filled trenches. Randall Klimer the schlep would be transformed into Randall Klimer, celebrity investigator.

After the morning's fiasco, Klimer was certain his years' worth of work had been lost. Who would have suspected that Peters would elude three armed FBI agents? No doubt the gods were taking care of him. When Lance White called and requested this meeting, the SEC investigator's hopes rose anew. Klimer told White he had a special file concerning Peters. In return for the information, White offered Klimer the chance to participate in locating the infamous trader. Klimer could not have been more excited. He raced back to JPL and found his way to Peters' cramped office. The splintered glass still surrounded the desk. A man stood in the debris examining the damaged poster.

"Are you Lance White?" Klimer asked calmly, professionally. White continued studying the picture. He spoke without turning. "Where are the files, Klimer?"

Klimer assumed this was to be a dialogue between equals. "Lance, I thought we were going to discuss my involvement in the Rick Peters investigation. I know your Agency is perfectly capable of locating..."

"The files," demanded White, "I want them. Now."

Klimer sensed danger. During their talk on the phone White seemed anxious for his help. This shift in attitude was not a good sign.

"These files contain sensitive material. I'll have to see some I.D."

White turned to the red-haired man and pulled a badge from his jacket. He didn't know how long he could stand being in the same room with this idiot.

"Here. Where are the files?"

Klimer squinted at the badge. It looked official, but the man was acting too aggressive, too superior. A check with the downtown office would be necessary before going any further. If he handed over Peters' files to the wrong person, his career could be ruined.

White abruptly reached inside his jacket and removed a small cellular phone, allowing Klimer a glimpse of a holstered gun. The short man walked out of the room without explanation.

"What is it?" asked White once he was in the hallway.

"Grady here. A man named Rick Peters rented a blue Taurus in Jackson, Wyoming about an hour ago. Two of the five scientists who sent the reports to Washington booked flights to Jackson this morning. The problem in the sky has intensified."

White hung up without saying a word. Time was at a premium. Northwestern Wyoming appeared to be a prime area for investigation.

He returned to the office and stood in front of the smashed poster. When he first saw the hole in the picture, he dismissed it as a ruse to be examined but not taken seriously. Like Ross' flight itinerary, the missing portion seemed too obvious, too contrived. With the information from Grady, White changed his mind. Tom Ross was smart. His files showed him to be a quick learner with an attitude. Ross had a plan. Rick Peters, on the other hand, was impulsive, didn't think ahead, acted on whims. He wasn't going to last long. White closed the door behind him.

"The files, Klimer. I have to leave."

"They're in my car. I'll give them to you, but only if I come along."

White's patience had been expended. Enough of this fool. He removed his gun from its holster. From his inside jacket pocket, he pulled out a silencer and quickly screwed it on the barrel of his automatic. Klimer's eyes bulged.

"You can't be serious. There's no way I give you the files under these circumstances."

White finished attaching the silencer and aimed the gun at Klimer. "Keys."

"Look, I've spent months chasing this guy. You can't trash my career like this."

Without the slightest hesitation, White fired. The slug passed through the fleshy part of Klimer's calf.

"Keys," White repeated.

Klimer crumpled to the floor. "Are you crazy!?" he yelled, holding his wounded leg.

White raised the gun and aimed at Klimer's head. "Not so loud, my friend. Where are the keys?"

"In my back pocket. The files are in the trunk," he said, grimacing in pain. "What are you going to do?"

White didn't bother to answer. He kept the gun aimed at Klimer's head, reached into the man's pocket and roughly pulled the keys out.

Klimer should be grateful. He could be missing both his kneecaps. There'd be an investigation, but it would be easy to blame the shooting on Rick Peters. Another discussion with Klimer would convince him to change his story. For now, it would suffice to have the files. It was time to get moving.

"Which key is it?"

"Red," gasped Klimer referring to the little plastic tops on the keys.

"Where's the car?"

"Out front. Green Dodge."

"You're a loser, Klimer," snarled White as he left the room. Stuffing the gun into his belt, he walked down the hallway to the entrance of the machine room. Standing in front of a glowing machine, bathed in green light, were a dozen management and research types. White brazenly walked into the room.

"Where's Keith Grunderson?" he demanded.

"In his office, two doors down on the right. You the government guy?"

White left the room without replying. He was sure Grunderson was gone. A quick check in the office confirmed his guess. On top of Grunderson's desk was a scribbled letter of resignation. The two suits tried to make excuses, but it was too late. Driving away from the facility, White called the office.

"Grady here."

"What happened with Grunderson?"

"We wired the house and planted a dozen homing devices. He took one of them with him. He's heading west on the 134 Freeway. Anderson and Oneida are two cars behind him. We're also tracking his phone."

"Good. Keep me informed." White sped up the freeway ramp, heading to the Burbank airport. Calling ahead, he made sure the Lear jet would be ready. Though Peters had a head start, the Lear could travel faster than a commercial jet and get a priority clearance to land ahead of other airliners in the traffic pattern. White had a reasonable chance of catching up to the fugitive, and when he did, Rick Peters was not going to enjoy his first meeting with Lance White.

JCS BRIEFING ROOM
WASHINGTON, D.C.
MONDAY, **SEPTEMBER** 13, **2027**
9:00 A.M. PST       10:00  A.M. MST       12:00 P.M. EST

The Joint Chiefs of Staff met promptly at noon. At the head of the large room was a computer-generated map. A thick red line indicated the projected path of the object. Containing information from the NRO, NSA, NASA and U.S. Space Command, the display showed that the object was tearing through space at just under seven million miles an hour. Within the last five minutes, Eagle, the object's newly acquired code name, had changed course.

Asteroids, comets and all naturally occurring events in space, even meteors, traveled according to strict laws of physics. Once located, their flight paths can be predicted. Considering the rate at which it was traveling and this recent maneuver, it was obvious that Eagle was not a natural phenomenon, but a spaceship heading directly at the Earth.

Priority orders were relayed to the country's most powerful intelligence-gathering satellites, maneuvering them to face away from the planet. The huge listening posts, positioned high above the Earth, located the quick-moving Eagle. Telemetry information streamed into the U.S. Space Command in Colorado.

The massive James Webb telescope focused on the alien, but could not locate it visually. An enterprising engineer from Goldstone, an old colleague of Keith Grunderson, backtracked Eagle's path and located its entrance into the solar system. It appeared just beyond the planet Pluto. When it arrived, it was traveling at slightly below the speed of light and had been decelerating ever since.

All military stations were coming to full war alert status, and with such increased military activity, there would be no way to avoid the press. However, until Eagle became an actual threat, all media communications would claim the military and the Administration had everything under control.

"Enough about the press. What about the five missing scientists, the ones who first reported the object?" demanded President William Lindon.

"Several of them traveled to the Jackson Hole area," replied Secretary of Defense Mark Trailer. "We're sending an Air Force search and rescue unit into northwestern Wyoming to locate them. We also have three top NSA tracking agents in Wyoming. Also, a Marine Expeditionary Force is being transported into the area. I assure you, we'll find them, sir."

"Can you can find them before Eagle arrives?" asked Lindon.

"The Marine Expeditionary Force and Air Force PJs are trained in locating and retrieving downed pilots behind enemy lines," replied Trailer. "Finding a couple of frightened civilians will be easy."

Lindon shook his head. "I am certain those men have information about this situation. We must talk to them."

"We'll find them, sir."

Lindon rested his chin on his folded hands. The Joint Chiefs waited. Then he rose and stood in front of the map, pointing at a flashing green square.

"Is this Eagle, General McKinley?"

"Yes, sir," replied the commander of the Air Force.

"How long before it arrives?"

The General conferred with his aide, then turned back to Lindon. "At its present rate, Eagle will be within the outer atmosphere by four tomorrow morning. However, it is slowing, so it could arrive as late as tomorrow afternoon."

"Can we communicate with it?"

"We've been sending signals on all radio frequencies, as well as VLF, ultrasound, laser and pulsars. Every known language as well as binary and hexadecimal code are being transmitted. They're not responding."

"I want to make it perfectly clear, there will be no offensive action taken toward this object without my authorization."

Nods around the table.

"I have no intention of starting a war with something we can't even see."

A PARKING LOT
TETON VILLAGE, WYOMING
SUNDAY, **SEPTEMBER** 12, **2027**
12:11 P.M. MST      2:11 P.M. EST

Rick drove into the small gravel-covered parking area at the base of the Jackson Hole Ski Area and parked the blue rental. Two ski shops, several real estate companies and a cluster of restaurants ringed the lot. In the center of the grouping was a barn-like structure that housed the Grand Teton Tramway. Rick purchased a one-way ticket and, along with fifteen tourists, boarded the red car.

During the ride to the top, Rick scanned the hillside, looking for the triangle shaped cluster of trees. Unfortunately, the area was hidden behind a small rise to the north, out of view from the tram. He raised his gaze and scanned the expansive view. He could see nothing unusual. The mountain looked solid and unmovable. The grass-covered slopes were peaceful and serene.

The tram gently pulled into the docking station at the barren mountaintop. First through the sliding doors, Rick clamored down the metal stairway and located the steep fire road that led away from the rock-strewn peak. A mile down the path, the vegetation returned, then the tall evergreens dotted the hillside. Birds flew from the trees as he approached. Unaccustomed to high altitude, Rick's body cried for oxygen. Out of breath, he was forced to stop.

At an elevation of eight thousand feet, the view was spectacular. Jackson Valley stretched for miles. To his right, miles in the distance, was the town of Jackson. In the center of the valley was a single strip of asphalt that marked the Jackson airport. Below him were narrow patches of pine trees that separated the grass-covered ski runs. The pale blue sky contrasted with tufts of golden aspen. Directly ahead three deer grazed in the middle of a hay-covered ski slope. It seemed so peaceful, so right, so powerful.

Halfway down the mountain, Rick left the dirt road and headed back in the direction of the tram lines. Checking the crumpled scrap of paper, he walked into a small indent in the ski run adjacent to a narrow sliver of evergreens.

As the distance between the trees and Rick narrowed, an odd feeling descended on him like a soft veil. He stopped and backed up. The emotion faded. Heading back toward the trees, the sensation returned. Expecting the sensation made it less of a surprise, but no more comfortable. As its intensity increased, Rick tried to identify the feeling. It wasn't unpleasant, it wasn't painful, but it was radically different.

He reached inside his jacket and wrapped his hand around his .454. Something was lurking in the darkness. What the hell was he doing? With steeled determination, he walked into the glen.

"You can stop right there," ordered a female voice.

"I've stopped," said Rick, standing still, half a dozen steps into the shaded glen.

"Why have you come?" came the voice.

Closely packed evergreen trees blocked the sunlight, making it difficult to see. Bubbling sounds from a nearby stream masked any sounds of movement. Over the months, Rick had been dealing with computers and printouts. Now another person was involved. He wasn't sure how to play this out.

"I was told to come," Rick replied. His mind raced. Sonya mentioned there was a woman traveling to meet him. Could this be her?

"Who told you to come <u>here</u>?" came the voice again. Definitely female, certainly not friendly.

"I guess you could say it was a sign, a vision. Glowing lights on a poster. I assume you're here because of a similar experience."

A movement to his left. Rick's hand closed on the handle of his Casull. The veil of emotion increased, blurring his vision. His thinking became muddled. He began to pull his revolver from his pocket when the sensation stopped. In front of him, partially hidden behind a large, moss-covered boulder was an attractive woman in a flannel jacket.

"What did the vision tell you?" she said. There was no warmth in her voice.

Rick shrugged his shoulders, his hands still buried in his pockets.

"1 was simply told to come," he said feeling strangely comfortable despite the stranger's edginess. In a momentary flash, he saw himself and the woman sitting next to the stream, talking as if they were old friends. Smiling and laughing, they seemed extraordinarily happy. Suddenly they stopped their conversation and with concerned expressions looked to the sky. With a flurry of movement, they gathered their belongings and raced out of the glen. Then the image disappeared.

"Did you see that?" she asked.

"What?"

"That picture of us talking by the stream."

It was Rick's turn to be cold. "Yeah, I saw it. What of it?"

"I've been waiting for over two years to get some straight answers. My name's Kim Callaway. Do you know what this is about?"

"Hello Kim. My name is Rick Peters and, yes, I've got a few ideas about what's going on. Do you mind if we get a little closer?"

"Stay where you are," she ordered, moving from behind the boulder. Her handgun was aimed at Rick's chest. He immediately recognized the weapon. It was identical to the one he was holding in his jacket pocket. A .454 Casull.

"Take your hands out of your pockets, Rick."

If he pulled his gun, he'd be dead in a second, unless she was a miserable shot. Perhaps it was time to have a little faith. After all, wasn't that why he was here in the first place?

"Suit yourself," said Rick, pressing his lips together in a welcome smile. He slowly removed his hands from his pockets.

Kim wasn't sure what to do with the tall man. From the moment she saw him approach, she sensed he was the reason she was in this secluded hiding place. Holding a gun on him seemed terribly wrong. Who would come to a swatch of trees on the side of this hill unless he was specifically looking for her? She'd have to lower her defenses if she was going to trust him.

Kim cautiously took a step toward him. They both felt it at the same time - a swelling inside their chests that rose and then fell, an amazing feeling that was physical as well as emotional, taking their breath away, a sensation as exhilarating as it was foreign. For a moment they realized there was nothing to fear, nothing to hide. The experience was so intense it left them speechless for minutes.

"I think we should talk about what's happening to us," Kim said in a much less intimidating voice.

"Get rid of the gun and I'll be glad to talk."

Kim lowered the weapon halfway.

"We don't have a lot of time," Rick warned her.

He was right on that count, but what were they supposed to do? Did Rick know?

"Kim, we've got to compare notes, exchange information. There's a puzzle here, and I think we were both given some of the pieces."

Callaway replaced her weapon in her holster quickly and professionally. Rick thanked God he didn't try to pull his gun. He wouldn't have had a chance. He held his hand out.

"Pleased to meet you, Kim."

She hesitated, then closed the distance and shook his hand. Like a massive wave of warm water, another relaxing swell washed over her body. A sensation of intense security surrounded her, and in that moment, she knew it would be all right to trust him, for now.

Over the next hour, hidden in the dark triangle of trees, Rick and Kim related the events that led them to the secluded sanctuary. Sitting by the stream, Rick told his story of the billboard, his winning day on the exchange, the vision of the windswept meadow and how he'd found a mysterious object ripping through the heavens, heading directly toward Earth.

Kim listened carefully, noting the similarities to her own experiences. She told him about her dinosaur dream and the vision where she traveled through a strange tunnel full of swirling bright colors as a stream yellow of material rushed past her.

"From what I saw," Kim said, "I'm not going to survive this ordeal."

A surge of sadness swept over her. The thought of dying without seeing her parents brought tears to her eyes. She'd tried to tell them she was involved in a dangerous mission, but they wouldn't listen. They kept trying to get her to go to a psychologist. No one understood what she'd gone through, except maybe Rick.

"So," she continued, "I'm prepared to die."

Rick nodded. He was in the same place.

Kim continued, relieved there was someone who could listen to her story and not make wild judgments about her sanity.

"There's this man. I don't know who he is, but he's got it out for me."

"Someone's got my number, too," said Rick remembering his own painful demise. "Is it in a meadow?"

"Yes. But it doesn't start out that way. First, I'm sucked up this elevator-like device. My body is stretched, then I come back together at the top and I'm inside this chamber, drifting, spinning among amazingly colorful clouds. I stop moving and directly in front of me is a dark red vortex, sucking this golden mist down a black hole. Something keeps screaming inside my head to fire my revolver into the tunnel over and over again, which I do. Then I'm on the ground, and there he is right in front of me, waiting..."

"Who?"

"The short guy I've been telling you about. I'm out of ammunition and he shoots me through the chest. The pain is incredible. After that, nothing. But this quiet voice keeps telling me to increase my stamina, the Casull is the only way out of the situation and somehow, if I believe what I hear, I can survive.

I've tried a number of options. I ducked, kept a single bullet in the chamber. I've even fired the revolver as I head back to the ground. Nothing works. He nails me every time."

Looking up, she locked onto Rick's emerald eyes. "What happened, Rick? What did we do to deserve this punishment?"

"I don't think it's a punishment, Kim. I think it's that we'll listen. Everyone has the ability to receive the messages, but they're too busy to stop and listen or they don't believe what they hear. For whatever reason, we were ready. Obviously the next twenty-four hours will be extremely dangerous, and whatever we decide will have far-reaching consequences. You must feel the same way or you wouldn't have been so ready to pull that gun on me."

"We're in it deep, Rick. What does the thing in the sky have to do with us?"

Rick shrugged. "I don't have a clue about it. All I know is I have to get to that light, no matter who tries to stop me."

He paused and looked into her green eyes. There was no denying her beauty. If he'd been anywhere else, he'd ask her out on a date. Kim seemed sensitive, attractive and accessible. He wished he had the time to get to know her better, but romance was out of the question.

"I'm glad you came, Kim."

"Why?"

"I've carried these feelings so long, hidden them from everyone. You're the only one who could possibly relate.

During those long days of looking through computer printouts and hiding my identity, I doubted my sanity. Wondered when I'd lose it. Being driven by a force that won't let you go, won't tell you what to do, yet demands total faith, makes you doubt yourself. Sitting next to you, I know I'm okay. It's a great feeling. Thanks."

Kim started to laugh. Rick had expressed her exact thoughts. Here was someone who could understand what she'd been going through, someone who'd lived through the same pressures, skepticism and fears she'd experienced, been given strange, obscure messages, told to be ready for an unknown event and sent to the middle of the country to meet another confused individual. Now she had a companion who'd been jerked around as much as she had.

"Wait!" Rick exclaimed, "We're in the image we saw an hour ago."

Kim continued to chuckle, "You're right. What do you think, Rick? Did we see the future? Or did we create it?"

"Well... if we've gotten our wish, that would mean we're controlling our future. We've created an image that came true. If we're merely seeing what's coming next, then we're following a predetermined path and have no say in the outcome. One way there's hope for survival; the other, we end up being killed by a stranger in a cloud-filled meadow."

Kim shook her head. "Those are pretty black-and-white observations. Perhaps there's a path in between where we bend the future, but don't control it."

"That sound's more plausible. When I was trading the stock...."

"We have to leave!" Kim was looking to the sky. Her body tensed.

"What's happening?" Rick stared through the canopy of branches. There was nothing unusual above them.

"You had another name, didn't you?" she demanded, returning her focus to Rick.

"I've used the name Rick Bradley since I started working at JPL."

"Why did you switch back?"

"It was the car rental," Rick said, remembering how relieved he was to use his name again, as if he'd written the name Peters for a specific reason.

"I was tired of hiding. I figured it wouldn't matter."

"Apparently it did. They'll be here in minutes."

"Who? Who will be here?"

"I don't know, but they're not friendly and they're coming fast."

The quickest route to the parking lot was straight down the grass-covered slope, but traveling the steep hillside was not as easy as it appeared. Kim was first to fall. Slipping on a small stone, her foot flew out from under her, slamming her butt to the ground. She slid several feet before stopping. Rick lost his balance and pitched sideways, rolling twenty feet.

The staff members manning the tram station couldn't help but notice the frantic couple scrambling down the hillside. Hiking was banned on the wide slopes as a precaution against erosion. Usually one of the staff would intercept, then warn the offenders. Before they could decide whose turn it was to perform the policing chores, Rick and Kim had stumbled down the incline and raced past the facility.

"What do you think they're up to?" asked Betsy, as she leaned on the metal railing.

"Beats me," replied Zachary, her co-worker. "I've never seen anyone run <u>away</u> from this place."

"My pack's in the car!" shouted Rick, heading for his Taurus.

"Leave it!"

"No way!" Rick raced to the rental, unlocked the trunk and pulled his backpack and duffel bag out of the car. Without bothering to close the lid, he dashed across the gravel lot and jumped into Kim's pickup truck, slinging the bags into the back seat.

"Here they come," said Kim, as Rick closed the door.

"Where?"

Kim nodded toward the horizon. Flying low and close to the ground, a black helicopter, its nose tilted downward, rushed toward the ski slope, passing directly over the pickup truck. The car shook with the beating of the rotors. Rick turned and watched out the back window.

"They seem to know where they're headed," he commented.

"There's another group coming by car," said Kim. "We'll have to pass them on the way out."

Kim drove down the road that connected the resort village with the main highway, keeping her speed relatively slow so as not to attract any unnecessary attention.

"There they are," she said, looking toward a single car traveling the main road.

"Guess it's time to disappear," he said, ducking below the dashboard. "Take a good look. We'll probably meet up with them again."

Keeping her eyes focused straight ahead, Kim tried not to appear too curious. As the car passed, she saw a woman driving with a male passenger. The woman stared intently at her, then looked away. Kim made a check in the rearview mirror, looking for brake lights. There were none.

"That was close." Kim turned to Rick. "They're taking your discovery very personally."

"I had to tell the authorities," Rick said defensively.

"So you say," she replied.

Rick had made several serious blunders. He used his real name to rent the car, his report to the government had alerted the authorities, and now, somehow, these people knew where she and Rick were. If another "accident" occurred, it would be time to part company, no matter how comfortable he made her feel.

"I can't promise you that those actions weren't part of a larger plan," said Rick. "I was told we had to stay together to survive."

"I wasn't."

Rick was shocked. He'd assumed Kim was going with him, that they were meant to be together until the situation was resolved. He stared at her while they were stopped at the main road. She was beautiful. Then his heart sank. How many others were supposed to meet him in the glen? Was he going to find himself alone in his strange venture? Kim was about to turn right, heading back to the town of Jackson.

"Take the left," he said. "It's a shortcut to Yellowstone."

"Who said we were going to Yellowstone?"

"I did." There was no doubt in Rick's mind about which direction they had to take.

"The helicopter will head south, but the car will continue to follow us."

Kim shot him a glance. She did not move the car. Rick knew he had to explain himself.

"I sense it, Kim. Going back into town will be a mistake, a really bad mistake."

Perhaps it was his turn to be the antenna, the one who knew the answers. Did she feel the same way when the voice came to her? How did she distinguish between whim and message?

"Kim, let me in on something."

"If I can," she replied, taking the left, heading north toward Yellowstone National Park.

"How did you know the helicopter was coming?"

Kim smiled and looked at him. "This is so much fun. Wait until you hear how it works."

JACKSON AIRPORT
JACKSON, WYOMING
MONDAY, **SEPTEMBER** 13, **2027**
1:20 P.M. MST        3:20 P.M. EST

By the time Lance White's Lear jet began its descent into Jackson, he'd pored over Peters' SEC files. Rick Peters was no Wall Street whiz-kid. Other than a single, spectacular day of trading, the man had barely made a two percent return on his investments. Not an impressive track record. However, he had bought and sold his clients' stocks frequently, creating a very comfortable income for himself.

Like Tom Ross, Keith Grunderson and Conrad Wiley, Peters was a capable man who'd never shown any sign of brilliance. According to his I.Q. test, Rick Peters was the least intelligent of the group. Yet, each of these individuals had timed their career changes so they could locate Eagle. Now it appeared they were heading to northwestern Wyoming.

Radioing ahead, White arranged for a helicopter to be standing by on the tarmac at Jackson airport. Washington had assigned additional agents. The two meddlers were on their way to Teton Village. The fact they'd sent a woman to do a man's job was even more infuriating.

The small helicopter covered the distance to the mountain in minutes. As the aircraft passed over the resort entrance, a calming sensation invaded White's body. The soothing feeling nearly hypnotized him. Steve Unger, the thirty-year-old pilot, felt it too. He glanced over to White with a goofy grin that annoyed the agent even more. This was no time for relaxing. Thankfully, the sensation dissipated as they neared the mountainside.

"Pull up to that stand of trees," White commanded over the intercom.

Unger surveyed the terrain White had indicated. "I can't land there. It's too steep."

"Fine. Get as close to the ground as you can. I'll jump. Wait for me."

Gun drawn, White opened the Plexiglas door and leapt to the hillside. The intense downwash tore at his clothes as he approached the protection of the evergreen trees. Although he considered Peters a clumsy amateur, White couldn't discount the possibility of an ambush.

He inched between the branches. The glen was quiet. Too quiet; made the skin on the back of his neck tingle. Circling a boulder, he came upon a clearing that bordered a quick-running stream. Footprints in the dirt told the story.

Someone had waited behind the rock. A second person had entered the small clearing. The two individuals met, then lingered near the stream. Overturned pine needles indicated they'd left in a hurry. White returned to the open field. As the throbbing from the helicopter assaulted his ears, he climbed the skid and returned to his seat.

Unger glanced at the weapon warily, then his eyes met White's for a brief moment.

"What's with the gun?" White could feel the man's fear, almost hear his thoughts: Please God, don't let this be one of those lunatics from California. White flashed his badge long enough for Unger to see the shield, but pulled it back before the pilot could read the NSA emblem.

"A couple from Los Angeles murdered a family in Montana. We're trying to stop them." White had used the lie many times over the years. Unger's look of dismay told him it had worked again.

"Did you find them?"

Nosy civilian bastard, thought White. "Not yet. Take it down to the base station," he ordered gruffly.

As the craft settled on the parking lot, White spotted two people running toward him. One was the new bitch, Janice Younger. A pudgy man followed her. He would be the second-rate field agent, Bruce Kirby. Getting rid of him would be easy. Younger was another matter.

"What'd you find, Kirby?" demanded White.

Younger knew she was being ignored. White was probably another insecure, macho men.

She answered the question without waiting for Kirby's response. "The tram operators saw them from the platform," she said. "The man grabbed a backpack from his car and went with the woman. It was probably Peters."

"Which direction, Kirby?"

This time Younger didn't reply. Kirby nervously glanced over to her.

Younger remained silent until White made eye contact. She'd heard about the hapless SEC employee who'd been shot at JPL a few hours ago. It fitted White's pattern of slash and burn. What a jerk, she thought, I'll just send him flying in the wrong direction.

"They headed south," she said with confidence. "In a red Land Cruiser."

"Good. Take Kirby and travel north."

Younger frowned. "They're not going to turn around. We should follow you on the ground."

"The man's an idiot," snapped White. "He could be in town, at this woman's place or driving in circles. Whatever he's doing, it's on a whim."

Younger knew that White considered her presence an intrusion. She tightened too-thin lips into a hard line to keep a violent outburst behind them.

"Rick Peters is no fool," she argued, towering over him, "He's left the area. Could be as far as Idaho by now."

"I don't care what you think. Cover the northern section of the valley. And keep in touch."

"You're in charge, Lance."

Younger and Kirby drove out of the small village and took the left, heading toward Yellowstone. She would have to get rid of Kirby as soon as possible. He was a liability. White, on the other hand, was dangerous. The Agency had made a serious mistake sending him to find Rick.

Rick Peters knew something about the object in the sky. He might even be in contact with it, but if Lance White found Peters before she did, the aggressive agent would resort to torture to obtain his information. Younger had other plans for the elusive stockbroker. She had to intercept him before White started doing what he did best: mangling innocent civilians in the name of national security.

Kirby glanced over to Younger. Her face was serious, eyes staring straight ahead, deep in thought. He was unsure if he should trust her. He'd heard nothing but rave reports about Younger's field operations as well as her fierce dedication to her partners. Lance White obviously had a different opinion of her. No matter what her disposition, Kirby's remaining silent would not help their situation.

"What's on your mind, Janice?"

Younger paused a moment before answering. "I think Peters will double back and head in our direction."

"Lance said..."

"Lance White thinks he's God. He's not. He's over the hill and far too prone to violence."

"I wouldn't let him know that's what you think."

"He knows what I think. He might be crazy, but he's not stupid."

A BACK WOODS ROAD
MOOSE, WYOMING
MONDAY, **SEPTEMBER** 13, **2027**
2:15 P.M. MST        4:15P.M.EST

Kim turned the oversized steering wheel at each curve. Stones pelted the underside of the pickup truck as the roadside meadow gave way to stands of spotted, white-barked aspen. Golden leaves pirouetted across the windshield. On the left, towering above the aspen and open meadows stood the majestic Grand Tetons; to the right, a continuous wall of evergreens.

"I've always had a voice inside my head that tells me what to do, when to act, how to dress" said Kim. "These messages sound different. They're quiet, less forceful, almost a whisper. If I get tense, or occupied, they disappear."

"Is that how you knew about the car rental?" asked Rick.

"That was different. I had a vision of you signing the contract, then I saw another pair of hands on a photocopy of the same piece of paper. I can't control those visions. They rip into my mind and cut me off from whatever I'm doing.

It's like what happened by the stream. I saw the helicopter coming and knew we had to leave, fast. If we didn't..." She paused, remembering the image of Rick lying on the ground with half a dozen holes in his chest and her being cruelly carved by the familiar short, squatty man.

"What would have happened?" asked Peters.

"He was going kill us."

"We're still alive. Maybe we are affecting the future. Still, it would be a good idea to steer clear of that guy."

"We will, if you stop leaving clues about where we are."

Kim was annoyed with his oversights, mistakes that could prove fatal.

Rick remained quiet. For the first time in years, he was in the company of a woman who interested him, both sexually and mentally. He found himself staring at her face, her shoulders, her hair. Every aspect of her existence fascinated him. He wanted to know everything about her, what she did in her teens, where she grew up, what she liked to eat. The loneliness he'd felt over the last year vanished, replaced by a warmth he attributed to his interest in Kim Callaway.

"What's next?" asked Kim, as she navigated the awkward pickup truck across a narrow wooden bridge.

"Yellowstone."

"Got that. Then what?"

"Try to find the meadow without being detained. My guess is the people following us think we're connected with the object in the sky."

"I wish they'd butt out," said Kim, spinning the wheel again.

"They've got their job to do," said Rick, "We've got ours."

"And exactly what is our job?"

"Protecting the Source," blurted Rick.

"Who's the Source?"

"It's under the ground, somewhere near here. There's a weak spot where it can be attacked..." Rick paused, suddenly confused.

"Damn, I had it there for a second. It was so clear. What the hell happened?"

"If it's important, it'll you'll remember it," Kim said optimistically. "Who else is in on this?"

"It appears that you and I are the chosen two."

Kim took a hard left and the truck bounced onto the pavement.

"You're kidding. We're already outnumbered."

Rick sighed. "I thought there were going to be more people involved."

"They could show up later," Kim offered.

"They'd better. We're going to need help. Lots of it."

As they entered Teton National Park, another flash image filled their minds. Kim sat on a wooden chair, inside a dingy tool shed, her hands bound behind her. The stocky man smiled as he placed his gun on a nearby bench. Raising his pant leg, he pulled a steel knife from its sheath. A wicked grin spread across his face as he walked toward her.

With a flick of the wrist, he ran the knife across Kim's thigh. Blood spurted from the deep gash. Kim was too shocked to scream. He struck again, slicing her arm. Suddenly a door burst open. Daylight filled the room. The short man swiveled, grabbed the gun, and fired several rounds.

Kim blinked. She was back driving the car.

"Look out!"

A huge RV camper filled the windshield. Kim jerked the car to the right. The two-ton giant ripped the mirror off the side of the car with an ear-splitting screech.

"Whoa!" yelled Rick, "too close!"

Kim regained control of the car. "That was the man! The guy in the field!"

"Who cares! Watch what you're doing!"

"Back off, Rick! I'm doing the best I can."

As Rick calmed down, he realized he'd seen the man in the shed before.

"That's the guy who's shoots me in the meadow. Well, now we know there's a shed involved. We know it's the same person who's after both of us. We should be able to avoid that situation...if we stay alert and don't get crushed in a car wreck."

THE OVAL OFFICE
WASHINGTON, D.C.
MONDAY, **SEPTEMBER** 13, **2027**
5:25 P.M. MST        7:25 P.M. EST

Franklin Turner, the President's oldest friend in the scientific community, arrived at the White House for his seven p.m. meeting. As head of NASA's High-Resolution Microwave Survey, Turner was a firm believer in extraterrestrial life. Although the bent sixty-year-old refused to accept the possibility that aliens had visited the Earth, simple mathematics dictated there had to be intelligence residing somewhere in the infinite reaches of space. He'd lectured extensively on this theory, but steadfastly refused to be swayed in his disbelief of alien abduction or believe in the UFO footage released by the military. At seven thirty-five he was ushered into the famous office.

The President met Turner at the tall double doors. "Glad you could make it, Franklin."

"It's always a pleasure to see you, Bill." Turner smiled, revealing his tobacco-stained teeth. "Sounds like you have your hands full with this one."

The two men sat in front of a planetary map spread across an eighteenth-century coffee table. A bright red line depicted Eagle's projected interception with Earth.

"Franklin, you've been predicting a situation like this for years. What do you think? Do we have a military problem in the making or is this something that will create a spectacular light show and pass us by?"

Franklin did not look at the chart. He knew Eagle's route. It was not passing by.

"Well," he began in his slow, deliberate manner of discussion, "Whatever it is, it is more powerful than anything we have experienced."

"So it's correct to assume you think this object contains intelligent life?"

"I have no idea what's inside, but Eagle is definitely a complex machine built by intelligent creatures."

"You're certain of this?"

Franklin pointed at the map. "This object has traveled across the solar system, altered its speed and made a course correction. This is not solar wind."

"All right. Let's assume a group of advanced beings is heading in our direction. There is no reason to assume they're friendly."

Deep ridges formed on Franklin's wrinkled forehead. "Were you thinking of trying to stop it?"

President Lindon smiled. "Our military complex has always been accused of creating fantastic scenarios for no apparent reason. Preparations have been made."

"A hostile move toward this force is inadvisable."

"What if its intentions are unfriendly?"

"I don't believe they are."

"There are many who disagree with you."

Turner stared at the President. "Be careful, my friend. I doubt you have anything in your secret arsenal that can affect this visitor."

"I can't wait around hoping the outcome of the next few days will be to our advantage. Military as well as diplomatic precautions must be taken."

Turner sat back on the couch. "Bill, an unprovoked attack on these beings could trigger a devastating reprisal. I am sure Eagle is carrying highly advanced weaponry."

The President paused. It was clear that Turner was afraid of a direct confrontation with the huge ship, but fearing the unknown was no excuse for being ill-prepared. Franklin dropped the subject. This was a discussion for his military advisors.

"What do you think about the scientists who first reported Eagle?"

"Oh, they know something," said Turner. When you consider how many directions one can look in the sky, how many possibilities there are, and yet these five people found a speeding, dark, object within hours of each other and sent their reports to a single man in Washington, my conclusion can only be that they're involved with each other and with Eagle."

"Do you think they're aliens?"

"Perhaps. Whatever their role, they'll probably be involved in the final outcome."

"We are making all attempts to locate them."

Turner nodded. "I think they will be at the center of any important activity."

As the President's eyes dropped to the map, Turner studied the former Governor. International disputes, political battles, even assassination attempts were expected when occupying the Chief Executive's office, but this was a challenge without precedent. No wonder he was turning to the military as his next move. It is impossible to negotiate with an adversary who won't communicate.

"You are in a difficult position, sir."

Linden stood, his paunchy frame taking on a presidential posture. "I will defend my people and my country."

Turner rose and shook his hand. "You have a lot to think about over the next few hours. I pray you use the powers at your command wisely."

"I'd like it if you'd keep in touch, Franklin. This is not an easy time."

"It might be easier than you think. I would avoid making any aggressive moves."

Turner took a long look at his old friend. Linden had aged noticeably.

"I'll make sure your office can reach me."

"Thank you for coming, Franklin."

"My pleasure, Bill. And good luck."

GRAND TETON NATIONAL PARK
TWENTY MILES NORTH OF JACKSON, WYOMING
MONDAY, **SEPTEMBER**, 13, **2027**
5:15 P.M. MST                     7:15 P.M. EST

Kim and Rick traveled the two-lane road that cut through the Teton Wilderness Park. Rick took notice of the numerous pickups on the road. This pleased him. The large number of similar vehicles would help keep their pursuers confused. He continued to check the skies for the bubble-shaped helicopter. "Did you ever consider that we're being manipulated by the bad guys?" he asked as he peered out the side window.

"All the time," replied Kim. "Sometimes I think we've been brainwashed, but I keep telling myself that I have to have faith what I'm doing is right. It's gotten me this far. Everything seems to be working out according to some plan, although it's not my idea of a vacation."

Despite Rick's earlier mistakes, Kim could not deny the extraordinary safety she felt when she was around him. It wasn't his looks or his attitude, it was his presence; being with him felt right.

"Did I tell you about the afternoon I discovered this whole episode was actually going to happen?"

"You only spoke about the dreams."

Kim glanced over and smiled. He wasn't bad looking, either. A little thin for her taste, but he felt so good. Soul mates.

"I was at a bar one afternoon having a drink with some friends. We'd been there about an hour when this gorgeous guy comes up and starts hitting on my friend, Renee. Five minutes later Renee and I both had a vision of a man killing someone.

"I was so confused, I had to leave. It turned out that Renee went home with him the following week. What we'd seen was her death. After that, I listened very carefully to the voice. I took pistol classes, stress reduction exercises and kept a strict jogging routine. If I do everything it tells me, my life runs like clockwork. Nothing gets in my way and nothing goes wrong."

"Doesn't help your driving much."

"We lost a mirror. Big deal." She paused to let a car pass, making sure it wasn't the couple from the ski area. "What day did you see the billboard?"

Rick sighed. She was so attractive. What rotten timing. Of course he had to meet her when he couldn't do anything about it.

"The billboard happened on April 11th, just after noon."

"I was in the bar on May 9th at about eleven at night."

"So much for the same-day same-time theory," Rick said as he made another sweep of the sky.

Kim liked talking to him. There were no stupid sexual innuendoes, no moronic jokes. Rick was pleasant and understanding. She knew he wouldn't make fun of her, no matter what she said.

"Did you see any dinosaurs or a massive storm in any of your dreams?"

Rick nodded. "I saw a storm, but nothing that resembled a dinosaur. There were plenty of Marines and that amazing pillar of light."

"I saw the pillar," said Kim, "In one of the dreams there were dinosaurs everywhere. And it took place in a swamp."

"What happens after the shaft disappears?"

Kim shuddered. "Tidal waves, incredible land upheavals, volcanoes. I still can't get used to it." She noticed a sign ahead announced the turnoff for Jenny Lake Lodge.

"You hungry?"

"Starved."

"I'll pull into the lodge. We can mingle with the crowd."

Rick was concerned. They couldn't afford to be caught.

"What if the park rangers have my photo?"

"Come on, Rick. This is America. Nobody works that fast."

"Those guys in the helicopter knew where we were."

Kim shot him a glance. "Because you told them where to find us. They don't know where we are now, do they?"

"No."

"You're sure?"

Kim's accusing tone annoyed him, but she had a point. The ripped poster in his office had probably led their pursuers right to the ski slope. How could he make such a foolish mistake? Everything else seemed so perfectly choreographed.

"I'm sure we're safe."

Tall spruce trees surrounded the huge wooden lodge. The trees provided excellent cover for the car. There would be no spotting the pickup truck from the air. Rick and Kim entered the log building and climbed a set of wide steps. On the second floor they were greeted by a fifty-foot-high window that revealed a breathtaking vista of fields and pines. Towering above the foliage stood the craggy peaks of the Grand Tetons.

After purchasing their sandwiches, Rick and Kim returned to the lobby. Tourists milled about, taking selfies with the fabulous scenery in the background. Rick watched Kim cross the room. She walked with such energy and determination. Her short blonde hair, trim build and casual confidence drew silent admiration from nearly everyone in the room. Heads turned.

A new awareness came over Kim. She felt someone's thoughts, thoughts about her. Turning around she realized Rick's eyes were locked on her body.

"What are you staring at?"

"Just looking."

"Sizing me up?"

"Not my choice of words," he said.

"Rick, just because we've been thrown together, for God knows what reason, that doesn't mean you get your hands on anything."

"I was merely enjoying the view. Don't take everything so personally."

Kim shot him a stem look. He smiled back.

When she turned her attention back to the breathtaking view, his mind wandered again. Kim's beauty was so enveloping, so subtly seductive. As she stood in the center of the huge lobby, he imagined they were alone in a backwoods cabin. He gently unbuttoned her soft flannel blouse.

Kim looked down at her chest, certain she was being undressed, yet her clothes remained unmoved. Turning around, she saw Rick staring again, definitely unfocused.

Could she feel what he was imagining? There'd been enough strange occurrences happening in her life today. It would make sense, considering the expression on Rick's face. There was one way to find out.

Rick fell to his knees. Without a sound, he grabbed his crotch as a look of intense pain spread across his face.

"What's wrong?" she asked innocently.

"I don't know," he gasped, "It felt like I got kicked...in the crotch."

Kim held back a chuckle. It always struck her as funny when men grabbed their privates, but Rick was obviously suffering. No sense in hurting his ego as well.

"Maybe you should be more selective about whom you're fantasizing. It appears you're able to project those thoughts extremely well."

"I didn't touch you, Kim."

"Neither did I."

Still suffering from the invisible blow, Rick looked up at her.

"I promise, I'll be more careful. You really felt that?"

Kim bent over and whispered gently in his ear. "Keep your hands to yourself."

Rick winced. "Trust me. Never again. I apologize."

"Good," she said, helping him to his feet.

Rick wasn't finished. He took a few steps away, then imagined kissing her on the cheek. The resulting slap across his face hit him with such force his head turned. Kim hadn't moved a muscle.

"Want more?"

"I had to make sure," he replied, rubbing the side of his head.

"Now you know. Was it worth it?"

"I think it was. It's a great way to communicate."

Kim frowned, her hands resting on her hips. "I find it personally invasive. A tap on the shoulder would have been adequate and resulted in much less pain on your part. Could we act a little more responsibly?"

He tapped her on the shoulder without lifting a finger.

"Rick, it works. Now cut it out."

"What do you think, Kim, can we do it to someone else?" He turned to face a uniformed guard and imagined tickling his ear. The guard didn't react. Rick was disappointed. "Didn't affect him in the least."

Kim was still annoyed. "What did you try to do, pull his fly down?"

"Tickle his ear."

"Let me do it," she said, deciding to join the game.

She tickled his ear.

"Did he move?" she asked without turning.

"No. How about both of us thinking the same thing at the same time. Maybe it takes the two."

"What do you want to do?"

Rick thought for a moment. "Kick him in the butt."

Kim chuckled. "On the count of three. One, two, three."

The guard jerked forward, then angrily turned around. Rick and Kim could barely stop from laughing. Covering their mouths, they left the lobby and headed back to the car.

"A tap on the shoulder would have been adequate," Rick chortled as they left the lodge.

INTERNATIONAL SPACE STATION
EARTH ORBIT
MONDAY, **SEPTEMBER** 13, **2027**
6:05 MST          8:05 P.M. EST

Ed Iris looked down at the Earth below his feet. He was living a dream he'd worked for the last twenty years - performing a spacewalk. Unfortunately, these circumstances were less than desirable. Iris and partner Hugh Smith had traveled into orbit to test their space laser two days ago, but it appeared their experiment was turning into a full-scale military attack on an alien ship, something their prototype was not designed to do. The generals in Washington probably thought this underpowered weapon could save the world. Yeah, right; and pigs could fly.

As Ed steadied the near-weightless behemoth, Hugh removed the last stays that attached the laser to the exterior of the space station. Next to the laser was a second weapon, a cluster of five small, nuclear-tipped missiles housed in a single canister. Eventually, hundreds of launchers like this would be parked in orbit, ready to fire their payload if the sentry satellites sensed a hostile missile launch. Even though Russia had ceased to be a major threat to the United States, North Korea and Iran had developed nuclear weapons along with sophisticated delivery systems. China had remained a threat since the political fallout from the Coronavirus outbreak of 2020.

Spaceborne defense systems were now a priority within the U.S. military complex. Today, there would be no satellites communicating with the launcher. The cluster would be manipulated by a crew deep inside Cheyenne Mountain, the location of the United States Space Command.

Commander Frederick Zyger watched Iris and Smith as they fired their jet packs pushing their laser further into space. Those were two individuals Zyger did not envy. The men had been the prime scientists during the design, testing and manufacture of the weapon. Now they were going into space, to do battle with a gigantic alien ship.

Zyger watched the two caretakers guide the fragile laser into the darkness. Hopefully they wouldn't be ordered to shoot. Even though Eagle would be traveling at a speed slow enough for the computers to plot an intercept solution, what happened after they fired on the ship would probably put an end to their careers.

ROUTE 191
FIFTY MILES SOUTH OF JACKSON, WYOMING
MONDAY, **SEPTEMBER** 13, **2027**
6:25 P.M. MST        8:25 P.M. EST

John Davis and his wife had spent five eye-opening days touring the thermal areas of Yellowstone Park. When the black helicopter landed on the road in front of them, they knew their holiday had taken a decidedly different turn. Out of the Plexiglas bubble jumped a short dark-haired man. It wasn't until he was at their windshield that they realized he was armed. Jamming the Land Cruiser in reverse, Davis attempted to back out of the situation, but a line of cars had formed behind him. Without a word, the stranger ran up to the car and peered into the back seat. Davis was certain he was going to die.

After circling the car once, the short man raced back to the helicopter. Moments later the craft took off and headed south. Lance White had located three Land Cruisers in his fast-moving search; none contained the elusive Rick Peters. He'd scoured the area from Teton Village to Jackson and all roads leading south. After buzzing the remaining five miles of road, he ordered Unger to drop the helicopter in a vacant field.

He opened his satellite phone and tried to contact Younger. No answer. He tried Kirby. No answer. The bitch was up to something. He called the Teton Village tram and asked to speak to the young woman who'd seen the fleeing campers.

"What type of vehicle did you say they were driving?"

"Like I told the woman, they left in a brown pickup truck."

"A pickup truck? Not a Land Cruiser?"

"It was a brown pickup truck, an old one," said the woman.

"And they headed back into town?" demanded White.

"I never said that. I told the woman they went north, toward Moose Junction."

"Is there anything else? Were they wearing unusual clothes? Did they have any rappelling or camping gear?"

"The woman had on a flannel jacket and carried a small day pack. The man wore jeans and a down vest. He ran to his car, pulled out a larger knapsack and brought it to the woman's truck. Come to think of it, they drove right under that helicopter. Oh, there's something else. It's kind of weird."

"Go on," he said as pleasantly as he could.

Younger had lied to him. Another filthy double-crosser, and a female no less. White was so angry he had difficulty listening to the tram attendant.

"When they ran by the station, I felt extremely comfortable. Like I was in church or meditating. Once they were gone, the feeling went away."

White terminated the call without thanking her. The description of the tram attendant's feelings triggered his memory. Could she be describing the same annoying sensation he had experienced as he'd flown toward the mountain? Could he have flown directly over Rick Peters?

If that's how it felt, he wouldn't need to look for the pickup truck, he merely had to pass over it. He would sense Peters beneath him. It didn't matter if the feeling was magic or magnetic; if it worked, his job would be that much easier. If it did work, it probably meant that Peters was an alien. White checked the sky. Not a lot of daylight left. A call to Washington informed him that an AWAC would be positioned above the park inside an hour, coordinating all communications within a four-hundred-mile radius. White smiled. The AWAC would allow him to access much more information and he could access it while in the helicopter.

The computer had more information. Eagle was still on course, and the White House was asking about the status of the missing scientists. White hung up. No sense talking to anyone until he had positive news.

Folding the phone, he returned to the helicopter.

# SEARCHING

ROUTE 89
NORTHWESTERN WYOMING
MONDAY, **SEPTEMBER** 14, **2027**
7:38 P.M. MST        9:38 P.M. EST

Twenty minutes after entering Yellowstone Park, Rick and Kim encountered huge stands of burned forest. To the right was the steep-walled Lewis Canyon. Normally hidden by the lush forest, the narrow gorge was easily visible from the road. To the left their vision was unobstructed for over half a mile. Burned, naked tree trunks stood by the thousands, like charcoaled sticks placed upright in the dirt.

"This is strange," said Kim, slowing to take a better look.

"Looks like hell."

"It does," replied Kim. "Apparently it's one of the ways the forest is replenished. If the fires are stopped, the trees become old and susceptible to beetle attack. The sap from young pine trees pushes the beetle out of the bark. There are several species of pine cones that won't open unless they're burned."

"No kidding."

"National Geographic wouldn't lie, Rick."

Life in the pickup truck calmed down. There'd been no signs of the helicopter, and neither Kim nor Rick had experienced any more flashes. Kim enjoyed being with the strong man sitting beside her. She especially liked his muscular forearms. Rick had obviously been training.

"You think the answer is in the shaft of light?" Kim asked.

"No doubt about it."

"I disagree," she said firmly. "It's the red mass I saw in my dream, the one where I was shooting down the dark hole."

"Any chance they could be one and the same?"

"I didn't notice any similarities. Whoa! Did you feel that?"

"Yeah, I did! Go back to that sign."

Kim turned the pickup around and pulled into a dirt parking lot. A large wooden marker boldly announced the Continental Divide.

"Is it strong for you?" she asked, looking over to Rick.

Rick nodded. His voice took on a serious tone. "Let's check it out."

As they approached the sign, a physical sensation tugged at their bodies.

"This is definitely bizarre," said Kim, rubbing her stomach. "Not that bizarre things haven't been happening."

"Walk around. Maybe it will tell us more."

Kim ducked into the woods while Rick wandered in front of the large brown sign, feeling the tingling sensation in his feet. The cold night air nipped at his face. Suddenly there was a sense of firmness beneath him. He moved to one side, then the other. The sensation underneath his feet faded. After finding it again, he put one foot in front of the other and, like a tightrope walker, crossed the road. He turned and walked in the opposite direction. Heading west was definitely more pleasant than heading east. He crossed the road again. He was so intent on his discovery, a Jeep ripped by and nearly ran him over.

Kim headed down an embankment, then walked between towering pines. The emotion beckoned, luring her deeper into the fragrant evergreens, but she missed the security she felt when near Rick. In minutes, she was deep into the dense forest. A noise in the undergrowth shook her out of her trance. She stopped. This was Wyoming, not Connecticut. The rugged wilderness surrounding her was mean and unforgiving. She was alone, without food and unprepared for any change in weather.

The sensation continued to pull her, tempting her to come further into the forest. She closed her eyes. West was the direction she wanted to travel. In her mind, she saw a line, twisted and bent, but immobile. She opened her eyes. It was time to get back to the car. She retraced her steps. Lost in thought, she didn't see the bear cub until she was almost upon it.

Every nerve in her body screamed danger. Bears, buffalo and moose were common in the preserve, but too many tourists made the mistake thinking park animals were friendly. The bear cub meant one thing: there was a protective female close by. Kim had to retreat, but in which direction?

Instinctively she pulled her Casull from her holster. A female grizzly was ornery enough, but if she thought her offspring was threatened, she would attempt to kill the offending animal. Kim quietly circled the small animal as her eyes darted in every direction. A bellowing howl came from behind. Kim whirled. A belligerent grizzly galloped toward her. She knew she couldn't outrun the huge animal. Bears could reach speeds of up to forty miles an hour.

Kim raised the revolver and fired a single shot in front of the beast. The blast reverberated throughout the forest, but the bear continued to charge. A second clamorous shot followed, but it wasn't from Kim's gun. This time the bear stopped. It stared at the human, then turned and ran to its cub. Together the animals made a hasty retreat.

Rick burst through the evergreens. Kim ran to him and threw her arms around him. Their eyes met, then Kim gently pulled herself away.

"I don't know how to thank you, Rick," she panted.

"No need. You'd do the same for me. I'm sure you'll have the opportunity soon enough."

They returned to the road and scampered up the slope.

"Did you find anything?" she asked.

Rick swept his arm to the west. "It's a line. It crosses the road and travels in that direction." He grabbed the map from the front seat of the pickup truck.

"I felt it, too, but nothing so precise." She examined the map, then she pointed to the bent red line tracing the Continental Divide.

"That's it. That's what I saw. It's the Divide."

Rick's finger traced the dotted line. "The road crosses it a couple more times. We should check out those places, too."

"I'd agree with that, pal," said Kim.

"Kick me in the crotch, and you ain't my pal, pal."

"I'm sorry, Rick. Another time and another place, we could have had some fun together." She paused for a moment, then hastily added, "But don't consider that an invitation."

"Didn't cross my mind."

"I know."

Eight miles later, they pulled over.

Kim felt the pull in her stomach, like a stabbing hunger pang. "It's stronger here."

Rick nodded. "It almost hurts. Let's drive to the next crossing."

"What time is it?" asked Kim, as she started the car and pulled onto the two-lane road.

"Seven-forty."

Rick glanced at the glowing horizon colored with hues of purple and orange. It reminded him of the evening he'd met Curt Smith on the softball field.

"We're running out of daylight," he said, returning his gaze to the park map.

Kim sighed impatiently. "We're running out of time."

Janice Younger pulled in front of a large sign indicating the Continental Divide. She left the lights aimed at the carved letters. Her oversized shadow moved across the words. There was something unusual about the area. She circled the parking lot, examining the ground. Unable to find anything about the location that warranted additional investigation, she returned to the car, unfolded her satellite phone.

"Younger, A459," she recited.

There was a brief pause as her voice was digitally encoded, scrambled, bounced off a satellite onto the receiving dish in Denver. From there the signal was routed to Washington via another uplink.

"What is your status, A420?" came the response.

The voice was generated by a computer in the East Coast headquarters of the NSA. A supervisor would be monitoring field communications, but this was not a human.

"Still tracking. Update subject 66, 67, 68, A400."

Requesting information about Grunderson, Peters and Wiley would raise no eyebrows. Asking about agent 400, Lance White, would eventually cause her trouble. Too bad. She was already in trouble.

The computerized response took only seconds. "66 took a flight to Salt Lake City arriving in one hour. Agents 28, 46 waiting there. Will track. 67 is at Teton Village in blue Hertz Taurus, Agent 400 in Jackson, Wyoming tracking. Subject 68 arrived Sunday 2 p.m. Jackson, Wyoming, US Air Flight 1432. AWAC in position over northwest Wyoming. Code red dog red. More info there."

Younger terminated the call. Circling above her was a Boeing 767, crammed with electronic sensing equipment and a radar complex as sensitive as any on the ground. There was no additional information concerning Peters. Grunderson was on a flight to Salt Lake and would be tailed the minute he left the plane. The only information on Conrad Wiley was he'd flown to Jackson the previous day. Younger redialed contacted the AWAC.

"Go ahead," came the digitized voice.

"Red dog red, A420." Younger said slowly and clearly. Sometimes the scrambler could confuse the voice I.D. equipment, especially on an AWAC.

"Go ahead."

"Ask information."

The computer took a moment to compile her information, then deleted any classified information that she was not eligible to receive.

"Marine contingent arriving West Yellowstone airstrip six hundred hours. NSA 400, 420, 708 tracking in area. Air Force PJs to arrive zero six fifteen, 9/15. Eagle nonresponsive. AWAC in position at nineteen hundred hours. Code DEFCON 1. Go ahead."

Younger loved this high-tech stuff. As long as she asked the right questions, information would be automatically fed to her. The AWAC had been in position for fifteen minutes. All military bases had come to imminent war status. Younger was sure Eagle would be attacked unless it started communicating.

Too bad Kirby was missing all the action. Younger had stopped for gas, and left him when he went inside to get a soda for her.

"Ask A400," she demanded.

"Contact at 7:45. Information asked A420, 708."

White had just checked in with the AWAC.

"Ask A420."

"Coordinates forty-four degrees twenty-one minutes north, one hundred eleven degrees, thirty-five minutes west. Asked info, 66, 67, 68, A400, AWAC, A420."

The AWAC's computers would dutifully tell White exactly where she was and what information she'd requested. She had to leave the area quickly.

"Tell AWAC."

"Go ahead."

"Subject 67 and female partner at Old Faithful. Bought gas. Changed cars. Subject 67 and female partner headed north toward Mammoth Hot Springs. Pursuing in rented Saturn."

Hopefully the misleading message would send White out of the area. Younger returned to the road and continued heading north. She had to find Rick Peters before Lance White got his hands on him.

UNITED AIRLINES FLIGHT 45
SOMEWHERE OVER UTAH
MONDAY, **SEPTEMBER** 13, **2027**
7:43 P.M. MST          9:43 P.M. EST

Keith Grunderson had sat in the narrow airline seat, fuming. He'd run a dozen red lights in a desperate race to catch this flight from Los Angeles to Salt Lake City. Although he'd made it to the gate in record time, as soon as the plane backed out of the terminal, it stopped. For nearly an hour the jet remained on the tarmac.

Grunderson was so frustrated, he ignored the equally provoked brunette sitting across the aisle from him. He noticed her when he first boarded the plane. Something about her long-braided hair had attracted him. She seemed intense, but approachable. He thought about starting a conversation, but when the delay was announced over the intercom, he forgot about her. This interruption would cause him to miss his connecting flight. Damn, if he hadn't stayed so long at JPL, he'd be on his way to Jackson.

By the time the jet touched down in Salt Lake, Grunderson had devised an alternative plan. Pushing his way past the sullen woman, he turned on his cell phone and Googled the nearest motorcycle dealers.

"Salt Lake Harley." The voice on the other end was slow, deliberate. Grunderson could tell he wasn't in Los Angeles anymore. "Do you have an off-road/on-road bike?"

"Harley only makes street bikes, sir," came the reply.

Grunderson dialed another number.

"Landers Suzuki." Another easy-going salesman. What was with these people? Didn't they have any energy? The stress level here was way too low.

"Do you have an off-road dirt bike that can also travel the highway?"

"Yes, sir, we do."

"Gas it up, will you? I'll buy it."

"I'm sorry sir, we're closed."

"I'll give you my credit card number. I need the bike tonight."

"Sir..."

"There's five hundred dollars cash for you if you stay open. How far are you from the airport?"

"Fifteen minutes." The man sounded a little more interested.

"I'll be there in ten."

Grunderson turned off his phone. No sense giving anyone an idea where he was. He also had the foresight to open a credit card in a different name for just this reason. Leaving JPL like he did was sure to raise suspicions. No telling what the United States government was doing now. Everyone had to know about the anomaly by now. He'd be one of the first people they would be looking for.

Within the hour, Grunderson owned an eight thousand-dollar Suzuki Dual Sport motorcycle. He threw his gear into the saddlebags and roared off, heading to the onramp of Interstate 15. A minute later, an unmarked National Security Agency car sped up the same ramp, following the transmission from the device sewn into the lining of Grunderson's duffel bag.

Barbara Whitten's entire existence had been permanently altered by her date with Rick Peters. Until that afternoon, her life had been orderly and predictable. The minute he dropped her off, her mind became consumed with the images she'd seen in Sonya's office. Throughout the weekend her nerves continued to be jumbled. Her life was in turmoil and her treasured appointment book rendered useless.

She tried to explain the scene she'd witnessed in Sonya's office to Ted and Gary. Her well-intentioned neighbors listened politely, but there was no convincing them what she'd experienced had changed her life or was even real. Although they'd insisted that she go sailing with Rick, they wanted no part of the results of that rendezvous.

"I want some of the drugs you're taking," commented Ted.

Barbara pointed a shaky finger at her neighbor. "You did this to me. If I hadn't agreed to your stupid blind date, I wouldn't be so...so...upset. This is your fault! I can't think straight. I can't talk about anything else. I can't do anything."

"Lighten up, Barbara. It was a bad dream. Have a drink and forget about it."

The images stayed with her late into the night. Over and over she saw Rick Peters running toward the shimmering column of light. Sleep became impossible, relaxation a faint memory. Exhausted and emotionally drained, she continued to play the scene in her mind, experiencing the wind, the luminous pillar and Rick Peters' death, until, at one point, she imagined being in the area.

Something changed. She ran the event again, altering her actions, running here, hiding there. By Monday morning she knew what she had to do, but wasn't about to act on it. She couldn't just fly to Wyoming to kill someone. This had to be a hormonal reaction, some kind of chemical imbalance.

Late Monday afternoon, when the Foundation's computers filled with alerts about an enormous space ship headed for Earth, Barbara realized she had no choice. She left work early, promising to return after taking care of a few errands. She packed her gear, and after a lightning run down the freeway, she boarded a flight to Salt Lake City. An equipment delay ruined her chances of connecting with the last flight to Jackson. As soon as she was on the ground, she headed for the car rental counter.

"Will you be returning the car here?" asked the Hertz agent.

Barbara smiled. You'll never see this car again, honey, she thought.

"Without a doubt," she said sweetly. "I'll only be needing it for three days."

"We have a special if you keep the car over a Saturday night."

There isn't going to be a Saturday night if you don't get moving. "No, thank you, but I do have to get going."

As she drove from the airport, Barbara noticed her hands were damp with perspiration. In the trunk was her fully loaded backpack and two high-powered rifles. After ten years of honing her shooting skills, becoming one of the best long-distance shooters in Southern California, she was heading to a Wyoming meadow to perform her first assassination.

CRAIG PASS
YELLOWSTONE NATIONAL PARK MONDAY,
**SEPTEMBER** 13, **2027**
8:10 P.M. MST          10:10 P.M.EST

The pickup truck's headlights illuminated the third sign that marked the Continental Divide. The sensation became stronger at each crossing.

Rick pointed up the road. "Let's keep going. When the feeling lessens, we'll know it's between the two points." Twenty minutes into Idaho they reached the next location where the Divide crossed the road.

Kim couldn't feel anything. "We're past it," she said without getting out of the car.

Rick nodded. "You're right, there's nothing here. We have to go back."

Kim pulled a U-turn in the middle of the two-lane road and headed in the opposite direction. After a few miles she pulled onto the shoulder.

"You have to drive, Rick. I can't focus anymore."

"No problem. We'll go back to the Madison Campground, catch a few hours of sleep and start fresh at dawn."

Kim shook her head in disagreement. "I think that's a bad move. Let's go to Old Faithful, find a trail and head in. I'll take a nap in the car."

"We should wait until daybreak. It's not safe out there, Kim."

"This isn't a vacation, Rick."

He checked his watch. "I think we should get some rest."

Kim laughed. "You just want to sleep with me. I know your type."

"Right. I'm dying to crawl into a tent with you and get kicked in the balls."

"I thought as much." Kim laughed. It was the first time she'd felt happy in years. "Rick, we can't pull into a campsite. It's the first place they'll look."

"We're fine among the tourists. We've tested that theory."

Kim shrugged her shoulders. She wasn't in the mood to argue. Maybe he'd change his mind. "Whatever. Let's go."

Rick slid behind the wheel. The fear had left him. Taking action eliminated his chronic feeling of helplessness. It brought back memories of when his Little League coach insisted that Rick swing at the ball, rather than waiting to be walked.

"You can't live your life waiting for others to screw up," the coach had told him. "There comes a point where you have to take control."

Rick glanced over to Kim, who was already asleep, resting her head against the car door. There was no keeping his eyes off her short blonde hair, her sculpted face. She filled his existence. Even when she was driving, he continually looked over at her, almost afraid she would disappear. Perhaps, if they survived this ordeal, she might consider spending some time with him. He had millions buried in the arroyo behind the Jet Propulsion Lab. Two people could have a lot of fun with that kind of money.

Rick slowed for the Madison Campground turnoff, hesitated, then continued down the main road. Kim was right. The sooner they headed into the forest, the better. He took the spur that led into the Old Faithful parking lot and pulled into one of the hundreds of parking spaces. He turned off the car and gently shook Kim awake. It was the first time he'd touched her. The sensation was electrifying.

"Are we okay?" she asked groggily.

"Everything's okay. I took your advice and kept going. We're at Old Faithful. It's a good place to pack up and head in."

"Fine by me."

The full moon shone down on the large parking lot. Kim and Rick studied the map under the illumination of the car's dome light. Rick sighed. He should have pulled off at Biscuit Basin. The Summit Lake Trail traveled directly to the Divide.

"You're right," Kim replied.

"I didn't say anything."

"But I heard you. We should go back and take the Summit Trail. The meadow is somewhere in here." Her finger circled the Madison Plateau.

"Are you sure?"

"Positive."

Why wasn't he told where they were going? Then the doubts began. What if Kim wasn't the woman he was supposed to meet? If she was connected with the people in the helicopter, she obviously would have known they were coming. Was she jeopardizing his plan or, even worse, leading him into a trap? Maybe it was time to split up. He had to get to that meadow. No matter how good she made him feel, he had a commitment to keep. Staying with her could be risky.

"That's enough," she said angrily. "I kept my temper when you screwed up, worked with you, saved your goddamned life on that ski slope, and now you suspect me of being the enemy? I'm out of here."

Kim opened the door and stormed away.

The emptiness returned, filling his heart with a cold wind. What was he thinking? Of course they had to stay together. He grabbed his down jacket, burst out of the pickup truck and raced across the nearly deserted parking lot. Would she have gone into the woods without him? She had her gun and heavy coat. Even with the light of the full moon, it would be impossible to locate her if she'd entered the forest.

He stopped, surrounded by acres of blacktop. She was gone. He stomped his feet. Damn. He might as well go home and watch the disaster unfold on TV like everyone else. Stupid messages and glowing balls of lights. Why did he think he could pull this off?

The familiar fear began to rise in his chest. What should he do? Where was the meadow? Could it be where Kim had indicated, was it back at the ski slope, or somewhere else?

Then he felt it, pulling him like a beacon. He followed the tugging sensation across the parking lot, down a concrete pathway. He found her sitting on one of the dozens of benches that ringed the famous Old Faithful geyser. He was only a few feet from her when the images attacked him.

The inside of the huge ship was dark. There was no console, no bridge, no sign of life. The machine hummed, and the deep rumble permeated his soul. Unfamiliar symbols covered walls. Information flooded Rick's mind, filling it with details and history. There were terrible weapons aboard, capable of defending the ship against any attacker.

It was a mining ship sent by a distant civilization which had tapped its own planet's Source, using it faster than it could replenish itself. Complicated organic computers ran the ship, guiding it to the few blessed planets that contained living organisms. The vessel's purpose was to mine the ethereal material that kept life safe and thriving on these globes, then return with it to the ship's makers.

Suddenly he was underground, inside a living organism, deep in a protected place. There was no doubting the wonderful strength that now surrounded him. It was not capable of fighting off the attacker. It possessed a different kind of power: nurturing, generative. Others had to physically preserve the entity's safety. Keep it safe. Keep it here. Although the alien ship was powerful, it could be defeated.

Rick listened. He would have to keep a strong, unwavering faith in order to survive. He needed to believe anything was possible. Without that faith, there could be no magic, no success, and the unthinkable would occur.

The images stopped and he was standing at Kim's side.

"We need to talk," he said, his body shaking from the intense experience.

"I'm listening," she said coldly.

Rick sat on the bench next to her. "I don't want to do this alone. I'm not even sure I can."

Kim stared at the white mound of sulfur deposits in front of her. Moments passed before she spoke.

"I won't put up with any more crap, Rick. If you want me to stick around, you have to trust me."

"You know what will happen if you give up."

"From what I've seen, the results are the same no matter what I do."

Rick stared through the darkness. Kim's face reflected the soft moonlight. Didn't she just see the ship or feel the amazing Source beneath them?

"No, I didn't see or hear anything. Rick, we're getting messages at different times. The only way we can possibly succeed is if we continuously communicate and let each other know what is happening. What did you find out?"

"The object in the sky is a ship. It's coming here to the park. It's coming to take the Source."

Kim frowned. "The Source of what?"

"Three, maybe four hundred miles underneath us is a huge, powerful...thing. If it's removed, this planet becomes a cold, hostile place. Horrible events will occur. Eventually the Source will regain its power, in about a million years. This ship travels the universe, mining planets that contain the Source. It was here once before.

"The dinosaurs. Is that what happened to them?"

"Perhaps. Anyway, by using the Casulls, we can defeat the ship. But we both know, before we get to the meadow, there's going to be a challenge, some kind of force that will split us up."

Kim scuffed her feet on the concrete. "Sounds like we're in the middle of that right now. Why didn't you tell me this earlier?"

"I swear I didn't know until a minute ago. I thought you saw it, too."

"Rick, we're supposed to be a team. Unbuttoning my clothes to test an amazing psychic ability, hiding important information and suspecting me of being your enemy are not helping. Either we work together or I'm out of here."

The moonlight fell on her short blonde hair and reflected into the crisp night, creating a halo over her head. He was so confused. Sonya told him that Kim held the key to his survival. He had to stay on course.

"Got that right," said Kim having heard his thoughts, "Straighten it out. I am not heading into the backwoods of Yellowstone with someone who thinks I'm the enemy."

It was so much easier working alone. No one to answer to, no communication problems, no distractions. If she'd been a man, this argument would never have occurred.

"Like hell," argued Kim. "If I were a man, I'd be history. That's what men do when they encounter a problem that involves emotion or consideration of other people: they bail."

"I didn't bail. I've made some errors, like remembering that you can read my thoughts..."

"Don't get caught up in the magic, Rick."

"And you say you're being honest."

"All right, I have developed an ability to hear what you're thinking."

"What else haven't you told me?"

Kim squinted at him. What a screwed-up mess. There had to be more qualified people trained to deal with situations like this. Why were she and Rick chosen for this thankless job?

"Okay. I didn't want to tell you, because it seemed so demoralizing. We won't be able to avoid the man in the field. He will catch up to us. We have to stay together or we'll die before the column of light appears. And no matter what you say, you're going to desert me when I need you the most."

Rick rubbed his chin. Did Kim have some special talent that would come into play at the meadow? Why was she here? Then he remembered. It was the hope he needed, the faith. He had to believe. That's how he'd made his millions of dollars. That's how he'd found the approaching spaceship, and that's why they'd run from the Teton mountainside. In each case, he'd believed. If he started doubting now, he was doomed.

Kim grabbed his hand. "You're right, Rick. That's all we have is our faith. But we are different people. I will act and react differently than you. That isn't to say either way is right or wrong. So what's your decision, Rick? Are we a team or do we split up?"

"We stay together."

"No more bull?"

Rick smiled. "Straight ahead and truthful."

"Great. And if that guy shows up, we'll have to kill him."

The ground began to tremble. Kim and Rick looked at each other.

"What now?"

Before Rick could answer, a loud hissing sound joined the shaking. A deep rumbling shook the ground. A white plume shot a hundred feet in the air. The burst of water caught the moonlight. It looked like a small volcano. Old Faithful was erupting.

Kim laughed, releasing the fear that had gripped her chest like a vise. "Oh my God, I thought it was over."

Rick was breathless. "Me, too," he said, suddenly aware of the crisp night air. He was alive. Kim was at his side. Life was never so precious as when it was coming to a close.

"I thought the earthquakes had started."

Kim put her arm over his shoulder. She really liked Rick. He was trying as best he could. So was she.

"We're going to make it, Rick. Somehow, we're going to be all right."

Marge McKinelly's Winnebago was parked at the edge of the parking lot. Though she didn't hear every word, she'd caught enough of the argument to know someone was going to the source and kill a man. This was a matter for the authorities. She quietly crept out of her camper and headed toward the ranger station.

The panicked vacationer received an understanding nod from the on-duty ranger. A bored housewife eavesdropping on a domestic dispute held no interest to the tired employee, but Lance White, an investigator from the Parks Department in Washington, had requested that any unusual activity be passed on to him. After the woman left, the bleary-eyed ranger called an 800-number and told the operator about the conversation.

CNN HEADQUARTERS
ATLANTA, GEORGIA
**TUESDAY**, SEPTEMBER 14, 2027
**12:15 A.M. MST**      2:15 A.M. EST

Just after midnight, the Atlanta office of Cable News Network received a call from Palomar Observatory. An anonymous scientist gave the news desk some sketchy details about a mammoth alien vessel approaching the planet. Shortly afterward, the network broadcast a story suggesting that an approaching intruder was related to the alarming national military alert. Once that news hit the wires, the media began circulating a barrage of conflicting information. Radio stations, cable and television networks stopped their normal broadcast schedules.

At three-fifteen a.m., a giant disk whisked directly in front of the full moon. Camera crews atop the CNN building captured ten seconds of spectacular footage that played throughout the early morning. Passing within five hundred miles of the silvery circle, Eagle cast a huge black shadow across the cratered surface. A local New York City station broadcast a rumor that the alien vessel was a scout ship, a precursor to a larger invasion. Clips from the movie "Independence Day" began playing on every station. By four in the morning, the three largest phone systems in the United States - AT&T, Verizon and T-Mobile, were overwhelmed by the volume of calls.

Two KH-12 satellites focused their powerful sensors on Eagle, then transmitted the information to the U.S. Space Command Center, ironically located a mere five hundred miles from Peters and Callaway.

After intensive computer analysis, the resulting picture showed a large black disk, without lights or protrusions. Comparing Eagle to the surrounding stars and planets, the size of the circular ship was estimated at eighteen miles in diameter. The photo was transferred to the Washington war room where the Joint Chiefs of Staff and their support personnel pored over the image.

Although the dimensions of the ship were alarming, there was new cause for concern. Eagle had altered the moon's orbit. There was also evidence that several large quakes had occurred on the moon's surface as the disk had passed. New fissures had appeared and an unusual amount of dust had risen. Close examination of Grunderson's gravity display convinced the experts that Eagle would trigger a series of deadly earthquakes and volcanic disruptions if it approached Earth. Secondary effects such as dam failures, toppling buildings, falling glass and tidal waves posed additional threats to the planet's population.

With this information, the Joint Chiefs of Staff concluded offensive weapons should be used if the ship continued to approach, regardless of the possibility of a counter-attack. All top-secret weapons were being readied for firing. The messages being sent into space were changed from a friendly greeting to a stem warning to steer clear or be attacked.

CAMP PENDELTON MARINE BASE
OCEANSIDE, CALIFORNIA
**TUESDAY**, SEPTEMBER 14, 2027
**3:19 A.M. PST**      4:19  A.M. MST      6:19 A.M. EST

Major Walter Glenhurst rushed into the mess hall and ripped into the large trash container at the end of the room. Four servicemen watched as the powerful and well-known commander pulled soda cans, half-eaten meals and food wrappers from the big plastic drum. After examining a soiled paper, he ran out of the room.

One of the privates looked over his shoulder. "Looks like Glenhurst has lost it. I always thought he was missing a few marbles."

"Don't let him hear you say that. He'll tear your head off. As a matter of fact, his whole crew is pretty weird."

Twenty minutes later, four CH53 Super Stallion helicopters were skimming across the Mojave Desert heading toward Wyoming. Glenhurst pulled the soiled paper from his pocket. Listed in a neat column were a series of events that now made too much sense. Glenhurst thanked God the kitchen crew hadn't emptied the trash.

When he first found the paper in his bag, Glenhurst had angrily crumpled it and tossed it away, knowing his daughter had planted it. When he and his men were gruffly ordered to find Rick Peters in northwestern Wyoming, Glenhurst realized that scrap of paper was as accurate as any intelligence report he'd ever received. The use of the space station weapons, the AWAC assigned to coordinate the communications of the area, even his own losing of the paper was listed, along with exact times.

It was the last item that concerned him the most. Separated from the list of events, underneath the carefully drawn map was an underlined command:

"Go into the light."

JACKSON AIRPORT
ELEVEN MILES NORTH OF JACKSON, WYOMING
**TUESDAY**, SEPTEMBER 14, 2027
**4:05 A.M. MST**      6:05A.M. EST

After refueling the helicopter for a third time at the Jackson airport, Lance White checked in with the AWAC.

In a brief phone conversation, White was informed of all the information about the current situation as well as details concerning his partners. Younger had deserted Bruce Kirby at a small gas station, but the relentless agent called Hertz and had them deliver a car. He'd also had the foresight to purchase a mobile CB radio from a traveler at Jenny Lake Lodge and was now communicating directly with the AWAC. The Marine contingent and Air Force PJs were on their way and would be arriving shortly. Eagle was rapidly approaching Earth. The military establishment was coming to a full wartime alert.

Finally, there was a message about a bickering couple in the Old Faithful parking lot. This sounded promising. White had the AWAC send a message to Kirby. He was to wait at the Old Faithful entrance. Then White directed his pilot to head for the geyser. It would be just like Younger to give him partially accurate information, hoping he would ignore it.

It took some time to reach the Old Faithful parking lot. White was concerned Peters and his girl might have left the area. As the helicopter approached the large expanse of blacktop, White felt the strange emotion again. Like the initial buzz from a strong drink, he felt giddy, almost happy.

Perfect. He had them now.

INTERSTATE 15
CENTRAL IDAHO
**TUESDAY**, SEPTEMBER 14, 2027
**4:05 AM. MST**      6:05  A.M. EST

Racing along Interstate 15, Keith Grunderson noticed a pair of headlights coming up on his tail. Nothing to really worry about; it was probably a late-night speeder. He opened the throttle, accelerating to ninety miles an hour. Grunderson sped past the lava fields north of Pocatello without noticing the cratered landscape on the opposite side of the river. The mysterious car stayed with him. Did someone follow him from Los Angeles? It seemed unlikely. Still, he wasn't going to take any chances.

At Idaho Falls he screamed off the freeway and took a right. The road quickly fell off into a relatively straight and deserted two-lane highway. At the town of Ashton, he took a hard right and roared up an even narrower road. The pursuit car was still with him, but was having difficulty staying with the swift-moving cycle. Grunderson let out a yell of victory. One more stretch of road and he would be home free. As soon as he lost these bozos, he could eat again.

OLD FAITHFUL PARKING LOT
NORTHWESTERN WYOMING
**TUESDAY**, SEPTEMBER 14, 2027
**4:15 A.M. MST**      6:15  A.M. EST
Kim and Rick heard the helicopter approach. Both tensed, ready to run, but the bubble-shaped shadow continued on its course, speeding southward.

Kim watched the lights disappear behind the trees. "Let's get out of here."

Rick nodded. "Time to head in."

Kim pointed upwards. "Look!"

A black circle moved rapidly across the center of the bright moon.

"Amazing," Rick said. "You know that sucker's big if we can see it from here."

They started back to the truck, crossing the unprotected space. A slight wind blew leaves across the asphalt top, bringing a fresh night scent of pine.

"What are you going to do when this is over, Kim?"

"I hadn't considered enjoying a future," said Rick.

"What if something happened to change that? Would you consider spending some time together?"

Kim continued walking without a pause. "Stop it, Rick. It's complicated enough."

SOUTH ENTRANCE YELLOWSTONE NATIONAL PARK
NORTHWESTERN WYOMING
**TUESDAY**, SEPTEMBER 14, 2027
**4:25 A.M. MST**      6:25A.M.EST

Grunderson roared past the Bechler River Ranger Station as the sun began to light the eastern sky. By the time the NSA agents realized they were on a dead-end road, Grunderson was a quarter mile up the well-marked Bechler Creek Trail. After traveling along the riverside, he stopped the bike.

Confident he'd lost his pursuers, he ripped into his duffel bag and wolfed down a Snickers candy bar and three Ding-Dongs. It was when he made a thorough search for any overlooked food that he discovered the homing device sewn into the nylon lining.

Taking his knife, he removed the metal disk, wrapped it in a resealable candy wrapper, and placed it gently into the Bechler River. Grunderson smiled. He was west of the Continental Divide. Perhaps the fools would track the device to the Pacific Ocean.

Grunderson unfolded a map and inspected his future route. He'd have to leave the trail, but there appeared to be plenty of open space up ahead. His biggest concern was driving into one of the fragile sulfur pits that dotted the park. In about a mile he'd begin bushwhacking across the Madison Plateau, heading for a clearing that lay directly above the Continental Divide.

OLD FAITHFUL PARKING LOT
NORTHWESTERN WYOMING
**TUESDAY**, SEPTEMBER 14, 2027
**4:40 A.M. MST**      6:40A.M. EST

"We're in trouble," said Rick as they approached the car. The horizon began to glow with the impending dawn. "We've got to leave, fast."

"How do you know?"

"Tuned into the right frequency, I guess," he said with a grin.

Kim smirked. "Don't get cocky, Rick. It'll be my turn soon enough."

Kim began stuffing her backpack with food, water and ammunition.

"We have to leave, Kim. I mean now!"

"I'm not ready. There's more ammunition and the extra water."

"There's no time. Follow me."

Grabbing his open pack, Rick left the car. Kim shook her head, muttering to herself. "We're going to need water and food, Rick. There's no telling how long we'll be up there."

She stuffed a second canteen, several bags of dehydrated food and a box of safety matches into the pack. After she secured the top straps, she threw the lightweight aluminum frame onto her shoulders. Now she was ready. Closing the trunk, she realized someone was at her side.

"We'd like you to come with us," said Lance White, flashing his revolver in her face.

On the other side of her, Bruce Kirby had his hand on a semiautomatic. "Put the pack down. Slowly."

"Guess this is the test," sighed Callaway, lowering the backpack with caution. As soon as the pack was off her shoulders, she threw an elbow into one man's crotch, eliminating him from further action. She went for the second, but the handle of his gun landed solidly on her skull, plunging her world into darkness.

"No," replied Lance White, standing over Callaway's inert body, "This is definitely not a test."

INTERNATIONAL SPACE STATION
EARTH ORBIT
**TUESDAY**, SEPTEMBER 14, 2027
**4:59 A.M. MST**      6:59 A.M. EST

A series of screaming alarms filled the small area of the Space Station. Simultaneously, a coded radio transmission was received by Commander Zyger. The Russians had launched fifteen nuclear missiles at the intruder. The alarms were automatically triggered by a sensor in the station specifically designed to sense any object that appeared in the station's path.

The Russians and the United States had mutually disarmed their automatic nuclear launch capability once Eagle's flight path was established. Leaders of both nations realized the incoming intruder would have set both countries' computers into a fit of retaliation. The disarmament also allowed the Russians to fire their battery of anti-asteroid missiles, devices that had been in development since the 1994 Shoemaker-Levy comet crashed into Jupiter. In the spring of 2022, they were quietly deployed. President Lindon thought he'd convinced the Russians not to take any offensive action against the ship. Word came back that an officer in charge at the Plesetsk missile complex had taken matters into his own hands.

Zyger looked out the porthole. He could see the exhaust trails of the missiles as they streaked through the atmosphere. The projectiles looked like a squadron of jets with accompanying vapor trails heading toward the distant vessel.

Suddenly, another set of alarms were triggered. Zyger snapped his head to the right where a series of computer displays lined the cabin wall. There had been a dramatic and sudden increase of radiation. All meters were far into the red. Luckily for the crew, there was a layer of lead built into the station's skin designed for unexpected solar radiation. The sensors were screaming at the crew to put on their space suits for added protection.

Zyger turned from the wall of red lights in time to see fifteen thin streaks of blue light reach out from the alien vessel and touch the Russian projectiles. There were fifteen silent explosions, each one representing the destruction of a nuclear-tipped missile in a colorful splash of light.

Zyger realized Iris and Smith were outside the ship. How much radiation had they received? A quick glance back to the meters told the story. Although the levels were intense, the wave of radiation had lasted only a few seconds. Iris and Smith were safe. Their protective suits had sufficiently shielded them.

"Guess that thing has some opinions about being attacked," commented Iris, who'd watched the awesome display of firepower.

"I would agree with that," responded Zyger.

"Maybe they used up all their battery power."

"Yeah, right..."

Another series of alarms went off. Seconds later, several dozen blue streaks flew from the ship to the Earth's surface.

"They're firing on Russia!" yelled Iris.

PLESETSK MISSILE COMPLEX
EASTERN RUSSIA
**TUESDAY**, SEPTEMBER 14, 2027
4:03 P.M. LOCAL TIME **5:03 A.M. MST** 7:03A.M. EST

The destructive bolts of light jumped from the leading edge of the disk and ripped through the Earth's atmosphere. Eagle had been monitoring all ground communications. As the missiles leapt into the air, the giant computer within the black ship focused on the exchange of voice and computer data in the area, then identified which facilities threatened its existence.

Ten separate targets were hit. Four of the Soviet's largest radio telescopes were cut to pieces by the twenty-foot-wide laser. The two-story control building and gantry of the Plesetsk launch facility were reduced to a pile of molten steel and concrete. Several targeting satellites were obliterated. The three supercomputers used to calculate the telemetry coordinates for the missiles were blasted.

The fifty technicians unlucky enough to be in the vicinity of the machines were incinerated. The third computer was hidden fifty feet beneath the Earth's surface in a hardened bunker. The blue ray cut through the spent uranium shielding like it was butter. Thirty seconds later, twenty billion dollars' worth of equipment had been destroyed and three hundred twenty people ceased to exist.

CNN HEADQUARTERS
ATLANTA, GEORGIA
**TUESDAY**, SEPTEMBER 14, 2027
**5:23 A.M. MST**      7:23 A.M. EST

CNN received the spectacular footage ten minutes after the alien attack. Raynek Tolneski, a vacationing videographer from the Russian town of Saint Petersburg, taped the steel-blue beams as they sliced through the night sky. Although he was too far away to photograph the rays touching the Earth, his built-in microphone dutifully recorded the thunderous reports that followed each blast.

A newly reformed capitalist, Tolneski drove to the nearest CNN bureau and sold the tape for the outrageous sum of ten thousand dollars.

TOM ROSS' CESSNA
8,000 FEET ABOVE NORTHWEST WYOMING
**TUESDAY**, SEPTEMBER 14, 2027
**6:45 A.M. MST**      8:45 A.M. EST
Tom Ross' twin-engine plane performed flawlessly. Pushed to its maximum cruising speed, the plane crossed two-thirds of the country with ease, despite strong headwinds. The plane's auxiliary fuel tanks had served their purpose in avoiding a time-consuming refueling stop. Long morning shadows pointed the way west.

By the time he reached Yellowstone, there would be plenty of light for his risky landing. He had never intended to approach Jackson airport or the West Yellowstone airstrip. He briefly considered dropping the Cessna onto the park's main road, but the chance of colliding with a surprised tourist was too great.

His original idea was still best: crash-land directly on the Madison Plateau. Ross checked his fuel gauge. Just about empty. Perfect. That would lower the risk of fire on impact. He watched as the Bighorn River passed beneath him. Ross had to smile. Was this his last stand? Probably, but things could be worse. He could still be an employee of the National Security Agency.

His altimeter registered eight thousand feet, as it had for the last hour. Throughout the night he'd followed easy-to-identify interstate highways until he reached the town of Gillette. From there he headed east-southeast, avoiding the Bighorn Mountains. Dollars to donuts the Cessna had already lit up somebody's radar screen. He took a long look at the Wyoming landscape. Lush, peaceful and teeming with life, this incredibly beautiful place was certainly worth protecting.

The next two hours were not going to be pleasant or painless. He pulled back on the wheel and started his last climb to clear the Absaroka Mountains. On the other side of the barrier was Yellowstone Lake. If he made it that far, he'd have a decent chance of surviving the first leg of his ordeal.

THE WAR ROOM
WASHINGTON, D.C.
**TUESDAY**, SEPTEMBER 14, 2027
**6:47 A.M. MST**      8:47A.M. EST

Ten floors beneath the Pentagon, the nerve center of the country's military crackled with intense energy. Dwarfed by giant screens displaying the global status of the nation's armed forces, seventy-five men and women kept a constant watch on Eagle's progress, relaying orders and coordinating the thousands of communications that were channeled to and from the chamber. In the center of the room, seated at an immense black slate table, were the Joint Chiefs of Staff, their assistants, a dozen aides, the Secretary of State, Secretary of Defense, thirty top-ranking congressmen and the President and Vice-President of the United States.

Word of the attack on Russia arrived seconds after the laser bolt struck the ground. President Lindon and the other key government members, including the Joint Chiefs of Staff, were whisked away from their vulnerable living quarters and brought to the bombproof war room, situated below eighty feet of lead-lined, reinforced concrete.

The uneasy group of leaders had viewed the CNN footage and were now watching video received from a recently launched Keyhole satellite. The high-altitude cameras taped the ominous beams mid-flight, then transmitted the pictures in realtime to a downlink in Europe. Moments later, the images were viewed both at the U.S. Space Command and in the war room.

"Mr. President," said General Moore, turning from the television screen, "We must fire the Strategic Defensive Initiative missiles across the bow of Eagle. If the moon was damaged by the ship's propulsion system, there's no telling what kind of havoc it will cause on our planet. Not only is

California at risk, but major faults crisscross the entire nation. We have to put these beings on notice that they're threatening our very existence. Once Eagle breaches the atmosphere, our defensive choices will be severely limited."

Everyone in uniform nodded agreement.

The civilians in the room weren't so eager to fire on the visitor. Senator Gunn from South Dakota scratched his head. "Shooting at this thing could result in a severe retaliation. Look what happened to the Russians."

Moore frowned at the slight man. Gunn had voted against every military funding bill over the last ten years. He was a diehard pacifist, democracy's worst enemy.

"Mr. Gunn, the Russians were trying to shoot at Eagle, not in front of it. If we don't warn Eagle off, it could turn the North American continent into a chain of islands."

"Come on. Is the situation really that bad, General Moore, or are you just playing soldier?"

Moore drilled Gunn with his intense brown eyes.

"It's that bad, sir."

Lindon glanced around the table. Most of the men surrounding him were warriors, trained to hide their emotions, but he sensed their concern. Their reconnaissance satellites were performing erratically, the Russians had been blasted, and the biggest goddamned machine they'd ever seen was ignoring their threats and treating them like children.

They were the underdogs. Linden was certain they were as frightened as he was. It was that constant fear that kept the United States the most powerful nation in the world. Fear of the Russians, fear of the Chinese, fear of the Communists and fear of the volatile Middle Eastern countries had oiled the mighty U.S. military machine for decades. But this adversary was carrying technology they didn't understand and possibly could not defeat.

"Have they responded to any of our communications?" asked Linden.

"No, sir," replied Moore.

"What about neutron bombs?"

Two dozen of the supposedly dismantled weapons had been secretly housed in strategic locations around the country.

"They are accessible and operational," replied George McKinley, commander of the Air Force. "Those devices are designed to kill humans. There's no telling what effect the radiation would have on these beings."

"Cut the theatrics, George," grumbled Mark Trailer, the Secretary of Defense. "Radiation kills everything."

"Everything on Earth," McKinley reminded him.

Lindon turned to General Bud Tracer, Commandant of the Marine Corps.

"What's the status of the men in Wyoming? Have we located those missing scientists?"

Tracer locked eyes with his boss. His men had not arrived in the area, but he'd received good news.

"Keith Grunderson's homing device just showed up on the AWAC's radar. We're sending one of Major Glenhurst's airships to intercept him. Rick Peters and Conrad Wiley are in the area, but we haven't located them yet."

Linden turned to General Moore. "How soon can we get a fully equipped battalion into northwestern Wyoming?"

"With all due respect, sir, there is no strategic target in that area," interrupted General Hood, commander of the United States Army. "I think the Marine contingent can handle anything that comes up in that part of the country."

General Moore jumped into the argument. "Mr. President, Eagle is an immediate threat. We must fire our missiles before the window of opportunity closes. Those scientists could be dead by the time we reach them. It is time to act, now."

Heads nodded. A uniformed messenger rushed into the room and delivered a note to Moore. The elder warrior scanned the memo, then looked up to find twenty-five men staring at him.

"More information from Yellowstone," he said in his raspy, monotone voice. "Grunderson is on a trail bike inside the park. The AWOL NSA analyst is flying his rented Cessna one hundred fifty miles east of the park boundary."

"I want a full battalion with tank reinforcements sent to the park immediately," ordered the frustrated President. "Get Ross or this guy Grunderson on some kind of communication device. I want to talk to them. There must be a radio in that plane. Maybe the AWAC can get him to respond." He turned to General McKinley. "How long until Eagle enters the atmosphere?"

"Less than two hours."

"Can you launch one of those missiles and detonate it in front of Eagle's path before then?"

"Yes, sir. That can be done."

"Do it. What other options are we exploring?"

Moore was quick to respond, hoping the President would abandon his fixation on the scientists.

"Five hundred fighters and bombers will be in the air between Japan and the West Coast, prepared to do whatever it takes to protect our borders. There are forty batteries of air-to-ground missiles along the coast that can send up a wall of armament in Eagle's path, if it gets that far. And we have the Strategic Defense Proton Accelerator in New Mexico that's being brought on-line."

"What's our next move?" asked Linden.

"The SDI missiles," answered General Moore. "If that fails, we'll use the space laser."

# CONFRONTATIONS

ABOVE THE LITTLE BIGHORN VALLEY
NORTHWESTERN WYOMING
TUESDAY, SEPTEMBER 14, 2027
**6:55 A.M. MST**      8:55A.M.EST

The circling AWAC spotted Ross' Cessna before he'd crossed half the state. The electronics-ladened jet identified and plotted the plane's location to within a few feet. The young, highly trained radar operators kept a careful watch over the tiny plane's movements, sending information to Major Glenhurst's command ship, as well as to the Pentagon.

A high-altitude check by a drone controlled from Beale Air Force Base verified the craft was the one Ross rented in Washington. An interception plan was immediately initiated. The Cessna flew too slow for Air Force jets, and the only operation they could perform was to shoot Ross down, an unacceptable option. Instead, the task was handed off to a couple of Apache helicopters racing from Fort Carson, Colorado. It would be their job to get Ross on the ground and into custody.

As he crossed the Shoshone National Forest, Ross noticed a reflection out of the corner of his eye. Something was behind him. Most likely a military aircraft. He checked his weapons. His two Casulls were loaded and ready. One was in his holster, the other on the copilot's seat. Speed loaders were full and tucked into his custom-made belt. Although the revolvers were not intended for self-defense, Ross knew he would have to use them if his path was blocked or he was about to be taken prisoner. Trying to shoot at another plane while flying was a ludicrous idea. He'd have to use the guns on the ground.

Maybe the plane behind him was a fixed-wing craft. An airplane probably wouldn't land in this rugged terrain. If it was a helicopter, there would be a chance of escape, if he landed close to a forested area where he could hide from his pursuers. A helicopter full of armed soldiers would be the worst situation, perhaps fatal. The best scenario Ross could conjure up would be a forestry plane with little interest other than shooing him away.

He opened the throttle, pushing the plane past its limits. No need to save this machine. He was going to crash-land on the Madison Plateau or be shot down. Either way the Cessna was history.

"Cessna 2428, this is a United States Air Force Airborne Warning and Control System," crackled Ross' radio. "You are entering a restricted air space. Please respond."

Ross chuckled to himself. Great, they're going to verbally abuse me. I should have brought a hall pass. Ross adjusted the microphone that curved in front of his mouth, took a breath and acted as irritated as he could.

"Get real, Airborne. This is America, Wyoming to be exact. This is not a restricted area. Piss off and play your war games somewhere else." Act arrogant and dumb, thought Ross. It might buy enough time to get to the meadow.

"I repeat: You are entering restricted air space. If you continue, you will be... Uh, Mr. Ross, President Lindon would like to talk to you, sir."

"Yeah, right, and Sandra Bullock is on call-waiting."

Ross nearly choked. Not only had they identified his plane, his report made it to the top of the military food chain. The big kahuna, the President of the United States, was requesting a conversation with him.

A broad grin spread across Ross' face. What a rush! Greenhorn technical specialist makes the grade after only one week on the job. But now what? Was the President going to quiz him or were they simply buying time until they could shoot him down? And what was he going to say to the man who was ultimately in control of his fate? Ross could imagine the conversation: President Linden, I'm extremely busy saving the world; could you call back tomorrow when I've got time to chat? Hardly. Reaching the meadow was the goal. If he had to talk to the President to gain a few precious minutes, so be it.

"Mister Ross? This is William Lindon, President of the United States."

"Good morning, Mr. President, if that is who you are. What's on your mind?"

"Where are you going, Tom?"

It sounded like the President. "You know perfectly well where I'm going, sir. The question is: Are you going to stop me?"

"That depends on how you answer my questions."

Ross checked behind him. This was bad news. Two Apache attack helicopters were coming up fast. Though they carried no troops, their nose-mounted machine guns could make Swiss cheese out of his thin-skinned plane.

"Ask away, sir."

"What is this object in the sky?"

"My best guess would be it's a large spaceship, sir."

"And its purpose?"

Ross adjusted his headset and paused for a moment. The job was to delay, waste time. Ten more miles and he'd be at the meadow. He was so close.

"I missed that, sir. Say again, please."

"What is the aliens' objective?"

"To attack the planet."

"Then why are you flying to Yellowstone?"

Should he tell the truth or lie his way out of the situation? Ross glanced behind him. The attack helicopters were within range. Better give them something to chew on, before they chewed on his defenseless Cessna.

"There are two people in the park who know how to stop the ship. I'm on my way to assist them. But I must warn you, if your forces get in the way, the ship will defeat us and everyone will lose."

"What do you mean, 'everyone will lose'?"

Lake Yellowstone was beneath him. Three more minutes, max. Keep them talking, Tom. They're still interested. String them along.

"The ship is a serious threat to the planet. It's come to rip the heart out of the Earth. The disk will stop somewhere over northwest Wyoming at approximately a quarter after eight. It will be at that location that the people who warned you about the ship will attempt a raid. Apparently, there's a way to disable the craft."

"Tell us how. I'm sure we can help."

"Sir, the men sitting with you are conventional warriors, the best on this planet. But to defeat this ship, radically different measures must be taken. This device is capable of stopping every one of your high-tech weapons before they're launched. Even the Advanced Tactical Fighter won't be able to fly near it. The ATF's dependence on computers for flight make them exceedingly vulnerable to the intense radiation that surrounds the ship. The only chance you have for survival is to call off the Apaches on my tail and tell your men in Yellowstone to take their orders directly from Rick Peters."

"I'll consider that option," said Lindon. Moore and the others were listening to the conversation on their headsets. The civilians were confused. Several of the Joint Chiefs were quietly arguing over Ross' sanity.

"You'd better do it now, sir. Once the ship reaches the coast, you won't be able to communicate with anyone in the northwest. You also might take another look at my report. You need to fire every weapon you have, especially ground-based artillery and missiles. Two particular times are mentioned. Coordinate your attacks at those precise moments and we will have a chance at defeating this monster. Once you lose a couple hundred of your F-14s, F-15s and F-llls, I think you'll consider this a valuable option."

Ross had achieved his purpose. He'd officially notified the military and was nearly to Yellowstone. Now it was only a matter of staying alive until he could get the Cessna on the ground.

"Gotta go, sir. Just remember, we're on your side. Wish us luck."

"Tom!"

Ross turned off the radio.

THE WAR ROOM
WASHINGTON, D.C.
TUESDAY, SEPTEMBER 14, 2027
**7:08 A.M. MST**       9:08 A.M. EST

"What do you think, gentlemen?" asked Lindon.

"May I speak frankly, sir?" offered General McKinley, commander-in-chief of the Air Force.

"You always do, George."

"Russia has been attacked and the structural integrity of Earth is in serious jeopardy. Spending valuable manpower and intelligence on these men is hurting us more than you realize. Forget Wyoming. Forget these scatterbrained civilians. We must deal with the issue of defending our nation's borders."

A loud, vocal agreement followed McKinley's speech.

The President nodded. "You have a point, George, but these men must be taken into custody and questioned."

"Absolutely," agreed Moore, placating the President to avoid further argument. "These men probably possess information that could be to our benefit, but we must focus our attention on the disk."

Again, agreements came from around the table.

"All right," sighed Lindon, "Let's get this intruder out of here."

INTERNATIONAL SPACE STATION
EARTH ORBIT
TUESDAY, SEPTEMBER 14, 2027
**7:09 A.M. MST**       9:09 A.M. EST

The deployment of the missile cluster went without a hitch. The cylindrical battery of five nuclear missiles floated eight thousand meters to the space station's starboard side, its stabilizers orienting the craft with coordinates fed by the supercomputers located at the U. S. Space Command. Commander Zyger looked around the cabin. Dressed in full space gear, the crew stared out the small windows at the alien vessel. Zyger's gaze was drawn to the rows of radiation gauges. If they indicated a change, he was sure Eagle would fire.

"We're into a launch cycle," announced Astronaut Mark Atkins, who was monitoring the missile cluster from within the space station.

Over the years, Zyger had been in a number of tight situations. In every instance he'd known going in that he was involved in a life-threatening mission. This trip had never been considered more dangerous than any other stay at the orbiting laboratory. Zyger was relieved he'd taken the time to say good-bye to his wife and two children before he left. His affairs were in order.

"Outer doors opening."

Zyger scanned the display panel. All meters were showing green.

"They're arming the boosters. Ten seconds to launch."

Alarms sounded. The control panel went crazy with red blinking lights.

"Tell them to shut the doors!"

"They can't! They only go one way!"

The radiation levels shot up. Atkins glanced over to Zyger. The computer specialist had his finger on the self-destruct switch with its plastic protective housing removed. The choice was Zyger's.

"Hit it! Destroy the cluster!"

"Too late!"

Zyger's vision was filled with a bright azure light. The alien beam surrounded then annihilated the tiny weapon.

"Damage report!" yelled Zyger, looking at the gauges that would reveal any breach of the station's hull. Nothing appeared out of the ordinary.

"There's no debris in our path," called out Atkins. "Everyone here is all right."

"Ed! Hugh?!" Zyger called into his suit's microphone.

"We're fine," Iris' voice boomed over Zyger's headset. "I guess that means we're up next."

Suddenly the warning panel lit up again. In a furious burst of energy, Eagle launched an attack on the United States. Zyger watched in horror as at least fifteen bolts of deadly blue light raked the country.

ABOVE YELLOWSTONE PARK
NORTHWESTERN WYOMING
TUESDAY, SEPTEMBER 14, 2027
**7:10 A.M. MST**      9:10A.M.EST

Tom Ross lowered the Cessna back to eight thousand feet. A wide meadow loomed directly ahead of him. Several miles short of his original goal, it would serve the purpose if he had to ditch early. Why were these jokers bothering with him at this late date? Didn't they have enough to worry about?

The two ugly Apache attack helicopters appeared on either side of the Cessna. Ross waved and smiled at the stern pilot to his right, then turned away without attempting any dialogue. The copters stayed with him. Their heavy rotors created a turbulence that bounced the tiny plane like a toy. From the comer of his eye Ross could see the Apache pilot vigorously pointing to the left. They wanted him to change course and follow, probably to West Yellowstone. No way would he buy into that plan. Ross turned and waved again. The Army pilot was not amused.

From the left, the second helicopter began move toward Ross in an attempt to force him to turn. Ross engaged the flaps. At the same time, he pushed the wheel forward and aimed at the ground. Both Apaches lowered with him. Then the helicopter on the left dropped even further, sliding underneath him.

Ross pointed at his instrument cluster, indicating that he'd encountered engine trouble. The Army pilot shook his head furiously and again signaled for Ross to follow. The nose gun swiveled toward him. Ross couldn't wait any longer. He shrugged and pushed the wheel forward. If the helicopter below him didn't move, his little Cessna would be chewed to bits. He throttled back and dropped another hundred feet. The second copter reappeared at his side. Ross smiled. Afraid to play a little chicken, eh, boys? They must have orders not to damage him. Great! He was safe. Maybe he should head for his original landing area.

Ross' enjoyment of the moment was shattered as a stream of thirty-caliber bullets ripped through the rear of his plane.

## A YELLOWSTONE PARK TOOLSHED
## NORTHWESTERN WYOMING
## TUESDAY, SEPTEMBER 14, 2027
## 7:12 A.M. MST        9:12 A.M. EST

Kim opened her eyes. The room came into focus. An incredible headache assaulted her. Worse than any hangover she'd ever experienced, the pounding in her skull was incredible. As she forced herself to look around, an intense fear pushed the pain from her consciousness. She was inside a dingy shed, bound to a chair, with a gag stuffed into her mouth. The place smelled musty, like a dirty old rag. The only source of light was a glowing bulb dangling from a frayed electrical cord. Her eyes darted from one side of the room to the other. A tall, goofy-looking man stood guard at the wooden doorway. A wave of relief washed over her. Thank God it wasn't him.

Her sense of comfort quickly disappeared. She was in this precarious situation because of her own stupidity. She'd failed to sense the danger, failed to listen to Rick's warning. Her frustration increased when she realized she might be sliced to death in a filthy shack, a few miles from her destination.

Kim shut her eyes. This was no time to lose control. An opportunity would present itself. She had to stay alert, certainly more alert than she'd been in the parking lot. Other than being bound and locked in an old shed, nothing traumatic had happened. The fact that she wasn't at Rick's side was irritating, not fatal.

Kim scanned the walls, trying to ignore the stabbing in her skull. Sharp gardening tools hung from the wooden beams, instruments that could be used as weapons. All she had to do was free herself. The bonds were tight. Coarse ropes bit into her skin. She heard something dripping on the floor. Looking down, she realized her blood had formed a pool beneath the chair.

The man noticed her move and darted outside. Good, that would give her some time alone. She leaned forward and tipped the chair. If she could hop to the other side of the narrow shed, she might be able to get hold of the clippers that hung on the nearby wall. Before she could shuffle more than a few feet, the door opened again. She let the chair fall flat. Her pulse pounded in her neck. Fear rose in her throat. It was the short man she'd seen so often. Far uglier than she'd imagined, he walked up to her and put his face directly in front of hers, nose to nose. His foul breath made her choke.

"Hello, Miss Callaway." He looked deep into her eyes, then turned to his accomplice. "Leave. I do not want to be disturbed."

Kirby left, closing the door behind him. White roughly removed her gag. Then, stepping back, he drew his gun and aimed it at her chest.

"Let's be civil for a moment, shall we, Kim? I took the liberty of examining your wallet. How else could I find out who you were? My name is Lance White. I am an agent of the United States Government. I have the authority to kill you, blind you, rape you, torture you, basically do anything I please to extract the information I need. I'm sort of like James Bond, except not quite as nice. We can complete this short question-and-answer session with little trouble, or you can resist and make it very, very ugly. The choice is yours."

He smiled lightly and cocked his head. "So, now you know the rules. I'll start by asking you the questions. Where is Rick Peters?"

Kim turned to the side and spit dirt from her mouth. Hope was the key. There would be a moment when he was vulnerable. She had to be ready for that opportunity. She faced him again.

"I don't know anyone by that name," she said. "There has been a terrible mistake."

"There's been no mistake." White's expression turned even happier. "Tell me what I need to know and you will feel little pain. If you continue to refuse me, in a short amount of time you will beg me to kill you to end the suffering. Quite honestly, at that point, I won't be very interested in helping you." He paused. His friendly grin grew full and genuine. "Don't fool yourself, Kim. I'm very good at this."

Keep believing, she told herself, there will be an opening. "You're talking to the wrong person."

"You can't say I didn't give you a choice." White removed a silk handkerchief from his pocket and wrapped it around his hand. "Where is Rick Peters?"

"I don't know a Rick Peters. I was going on a hike behind Old Faith-..."

A blur of flesh and fabric smashed into her chin. Blood trickled from her nose.

White's voice remained pleasant, almost gracious. "You are treating me like I'm stupid, Kim. Where is he?"

Kim didn't answer. His fist struck again. Her head screamed in agony. Her intense training had not prepared her for such a vicious, personal attack. Through the haze she saw him lay his gun on a nearby chair and pull a knife from a sheath strapped to his leg. Kim's pulse rose dramatically. Oh God, please let the vision be wrong.

"You're out of time, Kim," he said quietly. "You had your chance and you blew it."

Kim took a breath, hoping she was doing the right thing. In every other situation, honesty had proved the right choice in the long run. This time, she hoped it would act as a shield... or at least a delaying tactic.

"Rick is in the park," she slurred through her swollen lips.

"Where?"

"He needs your help."

White's eyes narrowed to a squint. "And how am I supposed to help Mr. Peters?"

"There's an alien ship coming here, to Yellowstone. Rick holds the key to defeating the intruder."

White's face lightened. She was making this so easy.

"Don't toy with me, Kim." His voice reeked with sweetness. "I don't care about your space fantasies. I want to know where Rick Peters is hiding."

Kim raised her head high. She had to stay strong. She had to believe.

"Rick Peters is your only chance for survival. Beating me will only waste both our lives. The weapons on the Space Station will fail to stop the incoming ship and the alien will retaliate. The Aurora won't survive because the leading shock wave and radiation will tear it to pieces. The alien knows when a weapon is locked on. It not only attacks the device, it destroys the source of the radar and its support equipment. Mr. White, this is a desperate situation. I'll be glad to tell you everything you want to know about Rick Peters, but I think it would be prudent to talk to your superiors as soon as you can about this information."

White stepped back and stared at her as he pondered his next move. He desperately wanted to punish her. Put some fear into her stubborn soul, let her know that he controlled her life, her pain and her limited future. The information concerning the possible danger to the Aurora and Eagle's reaction to a radar lock could be of help, if it was true. This woman probably possessed a great deal more vital information. It was time to rip it out of her.

This was where his two years of medical school came into play. White knew exactly where to cut and how deep. Avoiding arteries and slicing along the grain of the muscle, he could cut deep without killing. Not only was his method of torture extremely painful, it caused his victims intense mental distress.

"So, my life is being threatened, you know everything about this alien spaceship and Rick Peters is going to save my life. I think you're a very mixed-up little girl. We'll have to change that, won't we?"

A wicked grin spread across his face. With a flick of the wrist he ran the knife across her thigh. The blade sliced into her skin. Thick red blood spurted from the gash.

Kim looked down at the horrible wound. Searing pain shot up her leg as crimson liquid soaked her jeans. She was going to die. There was no way she could stop him and there would be no reasoning with him. He was enjoying himself too much. White raised his hand and struck again.

OUTSIDE THE EARTH'S ATMOSPHERE
TUESDAY, SEPTEMBER 14, 2027
**7:13 A.M. MST**                9:13        A.M. EST

It took Eagle a little over twenty seconds to target the telemetry, computer and communications devices involved in firing the missile cluster. The first hit burned a gigantic hole through the seventy-meter Deep Space Telescope outside Barstow, California. Then, in a series of quick sweeps, the bright ray sliced through the five-story parabola, cutting it into several pie-shaped pieces. A final pass reduced the rubble to a mound of boiling slag. The dozen men and women working at the facility were cremated at their posts.

Seconds later the downlinks at the Johnson Space Center were vaporized. Intense heat from the ray incinerated the trees surrounding the dishes, causing nearby buildings to spontaneously ignite. Six quick shots into space eliminated the communications satellites that relayed the firing instructions to the missile cluster. The last three bursts ripped into the center of North America, the location of the U.S. Space Command. The beam drilled through a half mile of solid stone like it was paper, melding the computers to the rock walls, consuming all the oxygen in the enclosed area. The tremendous heat caused by the laser overloaded the facility's redundant electrical systems and caused the self-propelled steel doors to close, trapping five hundred people inside the super-heated tomb.

YELLOWSTONE NATIONAL PARK
NORTHWESTERN WYOMING
TUESDAY, SEPTEMBER 14, 2027
**7:18 A.M. MST**        9:18  A.M. EST

Stopping his bike at the edge of a clearing, Grunderson heard the unmistakable sound of helicopters mixed with the drone of a small plane. A twin-engine Cessna was wedged between two fierce-looking helicopters, heading for the ground. Moments before the aircraft touched down, the two copters suddenly rose and tore off into the distance.

Tom Ross didn't notice the Apaches leave his side. He was busy preparing to land. He opened the cockpit door, so it wouldn't be jammed shut, then he pushed the stick forward and cut the throttle. He purposely bounced the plane twice to lose speed, then forced the craft down hard onto the field. The impact threw Ross against his seat belt as the pilot's door ripped off its hinges. The Cessna jostled across the rough ground until a rock crushed the right wheel. The plane did a single cartwheel across its nose and came to rest on its side.

Ross unbuckled his seat belt and grabbed his flight bag. He crawled over the seat and pulled himself out of the passenger door. A stream of blood flowed down the side of his head and his shoulder throbbed. Standing on the side of the plane, he rubbed his chest while he scanned the sky. No sign of the Apaches. He stuffed his second Casull into his backpack, threw it pack over his shoulder and leapt to the ground, sinking to his ankles in mud.

"Sure, Ross," he muttered, "You can drop a plane in the middle of a field, but you can't take a single step without embarrassing yourself."

The sound of a nearby motor startled him. From the other side of the narrow clearing, a long-haired, overweight biker bounced along on a motorcycle. He wasn't a military type, nor a camper nor a ranger. Must be one of us, thought Ross. He walked toward the biker.

Grunderson pulled up next to Ross. "Nice landing, buddy" grinned the rotund man, eyeing the crumpled airplane. "A few more lessons wouldn't hurt."

"Those jerks shot up my plane."

Grunderson noticed Ross' Casull tucked into a shoulder holster.

"What'd you do? Scare them off with your revolver?"

Ross shrugged. "I have no idea why they left. I'm Tom Ross, National Security Agency employee gone AWOL."

"AWOL?"

"Absent without leave."

Grunderson shook Ross' hand. "Pleased to meet you. Keith Grunderson, JPL scientist gone AWOL."

"Grunderson! Glad to meet you! Nice work on that gravitational display report. I'm the guy who made sure everyone in Washington took notice."

"Thanks...I think. Hey, you wouldn't have any food on you, like a Twinkie or a Mars bar?"

"Afraid not, Keith. I ate everything I had over Ohio."

The large man was clearly disappointed.

Ross checked the sky again, confused as to why the Apaches left so quickly.

"We've got to get a move on. I don't want to be hanging around in the open if those helicopters come back." As Ross swung his leg over the back tire, he spotted three parachutes floating toward a distant ridge. "We've got company," he pointed.

Grunderson shielded his eyes from the sun. "Where did those jokers come from?"

"Time to go," said Ross.

Grunderson opened the throttle and the two men bounced toward the shelter of the nearby pine trees.

THE WAR ROOM
WASHINGTON, D.C.
TUESDAY, SEPTEMBER 14, 2027
**7:18 A.M. MST**      9:18 A.M. EST

A distraught President Linden stared at the flickering red circle moving across the giant screen. "What are the Russians doing?"

"They're sending interceptors to confront the disk. They're also going to launch another battery of surface-to-air missiles."

"Those SAMs won't get off the ground," said General McKinley, looking at the map on the wall. "That thing knows what we're doing as soon as we do."

"Gentlemen," interrupted Linden. "How are we going to stop Eagle?"

"We'll have to see what the Russians do and how the ship responds. That will give us a better idea of what to do."

"Isn't that waiting a little too long? If those gravitational engines are as powerful as we think, believe me, we're in for a lot of trouble."

"We're already in a lot of trouble," muttered one of Linden's aides.

OLD FAITHFUL PARKING LOT
NORTHWESTERN WYOMING
TUESDAY, SEPTEMBER 14, 2027
**7:18 A.M. MST**      9:18A.M.EST

Rick hustled away from the pickup truck. Trouble was coming and he had no intention of being there when it arrived. Reaching a small cluster of campers, he ducked behind a Volkswagen van and watched Kim being taken away. Was he supposed to rescue her or continue to the meadow?

The voice told him to get her. His instinct wanted him to continue. Rick turned his back and headed west, wracked with guilt. He crossed through the narrow band of trees that separated the parking lot from the main road, but was forced to wait as a line of cars blocked the two-lane highway.

A single vehicle pulled out of the slow-moving traffic and headed for him. Probably a confused tourist. The woman driver lowered the electric window. Looking inside, Rick found himself staring down the barrel of an automatic.

"I've been looking for you, Rick Peters. Get in."

He cautiously entered the car, being careful not to make any unexpected moves.

"You're quite a popular man, Rick."

The stranger locked the doors with the remote at her side, then closed the windows, keeping the gun trained on him.

"The Marines, the President, two of my partners and a half dozen Air Force PJs are all very interested in talking to you."

Rick did not respond. He had to figure a way out of this situation, fast.

She continued. "You can't leave without her."

Peters stared into her dark brown eyes. How much did she know?

The woman's voice turned sharp. "No time for games, Rick. If you leave her behind you can't possibly succeed. The ship will be here in less than an hour. Where is she?"

Apparently she knew a great deal.

"I left her in the parking lot."

"You should have brought her with you."

"She wouldn't listen. Two men took her away at gunpoint."

"Jesus, Rick. What have you done? We've got to get her. My name is Janice Younger. I work for the NSA. When your report came into the Agency, three of us were assigned to find you."

"Why would you want to help us?"

He could jump and make a break for the meadow. But she knew about the meadow and Kim.

"Let's just say I had a few nasty dreams. I'm telling you, if you go to the meadow alone, it won't make a difference. She's the one who knows."

"Knows what?"

Could this be a trap or had this woman been living the same twisted life as he and Kim?

"Cut the crap, Rick. She knows how to defeat the ship and you don't have a clue what to do once you get to the light."

Younger lowered her gun and started the engine. "Don't jump out until you've heard everything. It could save your life."

She took the turn onto the access road, heading back to the parking lot. "How long ago did they take her?"

"Ten minutes at the most."

"There's a chance she's still alive. You have to find her. Then, there's another problem: Lance White."

"A small, kind of chunky guy?" asked Rick.

Younger nodded. "He is your greatest threat. I can only help you so much with him."

"And if I don't believe a word you're saying?"

Younger shrugged. "Then you'll both die before you reach the meadow. You know the rest."

# THE ATTACK

YELLOWSTONE PARK TOOL SHED
NORTHWESTERN WYOMING
TUESDAY, SEPTEMBER 14, 2027
**7:19 A.M. MST**      9:19A.M. EST

Kim's arms were bleeding severely. White had ripped into her biceps with the knife, cutting along the length of her muscles. He stepped back and admired his work. She was in pain, but still had an arrogant expression on her haggard face. She wasn't ready to talk. She had too much fight left in her.

A glazed expression spread over her face. Her head lowered to her chest.

"Oh, no, you don't, bitch. You're not getting away that easy!" White raised his fist to slice her again when a pair of hands wrapped around his neck. Instinctively, White jerked his short body forward to throw his attacker off balance, then grabbed for the expected elbow. It wasn't there.

The grip on his throat tightened. Staggering across the room, he managed to reach his Beretta. Three over-the-shoulder shots failed to stop the unseen attacker. His vision was failing. Whirling once again, White fired behind him. The slug passed through the wooden wall, but the hands stayed at his throat.

Kim did not watch the struggle. She only concentrated on Rick's thoughts. She felt him coming. The hum had returned. This was the opportunity she'd prayed for. She was ready.

"I'm outside the shed," Rick whispered in her ear. "He'll kill me if I try to come in. We have to choke him, like we kicked the guard at the lodge. Use two strong hands around his neck. Then tighten the grip. On the count of three. One, two, three! Don't let him breathe, Kim! Choke him. Tighter. Tighter!"

White turned to finish her. He dropped to his knees, gasping. If nothing else, he'd make Callaway pay for this embarrassment. The lock of the shed's door splintered. He summoned every ounce of strength he had and squeezed the trigger, but as the gun fired, something jerked the weapon from his hand, then a powerful blow to his head forced his body to the ground.

Rick raced into the room behind Younger. The agent kicked the gun from White's hand, causing the slug to smash harmlessly through the wall. The second blow, more forceful than the first, landed on White's neck, knocking him out. Rick began cutting Kim's bonds. By the time she was free, Younger had rifled through White's pockets. She grabbed his gun, his satellite phone and wallet.

"Damn it, Rick, move!" Younger glanced out the doorway. Satisfied there were no additional threats outside, she helped Rick carry Kim to the parking lot.

Bruce Kirby woke up in a dark broom closet. In seconds he'd smashed his way through the flimsy pine door and raced back to the shed. White was on the floor, bloodied. Callaway was gone.

Running out the door, he spotted three figures heading into the parking lot clogged with the vehicles. Kirby raised his gun to fire, but the trio reached a cluster of cars and ducked behind a large mobile home. He had no choice but to follow. Exploding into a full run, he raced after them. As they appeared on the other side of the RV, he recognized the third member of the group. Younger! The man with them must be Rick Peters.

Kirby dodged between the cars, quickly closing the distance. He had them now! They were approaching a deserted section of the large parking lot. There would be nowhere to hide.

Younger stopped and tossed a set of keys to Rick. "For the red Saturn. It's in Section B6."

"Where are you going?"

"I have to take care of our friend behind us. Get in the car and take care of her wounds. The bandages are in the back seat."

She glanced backwards. Kirby had disappeared. "Go!"

Rick scooped Kim into his arms and carried her to the car. Opening the door, he gently placed her on the back seat. The fabric immediately became stained with blood. Kim was moaning, her head lolled against the seat. A dreadful gash extended eight inches along her thigh, reaching down to the bone.

The pop-pop sounds of Younger's gun caught his attention. Rick glanced out the window. Younger and her pursuer were playing cat-and-mouse around a Winnebago.

"Who's the guardian angel?" asked Callaway, gritting her teeth against the incredible pain.

"She says she's a government agent who had some unusual dreams. Seems her task was to defend us."

"Did a damn nice job."

Rick checked the front seat. His backpack containing his Casulls was still on the floor.

"I was on my way to the meadow when she convinced me to come back. She said you knew how to defeat the ship."

"She lied."

Rick pulled the bandages from the bag. "She also said we can't possibly succeed if we split up."

"That sounds familiar."

"So, I'm not letting you out of my sight until it's over."

"Heard that one before, too," she said between clenched teeth.

Kirby chased Younger around several cars before he realized she was trying to divert him from Peters. He glanced in the direction the trio had been traveling. A hundred yards away was the rental car he and Younger had driven from the Jackson airport. Kirby ran for the Saturn.

Younger followed, separated by a row of parked cars. The thirty-six-year-old man was out of shape. Younger easily caught up to him. As she ran parallel to him with the vehicles serving as a shield. Kirby fired in her direction trying to scare her off. Younger stopped and squeezed off five well-aimed shots. Kirby was dead before his face hit the pavement.

The wild gunplay did not go unnoticed. Scores of tourists ran for cover. Several headed for the ranger station. By the time Kirby had fallen, park rangers were arming themselves with rifles and bulletproof vests. The supervisor notified the NSA and the state police.

As Lance White came to his senses, he heard gunfire outside the shed. He reached for his weapon. Gone, along with his phone and his wallet. Callaway's bonds hung from the chair. He raced out of the small building into the parking lot toward a small crowd. Pushing through the tight circle of horrified spectators, White discovered Kirby's body sprawled on the pavement. Without checking his condition, he grabbed the gun from the agent's clenched fist, burst from the cluster of onlookers and raced in the direction the calmer observers were pointing.

Janice Younger jumped into the back seat of the rental car. Rick was awkwardly trying to wrap the gauze around Kim's bloodied arms. Younger pulled a needle and thread from the first aid kit. With no regard for Kim's pain, she grabbed her leg, squeezed the sides of the deep cut together and began stitching the wound shut. "This will have to be cleaned and changed, but you'll be able to walk." Once the gash on her leg was closed, she pushed Rick out of the way and began working on her arms.

"Stay off the marked trails. That will force him to track you. It'll slow him down." She pulled a hypodermic needle from the bag.

Kim watched her fill the syringe. "I don't think..."

Younger jammed the needle into Kim's thigh. "It's the only way you're going to continue, girl."

Finally, she wrapped the gashes with a tight layer of gauze, securing the bandage with a double wrap of adhesive tape. As the drug took effect, Kim felt more confident. The hum of being near Rick helped. The pain faded.

"That should do it," Younger announced. "Let's get you out of here. The trailhead is at the end of that service road. Once you reach the falls, cross the stream and head uphill.

Don't look back, and most importantly, don't stop. I'll stall White as long as I can."

She opened the car door and disappeared.

Rick jumped into the driver's seat. "It's good to be near you again," he said.

"I'm glad you came back." Her voice was decidedly stronger. "Why didn't she kill him?"

Rick backed out of the parking space and headed for the service road.

"She said she couldn't do that. It has something to do with today's timing. If White dies, too many variables fall out of place. The entire event is orchestrated like a ballet."

"He's still coming for us, Rick, and that woman is going to be seriously hurt."

"There's nothing we can do about it. All we're concerned with is reaching the meadow, fast."

Rick climbed into the driver's seat and started the car.

Lance White spotted Younger's rental speeding across the blacktop. He took aim and pulled the trigger five times before a bullet hit him below his collar bone. The projectile kicked him back and pierced his windbreaker, but was stopped by his bulletproof vest.

White's shots shattered the windshield in front of Rick. Another slug ripped into the right back tire. The car swerved wildly, then straightened out as it entered a small service road. Rick regained control and headed down the narrow dirt road, missing several large trees. After crossing the main highway, he pulled over and located the path leading into the woods. The trail was well-marked, but the burned foliage offered little protection. They would be easy targets.

Rick helped her out of the car.

"We've got to get into some live forest."

Kim leaned heavily on him as they started up the dirt trail. The pain returned as soon as she put weight on her leg.

"That woman said there was a stream up the trail. I remember seeing the falls on the map. Oh, God, Rick, it hurts so much."

He carried as much of her weight as possible.
"You'll make it."

The small-caliber weapon didn't have the power to
penetrate White's Velkar vest. He turned and located his
assailant. Younger. Persistent bitch. White fired at her.

Younger heard the bullet whistle overhead as she ran past
a Jeep. The car's side window shattered as another shot
missed her. White was advancing, ignoring Rick and Kim's
escape. Good. That would give them a head start. Kim's
wounds were deep and damaging. They wouldn't be able to
travel fast or for very long. They were going to need every
second she could give them.

Using the parked cars to shield his approach, White
continued his pursuit. Peters and Callaway would not get far.
The Saturn was useless, and if they tried to travel on foot,
Callaway wouldn't stay conscious much longer. But as long
as Younger was alive, she remained a credible threat. She had
to be eliminated.

Younger paused and leaned against a pickup. The dreams
had been uncannily accurate, right down to the heavy traffic
that allowed her to snag Peters. Now it was a matter of
stalling. She knew White would continue to pursue her. Like
a shark, he was a predator operating on a predictable set of
instincts.

Younger crawled around the rear of the pickup, checking
under the car for White's feet. Nothing. He must be standing
behind a set of tires. She darted past two more vehicles. At the
far end of the large parking lot, she saw a cluster of park
rangers armed with shotguns. Hopefully they would block
White's escape. She checked under the cars again. Feet
running to the left. Younger popped up from behind a sedan
and let off three rounds at the figure, then ducked and rolled
behind the next car.

White fired back, aiming under the pickup. Bullet
fragments sprayed the area where Younger had just been
kneeling. Moving to the next car, she looked through the back
window. White had disappeared, probably sneaking around

the motor home to her right. Younger looked under the cars again. No sign of him. She had to keep moving, drawing him toward the rangers and away from the service road.

After waiting a beat, she made a dash to the next row of cars. The moment she left her cover, White appeared from behind a large camper. He took three steps into the middle of the open space and emptied a fresh clip at her.

Two of White's slugs found their mark. The first bullet passed under her arm, tearing a hole in her left lung and shattering two of her ribs. The second did the most damage, grazing her aorta.

The force of the bullets knocked her sideways and to the ground, her gun falling from her hand. Lying on the asphalt, Younger knew she was badly hurt. White would kill her as soon as he could put his hands on her. She tried to reach her weapon lying a few feet away. If she could grab it, she might be able to deprive the sadistic bastard his enjoyment of dispatching yet another partner, but her hands would not work.

White ran to Younger's body and roughly rolled her over, looking for his phone and gun. He found both. After pocketing her weapon, he grabbed her head and with a sharp motion snapped her neck, killing her instantly. He desperately wanted to cause her more pain, but there were more important issues at stake.

He raced back to Kirby's rental, avoiding the advancing park rangers. He whipped the car around and drove the same route as Peters. The abandoned Saturn was parked in front of a trailhead. Two sets of tracks led into the woods. He broke into a run, heading up the dirt path.

THE INTERNATIONAL SPACE STATION
EARTH ORBIT
TUESDAY, SEPTEMBER 14, 2027
**7:20 A.M. MST**        9:20 A.M. EST

Still floating in space Ed Iris looked out of his visor and scanned the laser's control panel. Reactor, receiving dish and diodes were operating perfectly. Though the contraption cost over a billion dollars, it looked like a howitzer built by a four-year-old. Tubes and support bars protruded from the sides of the device. The solar array and receiving dish stuck out at odd angles. The gray barrel, now fully extended, appeared as flimsy as the rest of the device. At the back, on either side of the weapon, two small rectangular slabs served as seats. Hugh Smith and Ed Iris, protected from the hostile space environment by their bulky space suits, sat on either side of the awkward space gun.

With Houston silenced by the blast from Eagle, the commands came from a quickly established link from Kennedy Space Center's emergency control room. Zyger relayed the message to Ed and Hugh: fire as soon as possible. With the Space Command off-line, the computers plotting the intercept solution were now located at the Livermore Laboratory in Palo Alto, California. The order to shoot across Eagle's bow had also been changed. This was a shoot to kill.

"More like a shoot to annoy," grumbled Iris.

On a separate channel, Zyger asked Mission Control if Smith and Iris should power down if the radiation levels increased. The word directly from the war room was definitely no. The laser must fire on Eagle, no matter what the circumstances or consequences.

Smith and Iris knew their chances of surviving this exercise were close to zero. Yet they performed the required checks and adjustments without a sign of fear or panic. Zyger was proud of the two scientists who conceived, designed and built the awkward weapon. They were staring at their own deaths and continued to operate as if this was like any other workday.

As if on cue, the alarms sounded. The wall lit up like a Christmas tree. Instead of reaching out to the laser, the shaft of light shot from the alien ship into the atmosphere. A large red glow emerged at the end of the shaft, somewhere in the Southwest.

Hugh Smith flipped a series of switches with his gloved hand, and the gun went into an automatic computer check and ramping of power.

"Two minutes before Eagle enters the atmosphere. Fire that laser!" came Kennedy's command.

Zyger relayed the message to the two men in space.

"Keep your suit on," shot back a frustrated Iris. "The reactor is just coming on-line."

Zyger shook his head. Iris never changed. Even before lift-off, the irritable inventor complained about the cramped quarters and uncomfortable helmets. Zyger looked over to his right. The gauges all were back to normal. So far, so good, but it took a minimum of forty seconds to get the reactor to supply the immense energy required to fire the laser. Thirty unbelievably long seconds passed. Zyger almost convinced himself that Smith and Iris were going to make it when the alarms sounded.

"Radiation's rising! You've only got a few seconds, guys! It's on automatic, let it go! Jump! Get off!"

Neither Smith nor Iris made a move. They continued to massage the huge weapon, coaxing it to perform. Three seconds before they could shoot, they became one with their machine. When the blue light receded, there was no sign of the laser or the men.

Zyger looked out of the portal and saw the air in front of the mammoth disk begin to glow as it encountered the Earth's atmosphere. Heading east, Eagle remained untouched by the fiery reentry. The familiar blaze was far in front of the actual ship.

Davison stared in amazement. "How do they do that?"

"Probably some kind of force field keeping the reentry heat in front of the vessel. That would eliminate the need for specialized skin and cooling equipment. Great idea. Too bad we can't do that."

The alarms sounded once more. Seconds later the blue shafts of light slashed into the night again. This time the rays came from the sides of the black oval and ripped through the reentry fireball. The Kennedy Space Center was raked by the searing ray, incinerating the radio dishes and long control building. A half dozen communications and guidance satellites were reduced to solar wind. The supercomputer located at Livermore was melted along with the transmitter that sent the data into space. The final blast did not touch the ground. Instead, the beam tore through the vacuum of space and annihilated the International Space Station.

YELLOWSTONE PARK, WYOMING
TUESDAY, SEPTEMBER 14, 2027
**7:35 A.M. MST**      9:35A.M.EST

Kim limped on her uninjured leg leaning heavily on Rick. The uphill trail had leveled, then turned to run parallel with a quick-running stream. A sign at the fork pointed down a steep hill to Fern Cascades.

Kim pointed to the opposite side of the ravine. "At the top of that rise we'll find some cover."

Rick looked down at the swift-running water. Small mountain streams were deceiving. Cold and forceful, they could easily knock a man over. The opposite side offered a steep climb through more charcoaled woods. Kim was much weaker than when they started. A glance to his right told him it would be wiser to change their point of crossing. Flat grassy areas on either side of the small river indicated the current would be less forceful.

"We should cross upstream."

"We don't have time. Let's go, Rick. Stop stalling."

They stumbled down the slope to the edge of the water. A fallen tree provided a narrow bridge.

"Are you going to make it?"

She managed a smile to counter his increasing doubts. "Sure."

Rick stepped in the water upstream of the fallen timber. The icy cold, snow-fed creek immediately numbed his ankles as the powerful current tried to dislodge his feet. Leaning against the log provided enough stability to brace against the flow and keep a grip around Kim's waist. He could barely watch as she crawled across the moss-covered log. Her arms and leg were drenched in blood, her face twisted in silent suffering.

She was so strong, so determined. He never realized that women like Kim existed. Leaving her in the parking lot had been a terrible mistake. He'd followed the voice throughout this entire ordeal, then ignored it when it came to her safety. It was time to put a stop to that. He would stay at her side until they were inside the light. He also made a silent promise to himself: if he had the chance, he would kill the man that had made her suffer so much.

Kim heard his anger, but had to concentrate on the damp wood in front of her. She couldn't be distracted, not now. Her purpose was to get across the log. The pain in her arms and leg helped her focus, but in the back of her mind she knew the man holding her had become more than a partner, his concern and compassion unquestionably deeper than she'd assumed.

The idea that she'd found someone who had the potential to be a good friend while on this death march was more than sad. He'd come back to save her, risked his life to get her away from White and was in the process of changing into a truly giving person. Yet here she was, bleeding to death in the wilds of Wyoming after finding the first decent man who cared for her. What a joke. A really bad joke.

Kim reached the opposite bank and fell onto the muddy slope. Rick pulled himself out of the powerful flow, then helped her climb up the slippery hillside. Once they'd passed the steep portion of the ravine, they moved a little quicker up the burned hill. Warm blood trickled into her shoe.

"Where is he?" she grunted, "He should be right on our tail."

"Maybe he didn't find the car. Or that NSA woman could have stopped him," offered Rick.

"We know that's not what happens. He won't stop until we're both dead."

"Or we eliminate him."

Yeah, right, thought Kim, glad that Rick couldn't read her mind.

"We've got to keep believing, Kim. We can make it."

Reaching the top of the rise, Kim twisted her neck to look behind her. There he was running between the trees they'd passed minutes earlier, about to cross the stream they'd struggled to traverse.

"Don't look. It'll slow us down. We'll lose him in the trees."

Kim was on the verge of tears. She didn't know which was worse: the unbelievable pain or the fear of what White would do if he caught them.

"Don't give up, Kim," Rick panted. He was dragging her as fast as he could manage. "We'll figure something out. Keep moving."

White was closing the gap quickly. He raced down the embankment to the small stream and jumped into the water, but underestimated the strength of the current. His feet were swept from underneath him. Lunging backward, he grabbed a cluster of bushes. The shallow roots began to give way, pulling out of the mud with a grotesque sucking sound.

Before the scrawny foliage released its grip, White managed to drag himself out of the greedy water. Angry he'd been fooled by the innocent-looking brook, he crawled across the moss-covered log. Scrambling up the other side of the ravine, he focused his hostility on the woman who continued to make him look like an amateur.

I will make sure Kim Callaway dies before the day ends, he promised himself, and she will suffer so much she'll be thankful to leave this existence.

His unchecked anger caused White more trouble. Though his powerful muscles saved him from being washed down the boiling falls, his lungs were unaccustomed to the thin mountain air. The weight of his soaked pants and bulletproof vest caused him to work that much harder. By the time he reached the crest of the gorge, he was winded and was forced to stop. The delay allowed Rick and Kim to reach the unburned section of the forest.

Now White had to follow their tracks. That slowed him even more, but he knew he was going to find them. He was looking forward to teaching this woman something about pain.

White chuckled to himself and continued into the woods. Half a mile into the Lodgepole pines, the footprints led him to a cluster of rocks. A single set of dirt-ladened tracks ended twenty feet later, atop a small boulder. Unbelievably, the two novices had tricked him.

ONE HUNDRED MILES ABOVE EARTH
TUESDAY, SEPTEMBER 14, 2027
**7:35 A.M. MST**        9:35 A.M. EST

The alien ship continued to ignore all known rules of space flight. Without establishing an orbit or firing rockets to slow it down, Eagle continued to descend into the atmosphere. The flaming spectacle was viewed by the entire European continent as the fireball turned night into day. The sonic boom that followed caused major damage throughout Russia and northern China.

Eagle's propulsion system began affecting geological flaws beneath the Earth's surface. Immense pressures that had built up over the decades were released as the disk passed overhead. Fourteen major tremors, ranging from 7.3 to 11.2 on the Richter scale, rattled eastern Russia, China and northern Mongolia.

A cluster of surface-to-air missiles rose from Russia's eastern batteries, along with a coordinated attack from three squadrons of MIG-29s. Eagle destroyed most of the SAMs two hundred feel off the ground. Once the incoming rockets were dispatched, Eagle eliminated the offending launch sites, fighters, radar installations and command centers.

Crossing over Japan, Eagle caused six immense earthquakes that rocked the densely populated islands. Multiple tsunamis swept over the low-lying coastal areas. As the huge ship dropped in altitude and continued to slow, its need for power diminished. As a result, the effects from

Eagle's engines weakened. That news offered little consolation to the inhabitants of Hawaii and Maui. Mauna Loa and Haleakala blasted open, pouring thousands of tons of lava onto the tourist getaways.

RECONNAISSANCE PLANE AURORA
GROOM LAKE, NEVADA
TUESDAY, SEPTEMBER 14, 2027
**7:38 A.M. MST**      9:38A.M. EST

Steve Lassil roared off the runway. The Aurora, a combination jet and rocket, was the cause of the mysterious "earthquakes" throughout Southern California during the early 2020s. Although its existence was consistently denied, the plane was secretly commissioned in late 2014. With its range of nine thousand miles and a top speed of eight times the speed of sound, it was the military's answer to a near-instantaneous reconnaissance photo. Where satellites had to be in the correct position to complete their radar, infrared and visual inspections, the Aurora could fly above any location in three hours and immediately send information via satellite anywhere in the world.

Lassil had his hands full preparing for his flyby of the giant disk. A check of the computer displays confirmed that the inlets were in their proper position, the automated cooling systems were working and the fuel flow through the skin of the ship was at its proper rate. The scramjets automatically kicked in, pushing Lassil back into his seat. At the same time, the plane's composite shield lowered, protecting the small window from the thousand-degree heat generated by the friction with the outside air.

Lassil's mission was to race directly at Eagle and take sensitive infrared, radar and video recordings from the rocketplane's battery of instruments. A KC-135 tanker and its escort of five F-111 Aardvarks would rendezvous with Lassil over the Pacific. Lassil would refuel, turn around and then pursue the massive ship. On the second pass he would attempt to fly directly above the ship, matching its speed.

Twenty minutes later, Lassil was streaking through the skies at seventy-two miles a minute. The intruder was traveling at approximately Mach 7. The combined pass-by speed would be Mach 20, almost thirteen thousand miles an hour. Not a lot of time to gather information. The Aurora was only three seconds from its pass-by when the shock wave hit. Although the composite fabric was stronger than any conventional airplane skin, the billion-dollar Aurora was shaken into thousands of pieces in a split second. Steve Lassil never knew what hit him.

THE COCKPIT OF A P-14 TOMCAT
SOMEWHERE OVER THE PACIFIC TUESDAY,
SEPTEMBER 14, 2027
**7:41 A.M. MST**      9:41A.M.EST

Johnson Coates pushed the throttle of his F-14 Tomcat, but the jet remained stationary. Suddenly Coates' plane catapulted across the carrier's deck. Pulling back on the stick, he angled the fighter into the sky as he and thirty-eight other fighters raced to intercept Eagle.

Five hundred miles east of him, Eagle continued to tear through the atmosphere. The alien ship was traveling too fast for an airborne pursuit. Even with full afterburners, the Tomcat's turbofans were only capable of driving the jet to a mere Mach 2.4, far too slow to keep pace with the disk. Interception would have to occur head on and only once.

The first ten planes raced ahead of Coates' group. They would be the lead group, probing the alien's defenses, looking for weaknesses and taking readings that would be analyzed by the carrier Independence. Five miles from the intruder, a powerful electromagnetic field reached out and scrambled every computer device aboard the advanced fighters. Without their computer chips to relay instructions to the wings and engines, the high-tech fighters became rocks in the sky, plummeting uncontrollably into the Pacific.

Coates gritted his teeth in anger as he fingered his weapons release. The aliens were minutes away from the United States mainland. Someone had to stop them. No way this thing could take on the mightiest military force in the world and waltz away unharmed. Damn, he thought, I should have gone to that meadow. That's where this thing is headed.

"Keep the radar off," he said to his Radio Intercept Officer, Greg Langley.

"Why?"

"Just a hunch," returned Coates. "There's something familiar about this thing." In his mind he saw a sea urchin surrounded by spines, except at the bottom.

Coates broke formation. It was underneath, the soft spot, where the ship was most vulnerable. Coates' F-14 went into a gut-wrenching dive, then pulled out and headed upward at the onrushing disk. Coates kept his thumb on the missile fire control.

"Radar on, Greg!"

"Radar on. We have positive lock!"

A sharp tone sounded in his ear. Before Coates could press his weapon release, the cockpit filled with a searing blue light.

THE WAR ROOM
WASHINGTON, D.C.
TUESDAY, SEPTEMBER 14, 2027
**7:43 A.M. MST**        9:43 A.M. EST

"What the hell is going on out there?" demanded President Linden.

The atmosphere in the war room had become increasingly brittle. Nothing seemed to affect the giant invader. General Moore stood in front of the wall-sized screen, staring at the large red dot that represented Eagle's position. "We've lost contact with Aurora, and a squadron of the Independence's fighters have been shot down."

"How many?"

"Fifty-two, sir."

"Fifty-two! How did that happen?" shouted the President.

"Apparently Eagle knows when a targeting device locks on it and immediately reacts."

Linden's clenched his fists. What would it take to stop this thing?

"Then fire the missiles manually!"

"Our missiles require a positive lock before they can be launched."

"Then bomb it. Knock that bastard out of the sky before it flies over the San Andreas fault and we lose California!"

Sweat beaded on Moore's forehead. Almost a thousand men had perished. The SDI space laser, the Grand Canyon Proton Accelerator, the International Space Station and over fifty fighters had been destroyed.

"We'll stop it, sir." His voice sounded strong, but the doubts had begun. All the weapons at his disposal were designed to attack specific types of ordnance. This black oval had no counterpart in the United States' arsenal. The missiles were shooting were too small and a nuclear weapon would cause too much ground destruction. Still, Moore refused to become discouraged. Every machine had its flaw, its weak point. It might take a single missile, or lucky bomb, but he would not give up until every possible avenue had been explored.

Admiral Forester offered an option. "The AEGIS missile cruiser Valley Forge has a small arsenal of experimental, extremely high-explosive missiles that can be sighted and launched manually. We could also reprogram our Tomahawks. We've got the Seawolf attack submarine directly in Eagle's path."

Moore looked confused. "Cruise missiles? What good are they?"

"If we program the targeting computer to detonate on an imaginary mountain in front of the disk, they'll pop up and explode underneath Eagle. The missiles wouldn't have the targeting signature that other lock-and-shoot devices have."

"Mr. President, may I speak?"

All eyes turned to Franklin Turner.

Linden waved a hand at the scientist. "Make it brief, Franklin."

Turner nodded, glancing around the table. "Eagle has only reacted to perceived threats. Not once has it taken an offensive action. You must cease your military actions or you'll be responsible for many more casualties.

General Moore looked at Turner in disbelief. "What are you suggesting, Turner? That we let it fly right over the continent?"

"That is exactly what I'm saying. I don't believe Eagle is the monster you're imagining."

Moore tried to contain his anger. Civilians did not have the stomach for military conflict. Turner was the worst kind, suggesting a unilateral surrender. He was not the type of person you wanted in a war room when your men were in a life-and-death struggle.

"Mr. Turner, these invaders have killed over nine hundred United States citizens not to mention the thousands of deaths caused by the earthquakes, volcanoes and tsunamis. Sitting around to see happens next is not an acceptable option."

"General, the alien has fired only in direct response to your aggressive actions."

Moore pointed an angry finger at Turner. "Destroying the U.S. Space Command was an offensive act."

Turner ignored the comment and shrugged. "That was a defensive maneuver. It destroyed a facility that was plotting its destruction."

"The entire Southwest could be lost if Eagle passes over it," argued Moore.

Turner smiled and pointed at the map. "An all-out offensive by this advanced warship would be far worse."

President Linden had heard enough. "Franklin, we will protect our borders."

"Eagle doesn't know about anybody's borders."

"It's going to find out."

Linden turned to Admiral Forester. "John, order your missile cruiser to launch everything it has. Follow it up with the sub's Tomahawks. General McKinley, what about bombing the alien?"

"We've got a squadron of B-52s on the way from Alaska. They have a load of ten thousand-pound bombs, as well as a complement of nuclear weapons. We can drop the conventional explosives in Eagle's path. Perhaps it will alter its course."

General Hood, commander of the Army, joined in. "Our batteries of Patriot missiles are in position along the West Coast."

Linden frowned. "They're no help. The Russians didn't get theirs off the ground. What else do we have?"

"The neutron and thermonuclear bombs."

Senator Downs was appalled. "A nuclear explosion would spread radiation across the entire northern half of the country."

General Moore acknowledged the Senator's fears without hesitation.

"The neutron bomb's radiation would be active for only four minutes and would be confined to a twenty-mile radius. A thermonuclear blast would create a cloud of lethal radiation downwind of the impact. We'd encounter a great number of civilian casualties."

The Secretary of State drummed his fingers on the table. "Maybe it's just going to fly by."

"Remove that imbecile from the room!" shouted the President.

GUIDED MISSILE SHIP VALLEY FORGE
FIVE HUNDRED MILES NORTHEAST OF HAWAII
TUESDAY, SEPTEMBER 14, 2027
**7:46 A.M. MST**      9:46A.M.EST

The guided missile ship Valley Forge shut down its radar as fifty lookouts scanned the horizon. When the black circle rose in the western sky, four dozen missiles leapt into the air. The slender projectiles reached an altitude of half a mile when they were blasted by the blue beam. Moments later, the circular shaft of light burned a twenty-foot hole through the center of the cruiser. With two quick passes, the laser sliced the ship from bow to stem, port to starboard. The four pieces immediately sank with all aboard.

OFF THE CALIFORNIA COAST
TUESDAY, SEPTEMBER 14, 2027
**7:46 A.M. MST        9:46A.M.EST**

A squadron of twenty B-52s reached their assigned position two hundred miles off the coast of Oregon, three minutes before Eagle arrived. The order relayed from the war room was to drop a large grouping of conventional bombs directly in front of the vessel's flight path. The alien ship would either move out of the way or plow directly into tons of explosives.

The bombs fell in perfect formation. Though the disk was traveling at Mach 6, it was impossible to miss. Dark clouds obscured the disk's front end as the huge warheads detonated. A group of F-111 pilots flying off to the side of the dark oval watched as the smoke and debris flowed harmlessly around the disk. The bombs never reached the hull of the ship. An envelope of clear air surrounded the intruder as it continued eastward. A physical force field protected the alien.

The twenty B-52s were eliminated seconds after the bombs exploded.

FIREHOLE MEADOW
YELLOWSTONE NATIONAL PARK, WYOMING
TUESDAY, SEPTEMBER 14, 2027
**7:46 A.M. MST        9:46A.M. EST**

Major Glenhurst's men scrambled across the meadow. Several large streams meandered through the middle of the field. As he watched the men take their positions, he sensed something was amiss. Although the Global Positioning System had led them to this location, there was no indication of any water on Sonya's diagram. Glenhurst signaled Larry Gott, his communications officer, and together they double-checked the maps.

The Madison Plateau contained a cluster of hot springs and a single spring-fed lake. It took Glenhurst a few seconds to find the problem. They were miles north of the meadow on Sonya's map.

"Get the men back in the choppers and over to the Madison Plateau."

"Yes, sir."

Glenhurst's remaining helicopter swooped over the trees, returning from its unsuccessful attempt at locating Keith Grunderson. The large craft was about to drop at the southern edge of the meadow when the pilot received the order to head south. The copter reversed direction.

"Sir, I've got Lance White on the radio, sir," called Gott.

Lance White wasn't on Sonya's list, but FORCECOM, the specified command for the defense of the continent, had informed him of the three NSA agents in the field of operation.

"I'll talk to him." Damn operatives, he thought, they always think they hold the fate of the world in their unaccountable hands.

Glenhurst grabbed the receiver. "What can I do for you, Mr. White?"

"Nice day for an invasion, eh, Glenhurst? Listen, one of our elusive scientists is about three miles ahead of me. I need one of your choppers. Fast."

Glenhurst wanted to blow him off, but priority remained with whoever could apprehend the missing men.

"You can have one of my Super Stallions for an hour. Where are you?"

"Three miles west of Old Faithful. The AWAC will give you my coordinates."

"The AWAC is a little confused at the moment," replied Glenhurst.

"I know, but they've got a fix on my phone."

Glenhurst glanced around the meadow. His men were climbing back into the choppers.

"Who have you located?"

"Rick Peters and Kim Callaway."

Glenhurst recognized Peters' name. Callaway was an addition.

"Your ride is on its way. An hour, no more."

"Thanks, Major."

Glenhurst turned to Gott. "Where's the rest of the unit?"

"An hour southwest of Yellowstone."

"Have all the men brought to the Plateau as soon as possible. Once we've reached the correct meadow, White can have his chopper. Send the other three Stallions back to West Yellowstone as soon we unload and get the rest of the company."

"What about the tanks, sir?"

"Have them take the park road. It'll be faster than cutting through the forest. The mortars, stingers and TOWs are to remain at the airstrip. They'll have a decent shot from there. Where are the para-jumpers?"

"They just arrived and are circling above us."

"Have four of them jump now. The others are to attempt entry to the disk. They'll get direct orders from FORCECOM. What's the status on the fugitives?"

"Ross crash-landed his plane eight miles southeast of us. The Apaches were trying to get him to turn. They shot up his tail, but were called off. The President ordered all aircraft to deal with Eagle's approach. It's two minutes from the Oregon coast."

THE OREGON COASTLINE
TUESDAY, SEPTEMBER 14, 2027
**7:47 A.M. MST**      9:47  A.M. EST

Thirty Tomahawks aboard the submarine Seawolf had been reprogrammed, targeted on a fictitious mountaintop ten miles off the west coast of Oregon. The submarine rocked as the missiles were launched. An emergency dive was initiated as soon as all missiles were airborne. The rockets rose one hundred feet, then arced over and skimmed across the waves. After several minutes, they rose from their sea-level trajectories and headed directly at Eagle's underside. The blue laser reached out and vaporized the weapons before they reached their target.

The retaliatory blast boiled millions of gallons of seawater above the diving submarine, but the liquid diluted the ray's intensity. A new weapon was employed. Eagle fired a blast of ultrasonic waves at the submerged boat. Although thousands of marine animals died instantly, the sub remained untouched as it continued to find safety in the black depths of the Pacific.

A third attack used a powerful magnetic tractor beam that latched onto the giant sub and yanked it to the surface so fast that the bowplanes and sail were ripped from the hull. As soon as the ship broke the surface, the tractor was disengaged and the blue laser quartered the ship.

YELLOWSTONE NATIONAL PARK, WYOMING
TUESDAY, SEPTEMBER 14, 2027
**7:53 A.M. MST**        9:53A.M. EST

Kim and Rick struggled across a small clearing. He could tell she was fading, unable to put any weight on her blood-soaked leg, barely able to limp on the other.

"I can't, Rick," she moaned.

Rick stopped a few feet into the forest and leaned against a fallen tree.

"We've got to get to the meadow, Kim. It can't be much further."

The pain had worked its way through the drug. Her legs refused to move. Her arms could no longer take the strain.

"You have to go on."

"Not acceptable." Rick was not going to leave her again. "How about climbing on my back? I'll carry you."

She could not hide the pain. Her voice trembled. "Okay. Let's try."

Rick lowered himself to his knees. Kim tried to wrap her arms around his neck. She screamed and fell to the ground.

"It's over, Rick," Kim panted, lying on her back. "I can't...go...any further."

"It's not over until the fat man sings," came a boisterous voice from behind the trees.

Rick pulled his Casull from his holster and leveled it at the shaking branches.

Tears streamed down Kim's face. It had to be Lance White. Oh, God, she thought, I can't take any more pain.

Two men pushed a cluster of limbs aside.

"Grunderson!" Rick lowered the gun and gave the husky man a hug. "I didn't expect to see you here!"

Grunderson nodded in acknowledgment. "I missed your face, Rick. Thought I'd drive up to the wild Rocky Mountains and join you in some fun. Tom Ross, this is Rick Bradley, another one of your scientists."

On hearing his JPL alias, Rick briefly considered telling Grunderson and Ross his real name, but decided it would only confuse the issue. He let it pass.

"Pleased to meet you, Rick." Ross' gaze dropped to Kim's bloodstained body. "Looks like you need a little help."

Kim stared up at the men, then passed out.

"We have to get her to the meadow," said Rick.

"You need to get her to a doctor."

"If we don't get to the meadow, there won't be any doctors."

"Got a point, Rick." Ross disappeared into the brush and returned with two long tree limbs. "Take your jackets off and help me strip these branches."

The men hastily removed the foliage, then slid the arms of their jackets onto the poles. After zipping the jackets closed, they carefully placed Kim onto the makeshift stretcher.

Grunderson picked up one end of the two branches. "Let's go. Not a lot of time left."

ABOVE YELLOWSTONE NATIONAL PARK
NORTHWESTERN WYOMING
TUESDAY, SEPTEMBER 14, 2027
**7:53 A.M. MST**      9:53  A.M. EST
When the C5A cargo plane lifted off, Dave Bartell was more than disappointed. He'd joined the Air Force to serve and protect his country. Being ordered to find some wacky scientists in a forest when the entire world was under attack frustrated him beyond belief. As the huge plane approached Yellowstone, Bartell realized his worries were totally unfounded. From the open cargo bay door he could see the alien disk approaching in the distance.

Bartell's orders were to take his platoon of seven men, jump onto the Madison Plateau, then locate and detain Rick Peters, Tom Ross, Keith Grunderson or Conrad Wiley. Under no circumstances were these men to be allowed near the alien ship, nor was he to believe anything they said about being part of an attack group.

Once an individual was in custody, the Marine command at West Yellowstone was to be notified. At that point, several intelligence officers would be transported to the location to interrogate the prisoners.

Fifteen minutes before reaching Wyoming, Bartell's orders were changed. Four of Bartell's men were to jump onto Eagle and attempt to gain entry. At its present rate of deceleration, the alien would be traveling at less than fifty miles an hour when it passed beneath Bartell's plane. If the PJs made it onto the alien vessel, three thousand paratroopers would join them. The remaining PJs, including Bartell, were to continue with the original mission: jump onto the meadow and locate the missing civilians.

Bartell was disappointed he hadn't been picked to take on the extraterrestrial, but he'd still be challenged. Word from the ground was that the civilians were armed and dangerous. Two NSA agents had already been murdered.

The light on the wall turned green. Bartell tightened his oxygen mask, walked to the gaping hole, and leapt out the back of the jet. The three hundred mile an hour wind jerked him away from the plane.

During the thirty-five-thousand-foot fall, Bartell kept a wary eye on the huge disk in the distance. Surrounded by hundreds of fighters and bombers, it looked like an animal being chased by a swarm of angry bees. At twenty thousand feet, Bartell shifted his concern to the land beneath him. In the distance he could see Tom Ross' damaged plane, but wouldn't be able to reach it. The C5A, forced to stay far from the disk, had dropped the PJs miles northeast of the park. It took a huge power glide to get near the Plateau. Bartell's chute opened automatically three thousand feet above the ground. Once he landed, he headed for Ross' damaged Cessna.

YELLOWSTONE NATIONAL
PARK NORTHWESTERN WYOMING
TUESDAY, SEPTEMBER 14, 2027
**8:11 A.M. MST**       10:11A.M. EST

Barbara Whitten reached the clearing without incident. She'd hiked the Summit Lake Trail until she spotted the small Continental Divide marker. Turning south, it took her another hour and a half to reach the meadow. Though she knew the others were watching from hidden positions, she boldly walked into the field and searched for a suitable location for her ambush. The civilians in the woods were of no consequence. They'd seen her and assumed she was one of them. Nothing could be further from the truth.

Examining the uneven ground near the edge of the meadow, Barbara found the small rise she was searching for. She removed a small, flat shovel from her backpack and dug a shallow indentation in the dark soil. After wrapping her custom-made Shilen in a sheath of plastic, she settled into the grave-like foxhole, covered herself with grass and put on her goggles. Now, all she had to do was wait.

Despite the level ground and lack of undergrowth to hamper his headway, Grunderson's chunky body couldn't take the stress of carrying Kim's stretcher. Covered in sweat, he handed his poles to Rick after only half a mile.

"Guess you didn't train for this one, Keith," grunted Ross.

"You flew here, Ross! I've been bouncing on my butt for hours."

"You should have chartered a plane. Would have been cheaper than the bike we just abandoned."

Deep furrows dug into Grunderson's forehead. "I never thought of that."

"Then again, you could have bought more gas. That would have helped."

"Lighten up, Ross. I was being followed."

"Who wasn't?"

"Besides," said Grunderson, running Ross' idea to its logical conclusion, "I don't think a pilot would have agreed to land the way you did."

"You're here, that's all that matters," said Rick.

"What matters is I might never get my hands on another Ding-Dong."

"Look, there it is!" exclaimed Ross.

All three men immediately recognized the small outcropping of lichen-covered boulders. Rick and Ross lowered Kim's stretcher.

Grunderson cupped his hands around his mouth. "Hey! Where is everyone?"

Ross shoved him sideways. "Ssshh! There are people here we don't want to meet."

Grunderson shrugged. "Oh, yeah. Sorry. Forgot."

A shadowy figure appeared from behind a cluster of trees and ran down a small incline. Rick and his companions pulled their Casulls and aimed at the approaching stranger.

The scruffy man with soiled jeans slid in the dirt, stopped at the bottom of the incline and put his hands in the air.

"Whoa, easy, boys." He looked at the revolvers. "Casulls. Glad to see you're on our side." His eyes lowered to Kim's blood-soaked body.

"What happened to her?"

Rick fingered the trigger of his Casull. "She ran into a cruel NSA agent. Have the Marines arrived?"

"A couple of military helicopters flew over a few minutes ago, but there's no sign of anyone on the ground. My name's Sean Sterling. We've got more people back by a small cave, but none of us know what to do."

"How many?"

"Twenty-nine. We met this morning and bushwhacked across the Plateau. We've got quite a diverse group: there's an actress, several businessmen, a cowboy, a film editor and two professional ballplayers and Robert Nordby is a park ranger. He led us around the hot springs that pepper the area. Watch your step. Those suckers will boil you alive."

Sterling stopped chatting and nodded at the guns. "I'd appreciate it if you put those revolvers away. There are twelve just like it aimed at you."

Ross looked around. He was surrounded by at least a dozen people scattered among the rocks and bushes. The men carefully replaced their guns.

"Pleased to meet you, Sean. I'm Tom Ross, National Security Agency Specialist. This is Keith Grunderson and Rick Bradley, both JPL scientists."

Sterling took a long look at Rick. "You're not a scientist. You're that stockbroker I read about last year. You're Rick Peters."

Rick nodded. There was no need to continue the charade. "That's right, Sean. I am Rick Peters."

"You blew up that plane."

"Relax, Sean. You don't know what you're talking about."

"Like hell I don't."

Rick's tone took on a harsh edge. "I didn't have anything to do with the plane."

Ross looked at Rick. "What's this jerk talking about?"

"Before I worked at JPL, I traded stocks for a living. About two years ago a plane was sabotaged, and I made a lot of money because I knew exactly when the plane was going down. What this gentleman doesn't know is I called the airlines. That's what got me into so much trouble. I warned them, but they chose to ignore me, just like your friend chose to ignore you."

Sterling visibly flinched.

Peters read the report about three people who refused to step foot on the plane. Sterling was one of them. His best friend laughed at him, called him a chicken and boarded the aircraft. That was the last time Sterling saw him.

"I'm sorry, Sean, I did what I could. I'm sure you did, too. No one believed us. Unfortunately, that hasn't changed. Does that ranger have a first aid kit?"

"There's a doctor here. He brought blood for a woman that was supposed to help us."

"Get him. Quick."

Sterling turned and disappeared among the boulders. Grunderson looked around, eyeing the semi-hidden pistols aimed at them. "What do you think, Tom?"

Ross rubbed his throbbing chest. "We look like a bunch of amateurs trying to save the world."

"We'll have to make it work," said Rick, putting his hands on his hips. "Sorry I didn't tell you about the name thing earlier."

"We all had a difficult time getting here, Rick. No need to apologize."

Raymond Holt ran down the small incline and knelt at Kim's side. Without bothering to introduce himself, he examined Kim's wounds, then removed an intravenous needle from his backpack and inserted it into Kim's uninjured thigh.

"I knew this was going to happen," he said, as he pulled a small cooler from his backpack. "I had these images of saving a woman in the woods, but I thought it was a subconscious wish to be a country doctor. It wasn't until yesterday I realized the dreams weren't symbolic."

"Did you see the pillar of light?"

Holt lifted a bag of blood from the ice chest. "At least a dozen times."

"And you weren't going to come?"

"Hell no, I wasn't going to come. Who'd believe that scene? It isn't going to happen, is it?"

"In about ten minutes."

Holt attached one of the blood bags to Kim's I.V. "We're in for some fun, aren't we?"

"Hardly," replied Rick, amazed that Kim's survival depended on a single man's whim. Or was it a single man? Younger had arrived at a critical moment, so had Grunderson and Ross. What did Younger say in the parking lot? If White died, too many variables would fall out of place. Maybe Kim had to be caught by White - if she wasn't delayed, perhaps other actions wouldn't occur.

Holt checked the blood flow in the I.V., then lifted Kim's eyelids. He grabbed a hypodermic needle from the backpack.

"Wait!" shouted Rick.

"It's for the pain."

"She has to be able to think clearly," said Rick firmly.

"She'll be lucid for a while, but I'm not sure what else I can do. It may be too late already."

Rick grabbed the end of Kim's stretcher. "Give me a hand, Ray. Grab the blood, Keith. We can't have her out in the open."

"Follow me," said Holt, "we'll put her in the cave."

The heavy beating of military rotors punctuated his command. "Hurry!"

Four CH53 Super Stallions roared into the meadow. Glenhurst directed the pilot to set down in the northeastern section. The three other choppers followed him in. As the huge transports bumped onto the ground, Glenhurst touched his shirt pocket. Who would have believed Sonya's absurd profession would have any kind of validity? He certainly didn't expect her work to affect his life. The Major made a mental note that if he survived the next few days, he'd have to find her and apologize. He hoped Sonya was more forgiving than he'd been.

"We're losing contact with the AWAC," said Gott. "Too much interference. Ground communications won't last much longer, either."

"Get hold of the PJs and give them our coordinates. I want those commandos here with us."

"What about the Apaches?"

Glenhurst had ordered the helicopters to cease their attack on Ross' Cessna and land at West Yellowstone.

"Have them join the offensive against Eagle, then see if you can raise FORCECOM. I want to know if there are other special forces in the area. Send Lance White his chopper. Damn, where's the rest of the unit? We need them here."

"Last report, they were ten miles north of Idaho Falls, about fifteen minutes from West Yellowstone."

"They'd better hurry or they're going to run into that disk."

Lance White waited impatiently in the small clearing, still puzzled at how Peters and Callaway could have evaded him. He'd been following such an obvious trail, then he'd become confident, almost to the point of being happy. And he'd lost them. How could two incompetent, wounded civilians fool him...of course! He felt happy just before he'd lost them. It was that same annoying emotion he'd experienced when he flew over the entrance to Teton Village, the same sensation he'd felt with Callaway in the shed. Somehow, Peters had the ability to deceive him.

White abruptly stopped pacing. If Peters could fool him into seeing or hearing anything, then he couldn't trust any of his senses. That was going to make locating the traitors extremely difficult. They could be in front of him and he'd never find them. The common factor was an intoxicating feeling of success. That was the giveaway. If he was too confident, Peters had to be close by.

The Super Stallion appeared above him. Its powerful rotors created a huge downdraft that bent the treetops. A rope ladder snaked out of the craft and was whipped around in the swirling winds. It took several attempts before White grabbed hold. He scrambled up the ladder, into the helicopter. Donning an offered headset, White barked his order: "Go west. Stay low."

The thirty-two-year-old Marine who'd pulled White aboard stared into the agent's cold eyes. As instructed, he offered White some information.

"Tom Ross' plane ditched about three miles west of here. Is that where you're heading?"

White couldn't help but smile. If Ross was headed west, he was probably close to Peters and Callaway. White took pause, noticing his own satisfaction. Was this the feeling? Could they be in the plane or in the clearing he'd just left? White glanced around the hold. No, they weren't here, and this wasn't the elation he'd felt before. Damn, these assholes were driving him crazy!

"Where's Eagle?" White yelled into the microphone. "Thirty-eight miles to the west."

"Drop me at the wreck."

White jumped out of the large helicopter before it touched the ground. In seconds he'd found the bike's trail and set off in a run. Half a mile into the forest he found the abandoned cycle. Following the sets of footprints was as easy as the bike tracks. When the trail led to a fallen tree, stained with blood, he knew Peters and the bitch were nearby. Three sets of prints left the area. They were carrying Callaway. He'd catch up to them in no time.

WEST YELLOWSTONE AIRSTRIP
NORTHWESTERN WYOMING
TUESDAY, SEPTEMBER 14, 2027
**8:11 A.M. MST**     10:11 A.M. EST
Three C5As landed at West Yellowstone three minutes ahead of Eagle's electromagnetic disturbance. The fourth plane was eleven miles from the runway when the electronic field swept across the huge jet, scrambling the plane's chips. The engine's computer-controlled fuel pumps immediately froze and the plane plummeted from the sky, crashing into the Grand Targhee National Forest. Ten badly wounded men survived the crash, but their emergency radios refused to work.

The transports that reached the landing strip were quickly unloaded. Four tanks set off down Route 20, on their way to the Old Faithful visitor center. The rest of the contingent split up. Half remained at the airstrip, securing it, setting up a command post and preparing the offensive equipment. The other group waited to be flown to the Plateau. The last communication received was an order from Major Glenhurst to fire at Eagle at two specific times. All Stinger, mortar, TOW and artillery were to participate in the strike.

Dave Bartell reached the wreck of the Cessna before the rest of his crew. Carefully examining the ground surrounding the plane, he found evidence of Grunderson's bike and another set of footprints within the tire tracks. Someone was following the bike. A fast-moving man, probably an NSA agent or a civilian. Bartell headed in the direction the bike had traveled.

Moments later he received a garbled message from the Marine Expeditionary Unit. Glenhurst was trying to gather the

PJs under his command. Bartell would have none of that. He'd heard about the Major's group, a highly unusual band of men who were known to have out-maneuvered smaller search and rescue units and performed exceptionally well in adverse conditions. Giving up his independence went against everything Bartell had been taught. He ignored the message and continued tracking.

The sky darkened. Gusts of wind grabbed at his uniform. An extremely forceful blast threw him to the ground. Bartell struggled to his feet and raced to the shelter of the woods, following deep footprints. The tracks lead him past an abandoned bike, to the opposite side of a wide strip of trees where he discovered a large, steam-covered field.

Bartell almost missed the flash of movement to his left. A rifle-toting Marine was making his way between the tree trunks. Bartell spotted another Marine on his right. Glenhurst's men were surrounding the meadow. He backed away from the edge of the trees and disappeared into the greenery. Rick Peters was here and Bartell was going to find him first.

MADISON PLATEAU
YELLOWSTONE NATIONAL PARK, WYOMING
TUESDAY, SEPTEMBER 14, 2027
**8:21 A.M. MST**      10:21A.M. EST

As Dr. Ray Holt worked feverishly to save Kim, the rest of the group gathered into a tight circle outside the small cave. Rick assumed command, standing in front of the crowd.

"We know we're supposed to go into the light. Does anyone have a clue what happens after that?"

Thirty confused individuals looked at one another. Sean Sterling stepped forward.

"We've been waiting for a woman. She's supposed to know the next step."

Everyone looked blankly at Rick.

"It's the red-shaped tunnel," came a voice from the cave.

Rick ran to the opening of the small den.

Holt gently placed his hand on her shoulder as he tried to keep her on the stretcher. "She's delirious," he explained.

Kim desperately looked at Rick. "It's the tunnel. You've got to fire the Casulls into the heart."

Inside Rick's head she said, "Believe me, I know what to do."

Rick finally understood. His job had been to make sure Kim made it to the meadow. He'd barely succeeded.

"Why, Kim?"

"The ship can't..." she took painful breath, "...handle the lead. It's not supposed to have anything solid inside."

Rick knelt at Kim's side and held her hand.

"It hurts, Rick. It hurts so bad."

Her face had aged. Rick wanted to cry, to hold her close, to make the pain go away.

She ignored his sadness and forced a smile.

"Get me to the light. I need to go first."

"Kim..."

"It's important, Rick."

"If that's what you want, Kim. You've got it."

She closed her eyes and a sense of relief came over her face. "Thanks. Thanks, Rick."

Holt grabbed Rick's arm and brought him outside. "She's not going to last much longer, even with the blood."

"There's got to be something you can do."

"Not here. I have no equipment, no medicine. We can only make her comfortable."

Rick looked to the northern edge of the meadow. "If we went to the Marines..."

Holt placed his bloody hands on his hips. "They've probably got medical equipment, but going to them would jeopardize everyone."

Ross overhead the conversation and approached the two men.

"We're here for a reason, Rick. Don't let your emotions cloud that issue."

"I was warned not to leave her side because she knew the answer."

"And she told you what to do, didn't she?"

"There might be more information than what she's told us. She goes first."

"That's fine with me, my friend," said Ross, his hand resting on his Casull, "But if you go anywhere near those Marines, I'll shoot you myself."

WEST YELLOWSTONE AIRSTRIP
NORTHWESTERN WYOMING
TUESDAY, SEPTEMBER 14, 2027
**8:23 A.M. MST**      10:23 A.M. EST

Four Super Stallions roared back to the West Yellowstone airstrip. One hundred forty Marines jumped into the helicopters which then lifted off and headed back to the Madison Plateau. The aircraft ripped across the terrain, skimming the treetops. They were minutes from the meadow when the controls of the lead helicopter began to go awry.

The pilot immediately began an emergency decent. He took no chances with his men or his craft. The soldiers could walk the remaining distance to the clearing. He managed to land hard, but upright. None of the troops were seriously injured. The second and third copters followed the first. The fourth pilot tried to squeeze another mile of flight before he landed. Suddenly every computer chip in the helicopter failed. The main rotor accelerated, tearing itself off the plane as the fuselage careened into the Earth.

MADISON PLATEAU
YELLOWSTONE NATIONAL PARK, WYOMING
TUESDAY, SEPTEMBER 14, 2027
**8:24 A.M. MST**      10:24  A.M. EST

Thirty civilians gathered around Kim's stretcher. The raucous wind forced Rick to shout as he addressed the small crowd.

"Spread out along the edge of the meadow. Once the yellow column appears, run for it. Kim says the heart is dark red and look like a tunnel. Fire your weapons into the heart. If we can get enough lead into the ship, it will self-destruct. Does anyone have any more information?"

"The Marines are going to try and stop us," yelled one of the women in the group.

"Right," agreed Rick. "Find a good hiding place and stay still until you see the pillar of light."

"How do we get up to the ship?" asked Sterling.

"I don't know. The key seems to be getting into the light. Good luck, everyone."

The group split up. Rick stayed at Kim's side.

"I'll help you carry her," said Holt.

"Thanks, Ray, but you'd better go ahead."

Holt looked at Rick, then to Kim's drained face. "This is where I belong."

Like a giant manhole cover, the disk slid across the sky, turning the forest black. As the light disappeared, the air grew cold. Wicked winds pushed sulfur steam in every direction. The stench filled the air. Small trees bent to the ground.

Glenhurst's Marines closed in on the cluster of ragtag warriors. Buried in leaves, wedged between rocks and crouched between bushes, the nervous civilians waited for the light.

Lance White had never seen anything so big. As the morning light disappeared, it came to him: Peters and Callaway must have known the invader was coming here. Peters, working at JPL, had fed vital defense information to the aliens and was preparing to return to his kind. White had to locate and terminate the traitors before they escaped into the ship.

30,000 FEET ABOVE SOUTHEASTERN MONTANA
TUESDAY, SEPTEMBER 14, 2027
**8:24 A.M. MST**        10:24 A.M. EST

The huge jet carrying the remaining PJs suddenly angled down as all four of its engines failed. The pilot aimed the falling plane away from the Wyoming border. At fifteen thousand feet he managed to restart two of the engines. Pulling up and away from the disk, he climbed back to thirty-eight thousand feet, but this time stayed far enough away from the interference to keep his plane in the air.

As soon as Eagle stopped moving, the four men were given the green light. Each of the PJs carried enough plastic explosives to level a medium-sized building. The four men leapt out of the back of the transport and began their power glide back into Wyoming. Four chutes opened and continued to float eastward. One by one, the skydivers crossed a powerful field of electrons that scrambled their delicate neurological systems. A second physical barrier prevented their lifeless bodies from touching the ship, deflecting them so they slid off the side of the disk, dropping to the ground, miles from the meadow.

The pilot watched the ill-fated heroes, then headed west to clear the electrical interference. He had to tell the officials at FORCECOM what had happened before thousands of Army paratroopers attempted the same deadly maneuver.

MADISON PLATEAU
YELLOWSTONE NATIONAL PARK, WYOMING
TUESDAY, SEPTEMBER 14, 2027
**8:28 A.M. MST**      10:28A.M. EST

The wind howled. Rick shielded his eyes from the swirling dust. Kim grabbed Rick's collar, pulling his head close to her lips.

"You have to continue the attack on the ship at all costs," she whispered hoarsely.

He looked at her weary face. "When does it start?"

Callaway did not respond. Her eyes rolled back in her head.

"Kim?"

He shook her gently. She couldn't leave him now.

"It's a machine," she said without speaking. "There's no one on board."

A deep rumbling could be heard over the howling of the wind. Spiraling like the shutter of a camera lens, a circular opening appeared in the bottom of the ship. A shaft of smoky green light burst from within the ship, reaching to the ground. Rick could once again see the entire meadow.

The Marines glanced around nervously. They'd been trained for unusual events, but nothing they'd experienced had prepared them for this.

Barbara Whitten watched patiently. The disk did not bother her in the least. Her target would come into view soon enough. Could she take another man's life because of what she'd seen in her mind?

Three Air Force PJs scurried to the coordinates radioed by Glenhurst. Perhaps the Major had received new information about the invader.

Dave Bartell resumed his cautious tracking of the three sets of footprints, determined to find Rick Peters. His country depended on his success.

Lance White edged further along the border of the field. Then he saw them. Rick Peters and another man were crouched next to the injured Callaway. Drawing his gun, White hid behind a pine tree. They were well within his range. His only consideration: the incredible gusts which would affect the bullets' trajectories. If he bracketed the stretcher with a full clip, he could be fairly certain of hitting them. No time for interrogation or torture; he had to finish these traitors before they could escape. White steadied himself against the trunk and took careful aim. As his index finger tightened, the cold steel of a knife touched his throat.

"Put the gun down!"

The voice was unemotional, professional. Callaway would have to wait until he took care of this diversion. Relaxing his body, he lowered his Beretta.

"Drop it!" the voice ordered.

White remained motionless. "I'm an agent of the U.S. government. You are interfering with my mission!" he yelled.

"Drop it now!" came the response.

White let his pistol fall. The moment the Beretta left his hand, he slammed his heel into his assailant's shin allowing him to grab the man's knife hand. White twisted the wrist away from his neck. Then, shifting his weight to the left, White pulled the man forward, flipping him into the base of the tree. A single kick to the neck and the Air Force PJ was dead.

"He's behind us," whispered Callaway.

"Who?"

"White."

Lance White looked around. He shifted one way, then the other, peering through the dim light. Satisfied the PJ was alone, he turned back to finish Callaway, but the stretcher was empty. He began to creep toward the clearing when a searing column of jasmine-colored light shot from the bottom of the ship and slammed into the ground so hard, he was knocked off his feet.

As the pillar drilled into the ground massive tremors rolled the Earth in two-foot waves. Steam frothed from fractured hot springs. Plumes of boiling water shot skyward. The shaking increased as the brilliant shaft continued to drill into the Earth. A swirling maelstrom pulled at everything in the meadow. Above, the ship remained motionless. The movement within the pillar slowed, then stopped. The quakes diminished, but winds continued to punish everything in the area.

Rick, Kim and Raymond Holt found a small thicket several yards from the stretcher. When the light stopped moving, Rick knew it was time.

"Let's go!"

The two men grabbed Kim and raced into the clearing. They'd only traveled a few feet when another earthquake hit. Kim shrieked in pain as they landed hard on the ground dropping her. More violent than the others, this tremor toppled dozens of trees and ripped a chasm down the far side of the clearing. A piercing scream, like the sound of thousands of animals crying in pain, could be heard over the howl of the wind.

The Earth continued to squirm as the golden stream began to flow again. Slowly at first, almost hesitantly, the current began to move upward toward the ship. As the tremors subsided, Rick and Holt grabbed Kim's limp body and they continued their run toward the light.

Rick quivered as he and Holt dragged Kim across the grass. These next few moments would tell if the future could be altered.

Fifty-four Marines, the three Air Force PJs, Major Glenhurst and Lance White spotted the trio stumbling toward the light. Glenhurst broke into a run, angled to intercept the three civilians. From the opposite direction, Lance White joined the pursuit.

The speed of the pillar's upward motion increased, causing the light to flicker. Elongated shadows cast by the men danced on the swirling steam like a bizarre puppet show.

To the left of the column, Lance White appeared, his face screwed in an angry expression as he squinted through the swirling dust. He raised his Beretta and aimed it at the three people. Despite the wind's roar, he heard the all too familiar sound of a bullet whizzing past his ear. Another projectile struck the dirt in front of him.

Ignoring the ambush, White raised his gun and began firing. Rick Peters and Raymond Holt veered to the right, pushed by another gust of wind. They held onto Kim as long as they could, then lost their footing and tumbled to the ground a second time. Before White could empty his gun at the fugitives, a slug tore into his shoulder, spinning him sideways.

Barbara Whitten was pleased. She could tell by the way the man jerked one of her shots had hit its mark. She'd accomplished the first part of her task. She'd saved Rick's life, but the short, squatty man was still alive. Her job was not over.

Rick was on the ground, as he expected. Even the dirt in his mouth tasted familiar. Something was missing, something substantial. The pain! He glanced at his chest. No blood. No wound. He was alive, unharmed. He jumped to his feet and grabbed Kim's arm. Holt stayed with him, helping drag Kim to the light. Ten feet from the column, they passed through a clear fluid wall and entered a belt of calm air that surrounded the roaring pillar. Rick looked into Kim's vacant eyes.

"I love you," he said, and shoved her into the golden river.

Glenhurst caught up to the men as the woman fell into the fiery light. He grabbed Peters and whirled him around. Twenty-five Marines rushed into the peaceful space and captured Raymond Holt.

Rick struggled with three powerful servicemen. "Don't!" he shouted, "It's taking the Source!"

Glenhurst tried to calm the frantic man. "Rick! Tell me what this is about. If you don't, we're going to stop your people. Look."

Rick turned his head. From all sides of the meadow, Marines and civilians emerged from the forest. One by one the civilians were intercepted by Glenhurst's men and disarmed. This was not how it was supposed to play out. He was supposed to be killed by the pint-sized shooter or make it to the light. Someone changed their mind.

"Major Glenhurst," Rick panted, "You must let us continue. Didn't you listen to Sonya? We only have a small window of opportunity. Don't stop us now!"

Glenhurst tried to hide his confusion. How did Peters know his daughter? Was an elaborate trick, an attempt to fool him into helping the aliens?

"This is no trick," shouted Peters, his eyes wide with energized emotion. "If this ship leaves with the Source, you will die, I will die, everyone on this planet will die."

"What do you mean, if it takes the Source?"

"This is a mining ship. It's stealing the Source. Order your men to jump into the light and shoot at the heart-shaped tunnel. There's no time to argue."

"I have all the time in the world," replied Glenhurst.

# THE LAST STAND

INSIDE THE ALIEN SHIP
ABOVE YELLOWSTONE NATIONAL PARK
TUESDAY, SEPTEMBER 14, 2027
**8:29 A.M. MST**        10:29 A.M. EST

Kim fell into the yellow stream. For a moment, she thought she would plunge down the bottomless shaft. Instead, she was held motionless in the swirling river. Then her pain and weakness disappeared as her head rocketed toward the ship. Below her, she could see Rick surrounded by a group of Marines. Her feet were still on the ground as she passed by the sides of the ship and entered the base of the gigantic disk. Seconds later, her body caught up with her head and she became whole again.

Inside, the light changed from a solid yellow to a vivid pattern of wildly gyrating colors. Nothing was familiar, nothing recognizable. She tumbled weightlessly through shifting hues, as yellow material raced by her. Suddenly, her body was grabbed, pulled downward and held tightly in place. She could feel some sort of scan run down her body from her head to her feet.

There it was! Off to her left was a deep reddish area. The yellow luminescent material was being sucked into an opening. In the distance was a dark, heart-shaped hole. The golden material rushed down the dark passage, into the portal. Kim tried to reach her gun, but couldn't move. The scan passed through her feet and her body was released.

She grabbed her gun and fired five shots down the shaft. As she pulled the trigger for the sixth time, her arm disappeared. The swirling colors vanished.

With a blinding flash she found herself standing in the meadow, facing the column of light. The winds ripped at her and pushed her back several steps. She checked to see if her hand was intact. It was. Her arms and legs were without pain. She looked at her tom pants. A long scar was the only evidence of Lance White's torture session.

MADISON PLATEAU YELLOWSTONE
NATIONAL PARK
TUESDAY, SEPTEMBER 14, 2027
**8:29 A.M. MST**       10:29 A.M. EST

Kim fought her way back toward the pillar. The Marines guarding Rick raised their weapons.

"No!" screamed Rick. "She's here to help!"

The shiny revolver she held in her hand indicated otherwise.

"Drop the gun, Kim!" yelled Rick in his mind.

Kim tucked the weapon into her belt and put her hands in the air. Several Marines grabbed her, took her gun and dragged her inside the protective shield.

"Kim! What happened?"

"It's there! I saw it! How long have I been gone?"

"Ten, maybe fifteen seconds."

Kim turned to the Major. "There's a heart-shaped funnel inside the ship. Introducing lead into the holding bin will cause a violent internal reaction and the ship will self-destruct. If we delay, the ship will leave with the Source. You saw me before I went in. I was nearly dead. Hang around in that stuff and you heal. It's the Source of life, and this ship is stealing it."

Rick joined the argument. "Sonya knew, Major. She told you to go into the light. The fact that you found us is proof you're supposed to help."

"Let us go!" shouted Holt, "There's no time for this!"

Rick looked at the blackened Marine faces that surrounded him. He had to convince these men what was about to happen.

"Kim, we have to show them!"

Kim knew what he meant. She closed her eyes. Not only did Rick and Kim affect Glenhurst, everyone within the circle witnessed the scene.

The roar of the golden pillar abruptly stopped and was drawn into the darkened ship. The disk rose and raced away, leaving behind a cloudless blue sky. The meadow was flooded with soft, warm sunlight. For a brief moment there was peace. Then, with a roar louder than the wind, the rip in the Earth widened, shattering the ground with a massive shock wave that leveled every standing tree. Glenhurst, Kim, Rick, everyone and everything, were swept into the angry caldera.

The vision shifted to miles above the scarred Earth. The continent writhed and twisted, mangled by a series of earthquakes and rising volcanoes. One area after area was engulfed. Islands disappeared. Coastal communities were swallowed by enormous tidal waves. No place was left untouched. There was nowhere to hide.

Glenhurst blinked his eyes in amazement. He was back next to the pillar.

"We're here to stop that from happening," Rick said forcefully. "We need your help."

Glenhurst looked at Rick, then Kim. These people had the ability to control his mind. Where they friend or foe? All of Sonya's predictions had come true. Why would she give him this information unless she wanted him to unwittingly help these people destroy the planet? But the disk had proved itself capable of accomplishing that task by itself.

Glenhurst took the soiled paper from his pocket. At the bottom of the page, underlined and in huge block letters, was Sonya's last command, "Go into the light."

"Hold them until I come back." He jumped into the golden river.

Barbara Whitten pulled herself out of the shallow foxhole. She'd failed to kill the short man who'd attacked Rick. Hopefully she'd be given another chance before it was too late. The ferocious wind pushed her braided hair straight behind her. She located another clump of grass and returned to her prone position.

Being out in the open with so much airborne debris could jam her sensitive rifle, but it was a risk she had to take. She watched another group of civilians break from the forest and run toward the column of light. The shimmering pillar did not concern her. Others were charged with the attack on the ship. Her job was simple and direct: kill the short man before he murdered Rick Peters.

INSIDE THE ALIEN SHIP
ABOVE YELLOWSTONE NATIONAL PARK
TUESDAY, SEPTEMBER 14, 2027
**8:32 A.M. MST**     10:32A.M.EST

Glenhurst traveled the same route as Kim. His body was elongated within the length of the pillar, then united within the body of the ship. Once whole, he drifted within a patchwork of colors until he was held stationary in front of the dark red tunnel. He felt the computer scan his body, head to toe, then the force released him. When he returned to the ground, he was a changed man. He felt stronger, more powerful, but most importantly, he knew why he'd come to the meadow.

Glenhurst rushed back to the pillar, fighting his way through the punishing wind.

"Let them go!" he shouted, bursting into the serene circle.

"We need our weapons!" demanded Kim.

Glenhurst turned to give the order, only to watch Rick Peters being grabbed from behind.

A Beretta was suddenly pointed at Rick's head.

"Nobody moves," said the Air Force PJ as he dragged Rick away from the light.

"Release that man!" ordered Glenhurst.

"This man is to be removed from the area," shouted Bartell.

"Son, you are highly outranked here. This man is here to help."

"My orders have not changed, sir. Nor have yours."

Rick struggled against his captor's grip. "We have to stop playing games!"

Glenhurst took a step toward the captain.

"Stay right there, sir."

Bartell knew he was in trouble. He was disobeying a superior officer, but he'd been specifically ordered not to let the civilians go into the light, nor believe any talk about attacking the ship. This was not the confrontation he had expected. Little green men with ray guns would have made more sense. At least then he would have known what to do.

Glenhurst sensed the man's indecision. "Soldier, there isn't a working radio within fifty miles. Nothing can fly anywhere near here. The rest of my unit is stranded at West Yellowstone. It's up to us to take on the ship."

Kim desperately wanted to help Rick, but valuable time was being wasted. At this point they all were expendable.

"Major, we have to continue. Don't worry about Rick. We have no time to argue. We have a job to accomplish."

Glenhurst realized Kim was right. They had to take on the ship. At this point, losing one or two men was immaterial, even if it was Peters.

"Suit yourself, son." He turned from the PJ and faced his men. "Let's get this assault underway!"

Rick stopped struggling and was pulled out of the haven into the maelstrom. Suddenly the grip on his chest was released. Rick turned to see four Marines wrestling the surprised PJ to the ground. Without waiting to witness the outcome of the lopsided struggle, he ran back to the safe zone.

"Thanks," said Rick to the Major.

Glenhurst nodded.

Kim took control. "Pull your people together. I'll explain what to do."

Glenhurst signaled to one of his men and a flare went up into the roaring wind. Though the glare was whipped across the meadow, the remainder of the elite recon team saw the burst of light and raced to the pillar. Rick grabbed his Casull and jumped into the light.

Kim turned to the Marines. "Here's the game. Remove your weapons from their holsters. Once you're in the column, you'll travel up the light into the ship, be turned around several times. You'll be held in place for a moment, then you'll be released. Once you're free, you have about three seconds to fire as many rounds as you can at the dark red heart. The ship will return you to the surface. As soon as you're on the ground, get back here, reload and do it again."

"This is a volunteer situation," added Glenhurst. "I can't force you to do this."

Without hesitation, two Marines leapt into the column with their M-16 rifles slung over their shoulders. The men hung suspended for moment, then in a single horrible second, they were transported upwards, while their rifles remained stationary. The straps ripped their bodies in half, then the remains disappeared up the shaft. The suspended M-16s were jettisoned from the pillar into the forest.

"Get rid of your rifles!" shouted Kim. "Revolvers only!"

The remainder of Glenhurst's group arrived at the protective area. They had two choices: stay and guard the Air Force PJ, or join the civilian rebels in their attack on the ship. Three chose to remain with PJ.

Two more men jumped into the light at the same time and were pulled upward. Another three followed right behind. Two more after them. The next group was about to leap when a soldier returned five feet outside the staging area with a heart embedded in his hip. The second serviceman appeared with a gaping hole in his chest. His lifeless body collapsed to the ground. The first soldier, unaware of the mishap, returned to the action. Rick and Kim stared at the grotesque organ gushing blood from the man's side. They recognized the problem at the same time and turned to the other members of the group.

"One at a time!" they shouted simultaneously.

The trio that leapt in together came down as a mass of flesh.

"We have to go slower!" yelled Glenhurst. "Wait until each man returns before jumping."

The round trip turned out to be just over twenty seconds.

"This isn't going to work," complained Kim. "It's taking too long. We have to shorten the time between people. Cut it down to fifteen seconds."

Glenhurst stared at her. He'd already lost seven men.

"It's not worth it," he said. "I can't send them in any closer together until I know we're doing something."

"Then we'll do it with our people," she said.

Fifteen seconds worked fine. Six of the disheveled civilians rode the golden river into the ship. Kim cut the time down to ten seconds, then six.

Sean Sterling made the ultimate sacrifice when Robert Nordby followed four seconds after Sterling. Sterling came back with an arm fused to his neck. Returning seconds after Sterling, Nordby saw the unfortunate writer blown over by a gust of wind. Then Nordby saw the protrusion sticking from Sterling's throat. Glancing down, Nordby realized his forearm was missing. Blood spurted from his truncated muscles. Screaming, he ran back to the staging area where a Dr. Holt immediately applied a tourniquet.

"We lost Sterling!" sobbed Nordby.

"I'm sorry, Robert," said Kim, "but he won't be the last to die."

She turned to Glenhurst. "If we go up at seven-second intervals we should be safe. Are you ready to commit your men?"

Glenhurst nodded.

"How many shots did you fire, Robert?"

Nordby was still staring at his severed arm. "Th..th... three," he stammered.

"Damn. Not enough. Let's go!" she shouted. "Load your weapons as soon as you come down!"

THE WAR ROOM
WASHINGTON, D.C.
TUESDAY, SEPTEMBER 14, 2027
**8:31 A.M. MST**          10:31A.M.EST

Reports of the bright yellow beam reached Washington moments after it appeared. It was obvious the alien ship was doing something to the Earth.

"It's attacking a patch of dirt!" shouted the Secretary of Defense.

"These aliens didn't travel hundreds of light years to do a bizarre trick in the middle of Wyoming," countered General Moore. "Whatever it's doing, we've got to stop it! Nuke it now!"

"What about the radiation? We'll kill millions!"

"It's not doing anything to the planet!"

"It's drilling for something!"

"It could be a trick."

"It's out in the god-forsaken wilderness. It's got to be off-course."

"They know exactly what they're doing! We're the ignorant ones!"

"Tell the B-52s to arm and drop the neutron bomb," interrupted the President.

"What about the Ross report?" shouted McKinley. "Everything he said has come true. Maybe he was right about firing everything we have at two separate intervals."

The men shuffled through their piles of papers and messages.

"I've got it here!" shouted Franklin Turner. "He wants us to attack in eight minutes. He says a coordinated strike will overwhelm the alien's defensive systems, especially if small rockets, stingers and mortars are used. Two separate attacks need to be made. The second has to occur ten seconds after the first. As the disk prepares its retaliation, it'll be too occupied to deal with the second offensive.

"All right," agreed Linden, "But if that doesn't work, we'll use the nukes."

Every available plane, stinger missile, tank, helicopter, fighter and military officer within range of the leviathan and still in contact with the AWAC was informed of the plan. Howitzers, small arms, sidewinders, TOWs Patriots, MX, Peacekeepers, and every working weapon were to be used.

Minutes later, fifteen thousand weapons were fired. The blue light sliced through the air, vaporizing missiles, Sidewinders, Stingers and anti-tank weapons. The beam slashed in all directions, creating a laser show that could be seen for hundreds of miles. The few armaments that were not destroyed mid-flight were rendered useless by the electronic force field or exploded harmlessly against a physical barrier five hundred feet outside the ship's hull.

The second strike proved more promising. Although only four dozen missiles impacted harmlessly onto the outside of the ship, the retaliation was inaccurate and incomplete. Seventy-two additional aircraft were destroyed, but the majority of the armada remained intact.

Kim entered the alien ship as the first attack began. The amount of computer time required to track and destroy all of the missiles and projectiles halted Kim's scan. Suddenly she was able to move. Raising her Casull, she unloaded her six shots. A creaking sound emanated from the tunnel. Still floating free, she used the speed loader on her belt and reloaded. Within seconds she'd fired another six rounds into the holding bin. This time the groan was louder. She managed to reload six more times, sending a total of thirty-six heavyweight shells into the ship before she found herself back on the ground.

Tom Ross had taken his turn just before Kim. Still unaccustomed to the wild ride, he only managed to get a single shot off before being returned to the ground directly in front of wounded Lance White. White recognized the NSA technical specialist. The flash of the agent's gun was the last thing Ross saw. He dropped to the ground with a hole in his heart.

Platoon leaders were acting as traffic police, waiting the required seven seconds before sending the next man up. Rick had just taken his place at the back of the line when another earthquake struck. The ground beneath the small army rose ten feet in the air, then fell back twenty.

The rip in the center of the field widened, swallowing three civilians as they headed back to the staging area. Conrad Wiley, the man who'd commandeered the Very Large Array in New Mexico, materialized on ground that had vanished a second earlier. He plummeted two hundred feet to his death.

The quake was felt around the world. More eerie, though, was the sound. The massive groan welled from the center of the Earth. Almost human in its sorrow, it sounded like a dying beast.

THE WAR ROOM
WASHINGTON, D.C.
TUESDAY, SEPTEMBER 14, 2027
**8:35 A.M. MST**      10:35A.M. EST
The failure to affect the alien ship was transmitted to Washington. The global earthquake convinced the National Command Authority to give the President the official authority to drop a single neutron bomb. Another coordinated attack would coincide with the bombing. The majority of the Joint Chiefs of Staff secretly wished the alien would be stopped by the blast. Their next option would be to use a tactical nuclear device.

29,000 FEET ABOVE NORTHWEST WYOMING
TUESDAY, SEPTEMBER 14, 2027
**8:37 MST A.M.**      10:37A.M. EST
The lone B-52 circled high above the disk. Once the drop code was received, the nervous but professional Air Force bombardier released the deadly weapon. Set to detonate a mile above the disk's electromagnetic field, the explosive fell carelessly away from the jet. The Joint Chiefs of Staff figured the disk would not recognize the falling object as a weapon, especially if another synchronized offensive was in progress as the bombs fell.

Although it took almost fifteen seconds to dispatch the twelve hundred missiles and other projectiles that had been launched, the nuclear explosive was consumed by the blue laser moments before it was to detonate. Once the bombs, missiles and artillery shells had been dispatched, the B-52 was surgically removed from the sky.

MADISON PLATEAU
YELLOWSTONE NATIONAL PARK
TUESDAY, SEPTEMBER 14, 2027
**8:41 A.M. MST**          10:41A.M. EST
Lance White redefined his mission. The Marines and PJs had clearly been turned by Peters and Callaway. Soldiers were leaping into the river of light, then being magically returned, probably reprogrammed for a ground assault. Walking from position to position, White dispatched the Marines as fast as they appeared.

Once a person materialized, White would run to him. The unsuspecting warrior would approach the short, squatty man, expecting help or new information. Twenty dazed militiamen died at White's hand before Kim reappeared from her lengthy attack on the ship.

White's eyes widened. This time the bitch would not escape. He fingered the trigger on his Beretta, knowing his aim would not be as effective with his left hand. He would have to be extremely close to make sure he could finish the job.

Kim saw White heading toward her. This was the final test, but the situation seemed different. In her dream, she appeared and was immediately shot. In reality, she had time to react and White appeared to be wounded. Kim grabbed the last of her speed loaders and pulled the cylinder release on her Casull.

White saw Callaway shoving a fresh load of shells into her revolver. He raised his Beretta. Again, puffs of dirt appeared in front of him. Someone was shooting at him. He wasn't going to stop now. Before Kim could slap the cylinder closed, White fired a spread of shots. A single slug entered Kim's chest.

The pain was intense. Slumping to her knees, she knew she was dying. It had been as she had imagined.

Barbara Whitten continued to shoot even after Kim fell. Bullet after bullet was loaded into the Shilen's chamber. Though the wind sent her shots far off their mark, she remained calm and kept firing. Finally, one of her shells caught the man in the leg.

Standing in line to ride the column, Rick felt Kim's fear. He raced into the windstorm. Shielding his eyes, he saw the orange flashes coming from White's gun, then he saw Kim fall to the ground. Rick became insane, unable to control himself. He raced at White without thinking about the danger.

White was limping away from Callaway when he spotted Peters. With a wicked grin White raised his gun. What a pleasant surprise. The fool was going to die for his stupidity. The winds would not save him this time. White squeezed the trigger, but the hammer closed on air. He'd emptied the clip firing at Callaway. He dropped the Beretta and pulled Younger's pistol from his belt.

Rick saw White produce the second gun. Before the agent could fire, Rick jerked the trigger of his Casull three times. One of the large rounds shattered White's left elbow.

The gun dropped from White's hand. He turned and limped toward the edge of the meadow, hoping Peters would go to his partner rather than pursue him.

But Rick did not stop. The world might be destroyed in the next half hour, but this animal who'd caused Kim so much pain was going to die alone.

Rick was only ten feet from him when the ground gave way under the agent's feet. White fell through the crust of a boiling sulfur pit. Up to his waist in the scalding, corrosive water, the injured agent screamed as his legs dissolved beneath him. Rick's anger turned to repulsion as he watched the man's face turn red, then white as he was boiled alive. The limp body fell face first into the acerbic liquid, surrounded by a flurry of bubbles and steam.

Rick left the killing pool and rushed to Kim's side. Gently turning her over he put his mouth to her ear. "Hang on, Kim. I'll get you back to the light."

He picked her up and headed toward the column. He'd only taken three steps when her body went limp. The hum inside his head disappeared and he knew she was gone. He carefully laid her on the ground and kissed her lips, then returned to the battle.

The number of people who returned to ride the light had been severely depleted. Over two dozen men had been killed by White. Nine more had fallen into the widening crevasse in the center of the meadow. Three had been transported into the deep pit, succumbing in the scalding water that filled the large jagged hole. But now, with their timing down to the second, the remaining twenty-four Marines and ten civilians were accustomed to the frightening ride up the shimmering column and were hitting their mark on each trip. Hundreds of rounds were fired into the ship's hold.

ALONG ROUTE 89
YELLOWSTONE NATIONAL PARK
TUESDAY, SEPTEMBER 14, 2027
**8:43 A.M. MST**      10:43 A.M. EST
Craig Price guided his contingent of four tanks down the park's main road, shocking hundreds of already panicked tourists. He made the turn south and was only two miles from Old Faithful when the electrical disturbance shut down his tank. As the circular opening appeared at the bottom of the ship, Price knew it was time to act. The crew left the safety of the tank compartment and manually positioned the barrel to shoot into the origination of the light. Swiveling the heavy turrets took almost ten minutes. Once the barrel was aimed at the base of the alien ship, explosive shells were loaded into the gun's firing chamber.

With no prior electronic warning, the alien defense system was not expecting an attack from below, but it did detect the incoming artillery. Three of the four shells were destroyed mid-flight. The fourth passed through the electronic barrier to explode on the physical force field, rupturing the membrane for a split second. The ship plotted the original source of the projectiles and quickly vaporized the tanks along with their crews.

Although the attack appeared to have been useless, the ship's computers had been caught off-guard. During that five-second interval, Rick managed to unload three full cylinders into the red tunnel. When he returned to the ground he was immediately blown over by a powerful gust. Wiping the dirt from his eyes, he looked up and saw the ship wobble. The yellow flow from the ground seemed to falter. Perhaps the last eighteen slugs had affected the alien's threshold of tolerance, but the ship steadied and the upward movement within the golden pillar resumed its quick rate.

THE WAR ROOM
WASHINGTON, D.C.
TUESDAY, SEPTEMBER 14, 2027
**8:48 A.M. MST**       10:48A.M.EST
The United States' best fighting machines proved no match for the invader that boldly and arrogantly drifted above the country. The once undefeatable protectors of peace were being routed on their home turf. Even the seventeen unauthorized kamikaze attacks had been quickly and effectively thwarted by the blue laser. A few of the men that sat at the huge table remained optimistic.

"It's not doing anything destructive," argued General Hood, commander of the Army. "We've seen no damage. Granted, there have been major earthquakes, but there is a possibility this visitor is not detrimental to our existence. It could be simply refueling."

His comments were answered with a low rolling motion. The room rocked for thirty long seconds. Pencils rolled across the black slate table, coffee rocked in cups, terrified soldiers held onto walls and desks. Seconds after the shaking stopped, reports flooded into the command post. The epicenter was located approximately three hundred and fifty miles under the surface of the Earth, six miles west of Old Faithful.

The shock wave was felt everywhere on the planet.

MADISON PLATEAU
YELLOWSTONE NATIONAL PARK
TUESDAY, SEPTEMBER 14, 2027
**8:52 A.M. MST**       10:52 A.M. EST

The next quake was the worst. The Earth heaved and pitched like an out-of-control roller coaster, rising and falling over thirty feet. The meadow split into five pie-shaped slices. Two-hundred-foot-high cliffs plunged into a rapidly filling pool of scalding sulfuric water. Despite the loss of five additional men who fell into the pit, the attack on the alien continued.

Rick leapt into the pillar again, was elongated and pulled into the ship. As soon as he was released by the computer scan, he emptied his revolver directly into the dark red pattern in front of him. This time a new sound emanated from the bowels of the ship. A grating screech ripped through his head. The return to the surface took longer. Something had been damaged.

Rick found himself on one of the slivers of land that ended abruptly in the middle of the meadow. There was no returning to the light. Realizing he was standing on a five-foot strip of dirt, he turned around and headed back to the forest. On the way he discovered Kim's inert body. Before another quake could shake her over the edge, he picked her up and carried her to the meadow's border. He held her in his arms and watched as the remaining warriors took turns leaping into the column.

Rick witnessed twelve more attacks until one of the Marines jumped into the beam. Instead of being transported, he stayed inside the column. Suddenly the yellow pillar was sucked back into the ship, leaving the soldier standing above a giant hole. For a brief moment he stood suspended in space, then he fell out of sight.

Rick looked skyward. It was over. Eighteen months of his life had been dedicated to this last half hour. All that remained was the final disaster. He gripped Kim's lifeless body and began to sob. If they'd been better prepared or had more help, the terrible onslaught that was about to occur could have been avoided. At least he'd made the attempt.

Thousands of people must have ignored the responsibility and the challenge. They'd heard the call; most probably had had a lucky break put in front of their noses, like he had, but they'd taken the money, the fame, the happiness and turned their backs on what brought them their wishes. The only regret Rick had was he didn't get to know Kim better. Tears flowed as he waited for the end.

Keith Grunderson was the last to successfully travel the pillar. He was inside the ship when the fifteen remaining Marines, along with Raymond Holt, watched the light being sucked back into the ship. The soft green illumination from the opening flickered wildly, alternately plunging the area into pitch black then flooding the meadow with an emerald glow. The circular door started to close. Halfway through the cycle, the ship began to rock from side to side. With a massive grinding noise, the portal abruptly reversed direction and ripped open. The edges of the giant ship dipped like a top losing energy.

"Get to the forest!!" screamed Holt. He led the commandos across the narrow strip of land all running for their lives.

From the bottom of the craft came a tremendous outpouring. The force of the downwash created a suction that drew everything toward the vortex. Two of the marines were sucked into the whirlpool of blazing light. Rick watched as the last eight men ran into the dense forest on the opposite side of the chasm.

He knew he couldn't stay where he was and survive, but had no fight left. He'd already seen how it would end. Running seemed pointless.

Keith Grunderson returned from the ship standing next to Rick. Rick raised his eyes and stared up at his friend.

Grunderson shook his shoulder "Rick, come on, let's get out of here!"

Grunderson tried to pry his friend's arms loose, but Rick refused to release his grip on her.

"Let her go, Rick! She's gone."

Grunderson grabbed him from behind and dragged the two bodies toward the woods as the yellow outpouring spread from the center of the meadow. Exhausted, Grunderson collapsed on the ground next to Rick.

"I can't pull you any further, buddy. If you don't want to move, that's your decision."

Rick did not respond. Grunderson patted his friend on the back and crawled into the forest.

The berserk stream increased in intensity, closing on Rick, ripping into the Earth in front of him. Wind and dust peppered his face, forcing him to close his eyes. At least he would die with someone he cared for, someone he could have spent the rest of his life with. Even with his eyes closed, the yellow light filled his mind. The roar filled his head. Then he felt the stream envelop his body, and he was falling.

30,000 FEET ABOVE NORTHWEST MONTANA
TUESDAY, SEPTEMBER 14, 2027
**9:01 A.M. MST**       11:01A.M. EST

The AWAC retreated hundreds of miles into Montana, still helping to coordinate the massive collection of military hardware. There had been no change in the alien ship's position since it had arrived over Summit Lake. Like a rock, it had withstood every type of attack the United States had thrown.

Suddenly the displays in the back of the ship shot off the scale. Radar, infrared, communications and low frequency displays showed incredibly unstable fluctuations. From the flight deck, the pilot saw the disk begin to tilt first to one side, then to the other. The pitching continued to increase. It was the first time this kind of reading had been recorded since Eagle had been tracked. A call came from the intelligence officer in the back of the AWAC.

"Get us out of here! That thing is going to blow!"

Eagle had been damaged. Rick and his renegade commandos had thrown enough lead into the fragile holding bay to damage its sophisticated anti-matter containment system. The ship's computers, unable to control the resulting reaction, went into an emergency cycle, jettisoning the precious cargo it had traveled billions of miles to steal.

System after system failed as the ship's instruments tried to thwart the contamination. According to its programming, once the holding bin was emptied, additional procedures were made in an attempt to return the damaged ship to its makers.

Orders came from the war room to stop firing until the intruder reached the Atlantic. At that point a decision would be made whether to allow the mammoth ship to flee or take it down. Most of the generals supported the idea of finishing the ship off. A small minority feared that if the disk crashed, a lethal self-destruct system could be engaged. There was also the possibility that the alien power system might contain toxins that could contaminate the planet.

The AWAC broke from its circling pattern. With full power from its Pratt and Whitney engines, it sped away from the disk. At the same time, warnings were sent to all aircraft that the alien craft appeared in imminent danger of exploding.

Slowly and unsurely, the gargantuan ship rose from the meadow. Several cocky F-18 pilots launched their remaining Sidewinders. The slender missiles passed unharmed through the electromagnetic and physical force fields, scoring direct hits on the outside of the disk, damaging the hull. The retaliatory laser fire missed the jets completely.

Seconds later a barrage of anti-aircraft and air-to-air missiles erupted, smashing onto the thick skin of the easy-to-hit target. The ship returned the fire, but the blue laser bolts flew wild. Reaching an altitude of ten miles, the alien craft seemed to stabilize when it lost power and headed directly toward Chicago. All aggression ceased as the disk plummeted toward the city. At two thousand feet the ship began to climb unsteadily into the sky.

The tiny jet planes that flanked the disk retreated at top speed, scattering like flies. Eagle's electronic force field was restored, along with the physical force field, as the craft regained its upward momentum.

An immense sonic boom signaled Eagle's astonishing increase in speed. By the time it reached the Atlantic, the disk appeared to have recovered much of its vitality. Two ships off the coast of New Jersey were damaged as they locked and armed their missiles, but the blue light that shot through the atmosphere was not strong enough to sink the vessels.

Fifty miles off the New England coast, Eagle reached escape velocity. Freed from its ties with Earth, the ship shot into space.

# DEPARTURES

MADISON PLATEAU
YELLOWSTONE NATIONAL PARK
TUESDAY, SEPTEMBER 14, 2027
**9:15 A.M. MST**      11:15  A.M. EST

A huge contingent of helicopters, mobile vehicles and Army paratroopers converged on the battle site. A ground crew came across Rick and Kim at the edge of the crater. The white-suited team carefully approached the two bodies.

Lush vegetation, growing centimeters a minute, surrounded the gaping hole. Expecting the worst, the decontamination team took half an hour to cross the thirty feet, at each step taking careful readings for radiation, heat and possible bacterial and viral mutations.

When they finally reached the unconscious couple, the men discovered Rick and Kim fiercely clutching each other. Both were unconscious, but very much alive. With some effort they pried them apart and carried them back to the staging site on the other side of the ridge.

ABOVE THE EARTH
TUESDAY, SEPTEMBER 14, 2027
**9:18 A.M. MST**      11:18  A.M. EST

The metallic disk sped into space. Although its motion continued to be unreliable, its speed increased rapidly, as if acceleration would solve its internal problems. Two hundred thousand miles from Earth, an internal explosion occurred. Huge orange flames could be seen spreading along the edge of the ship.

As Eagle headed for the inside track of the moon, its shaking became so severe, the ship began to tumble end over end. The moon, having pulled the oceans and affected people's emotions for millions of years, subtly lured the speeding spacecraft closer and closer.

Totally out of control, the alien craft crashed into the moon's surface. The impact raised a cloud of dust that lingered for the next two months.

MADISON PLATEAU
YELLOWSTONE NATIONAL PARK
TUESDAY, SEPTEMBER 14, 2027
**12:19 P.M. MST**     2:19 P.M. EST

Rick Peters woke on his back, staring at a cloudless blue sky. He slowly propped himself on one elbow and surveyed the area. Dozens of helicopters were landing and taking off. Stretchers dotted the ground, surrounded by men in helmets and decontamination gear. More injured men were being carried from the forest.

Several men in the bulky white outfits noticed Rick's movement and rushed to his side. They leaned over, looked at him, then stood up and talked to each other through an electronic device inside their helmets. After taking several readings with their awkward equipment they had another lengthy discussion. When they were through, they turned back to him.

"Are you Rick Peters?" asked one of the men through a small speaker in the front of his suit.

The time for hiding was over.

"Yes, that's me." He was alive. That could only mean one thing – they'd succeeded.

"Where's the disk?"

The two men had another lengthy conversation, then turned back to face him.

"It's gone."

"Where's Major Glenhurst? Did he survive?"

The bulky Marine appeared, pushing the two men aside.

"I'm here, Rick. Are you all right?"

"Seem to be. I feel... great."

"There's someone you should know about." Glenhurst pointed to a nearby stretcher. Two more of the white-suited men hovered over an inert body. It was Kim.

"I know. I was holding her when it happened."

Glenhurst smiled. "Guess again, big guy. She's alive."

Rick jumped to his feet and ran to her. The two men at his side moved to stop him, but Glenhurst reached out and grabbed the backs of their loose clothing holding them in place.

"Leave him be," he ordered. "He's not going anywhere."

Kim was breathing, but unconscious. Rick knelt at her side and took her hand. Glenhurst came up behind him.

"She's been like that since they found the two of you at the edge of the meadow. Another foot and you would have been in that pit."

"Something pushed me back," said Rick.

"Me, too," said Glenhurst, "I was running for the trees. Next thing I knew I was lying on the ground over there. Pretty wild stuff."

Rick squeezed her hand. "Kim. It's me, Rick."

A low rumble caught their attention.

"Hold on," said Glenhurst, as the ground trembled. "The decontamination unit won't let us go until they're sure we're clean."

"What happened to the disk?"

Trees swayed. Helicopters rocked back and forth. The sun was shining.

"Destroyed. Crashed."

"Where?"

"Into the moon. Made quite a mess."

"Phone for you, Major," interrupted one of the suits.

Glenhurst took the mobile receiver and left Rick and Kim to themselves.

Kim's eyes opened and slowly focused.

"Rick!" She wrapped her arms around him. "I thought I was dead."

Rick held her. "You were. I think the Source threw some life back into you."

Glenhurst rejoined Rick and Kim.

"The President is mighty pissed," Glenhurst said, chuckling to himself. "He wanted to order a battalion into the area, but the JCS talked him out of it. He wants to know what happened."

"What'd you tell him?" Kim said, feeling stronger than she'd ever felt in her life

"I made up some bullshit about the aliens beginning an all-out attack and described in gory detail how we defended the planet with our lives."

Glenhurst ran his blackened hands through his crew cut. "Funny thing, though…I could have sworn we lost a lot more people. Most of my crew is here. Some are unconscious, but most of them are alert, unharmed, and feeling great."

Kim unbuttoned her tattered shirt. "Whoa, look at that." In the center of her cleavage was a neat round scar the size of a dime.

Glenhurst examined the wound, then turned to Rick. "Do you have any idea what happened to Lance White?"

"He fell into a sulfur pit. It was not a pretty sight."

Rick wasn't about to admit his involvement in White's demise.

Kim glanced at the scar that ran the length of her thigh.

"Did he suffer?"

"I'm afraid he did. A lot."

Glenhurst was confused. "Why wouldn't he come back, if the rest of us did?"

Rick instinctively looked behind him. "You've got a point. I don't know."

Glenhurst pointed in the direction of the busy landing area. "I saw that other NSA guy, Tom Ross, about half an hour ago. He's got three nasty holes in his chest. It seems he was shot, too, but he's in fine shape. He's over there with that fat guy eating everything they can stuff in their mouths. What a pair."

Kim shuddered. "If all these people survived, White could be lurking nearby. Rick, he'll never let us live in peace."

"He's gone, Kim. I saw him die."

"You saw me die."

"Forget him," said Rick.

"I'll never forget that man." Kim glanced at the men in the white suits who'd been listening to their conversation. "This place gives me the creeps. Can we leave now?"

The men talked among themselves, then nodded in the affirmative.

"We're all leaving," said Glenhurst, "I'm afraid you won't be going home right away. There are a lot of questions to be answered. It'll probably take a few weeks."

Kim turned to Rick and realized she wasn't hearing his thoughts any longer; the hum she'd become so accustomed to over the past day had disappeared. Even the quiet voice seemed to have left her head.

Keith Grunderson and Tom Ross sauntered across the clearing and joined the small group. Their arms were loaded with half-eaten Army rations. Grunderson looked ten pounds lighter and healthier than Rick remembered.

"Major Glenhurst, could we get our hands on some real food? This stuff is terrible."

Glenhurst slapped Grunderson on the back. "Nice fighting, soldier. Never seen a big guy like you run so fast."

"Fear does strange things, doesn't it?"

"You're not kidding," came a female voice.

"Barbara Whitten," Rick said softly as the brunette approached. "It was you shooting at the NSA agent, wasn't it?"

"Someone had to play defense. Not that I didn't try to avoid the issue. After you left last Saturday, those images wouldn't leave me alone. I think it would be fair to say you ruined my weekend."

Rick stood up and hugged her. "You saved my life, Barbara. I owe you for that."

Barbara returned the hug. "You and your friends saved our lives, Rick. We owe *you*, big time."

ABOARD A SUPER STALLION
ABOVE THE MADISON PLATEAU
TUESDAY, SEPTEMBER 14, 2027
**12:28 P.M. MST**    2:28  P.M. EST

As the Super Stallion rose from the meadow, Rick and Kim stared out the portal into the simmering hole where the meadow once stood. Clouds of steam drifted toward the sky.

Rick shook his head. "How many others ignored the messages? There must have been so many…"

Kim looked into the simmering pit below. "We could have used more help."

Rick noticed the bright green vegetation that bordered the pit. It was still expanding.

"Sooner or later someone's going to miss that ship."

Kim's eyes rose to meet Rick's. "Unless they needed the Source to survive."

Rick shook his head. "We'll probably do the same thing, now that we know where it is."

There was an awkward pause, then Kim spoke.

"Have you thought about what you're going to do when they let you go?"

Rick answered with a quiet voice. "I'm going to do a little traveling, take some photography classes and enjoy the good things life has to offer."

"Last night you were talking about spending some time with me."

"I remember," he said.

It was hard to believe that conversation took place only twelve hours ago. So much had happened. Twice he thought he'd lost Kim. Twice he'd been wrong.

"Does the invitation still stand?" she asked.

The thrumming helicopter changed pitch as it approached the West Yellowstone airport. Rick turned to Kim. He wasn't about to lose her again.

"Yes, it does. I think we make a good team."

"We do, don't we?"

Maybe she'd wait a day or two before telling him that her psychic abilities had vanished, that she'd returned to being a normal human.

A huge smile spread across Rick's face. "I already know."

Kim laughed. Being with Rick was going to be fun.


### THE END

About the Author

Steven E. Browne resides in Southern California where he writes and works in motion picture movie promotion.

www.ingramcontent.com/pod-product-compliance
Lightning Source LLC
Chambersburg PA
CBHW021230130626
46554CB00004B/1417